Red Hands

Red Hands

COLIN W. SARGENT

BARBICAN PRESS

First published in Great Britain by Barbican Press in 2020

Copyright © Colin W. Sargent, 2020

Registered office: 1 Ashenden Road, London E5 0DP

www.barbicanpress.com

@barbicanpress1

Cover by Rawshock Design

A CIP catalogue for this book is available from the British Library

ISBN: 978-1-909954-39-7

Typeset in Adobe Garamond

Typeset by Imprint Digital Ltd

Printed and bound by CPI Group (UK) Ltd, Croydon CR0 4YY

To Colin Sterling Sargent, son and friend,
with love

Prologue

Portland, Maine, USA

Truth lies at the bottom of the well

Tires screeched on the usually quiet street. A car door slammed. I pushed myself away from my desk and wheeled to the library window. An intruder with a knitted cap pulled low blew past the gate and started up the brick walkway. I headed toward the stairwell and leaned over the banister, trying to gauge if I could duck this fresh hell. He rattled the door knob and with cupped hands peered into the sidelight. As he banged the glass, a Rolex flashed on his wrist. Late forties, roughly five-ten, dark curls brushing the collar of his fitted leather jacket like a 1960s movie star. His jawline was vaguely familiar, the extravagant watch a dead giveaway. The former race driver Catalin Tutunaru wasn't going to be put off.

"Colin. I know you're in there. Your car is in the driveway."

I moved from the stairwell to the door. "How did you find out where I live?"

"I asked at your office."

"They shouldn't have told you."

"Are you going to let me in?"

"I'm deciding."

"Aw, come on, man, don't I bring you scoops?"

CATALIN AND I had met when I wrote a review of the Romanian sport-utility vehicle dealership he was launching outside of town. The four-wheel-drives were rugged, cool, and never failed to turn heads and elicit a "nice rig" from teenagers. I overcame my skepticism. Maine just might prove a good beachhead to sell these Cold War souvenirs. The self-indulgent market, always on the hunt for the next new thing in post-Revolutionary chic, would surely snap up these relics.

Catalin embraced his interview experience, perhaps because he'd been out of the limelight a few years and missed the celebrity status. He even forgave me a gaffe: I'd asked if his Auto Romania vehicles–originally designed for soldiers and now Warsaw Pact surplus–had "Soviet" styling.

"Soviet!?" Catalin jumped to his feet, his hand on his heart. "AROs are the product of a free Romania!"

It struck me that I didn't know much about his homeland, beyond having seen *The Prince and the Showgirl* and the Marx Brothers in *Duck Soup*.

During the interview, Catalin took off his jacket and folded it neatly over the back of his desk chair. "One moment, please." He pulled up his shirt. With a manicured index finger he pointed to a depression on his lower torso where a tiny devil had dug something out of his side. The crater was two inches deep, three inches wide, the excavation surgery ragged and rushed. The skin had healed to a pearly shade. "This too is a souvenir of my homeland."

"In Maine, we'd call that a hunting accident," I said. But it didn't look like something a deer rifle would do.

"Good one," Catalin said. "I'm going to use that."

So HERE was Catalin now, standing in my foyer, grinning. No question about how he'd earned his nickname, The Cat.

"Well, this is weird," I said. "What's up?"

"Do you know anything about the Ceausescus?" Catalin asked.

"The dictators? Nothing beyond what I've seen on CNN."

"Perfect. There's someone I'd like you to meet." He crossed his arms and motioned with a quick jerk of his head toward his Porsche, which looked like a spaceship that had landed in my Victorian neighborhood. I could see a shadowy figure hunched down in the passenger seat.

"I've brought a friend who needs a friend," Catalin said. "But if I introduce you to this person, you have to swear to secrecy. No story here for your magazine. She is in great danger. Many people would like to hurt her. No one in the world knows she's anywhere near this continent at this moment."

"Then why are you doing this?" I asked.

"Because she needs to tell someone her story so that if something happens to her, the truth will have been told." Catalin clapped me on the shoulder. "Besides, she said you got me just right. Or, we can stop right now. This will never have happened." He dropped to a whisper. "She wants to be heard, but her peculiar circumstances have made that... problematic."

"Okay," I said. "I'll tell no one she's here now." I regarded the shadow in the car. "Please bring her in. I'll put on some coffee."

When I returned from the kitchen, Catalin was already helping a specter with enormous dark glasses–even though it was one of those early winter days where the sun was threatening never to appear–up the front steps. She was nervous and gaunt. Her chestnut hair, elegantly dressed, was slightly streaked with gray.

"Iordana Ceausescu, this is Colin, the writer I told you about," Catalin said.

When I shook her outstretched icy hand, I had the sense she was a bird poised to take flight in a split second.

"Borila," she said.

I wasn't sure if this was a correction or command.

"Iordana Borila Ceausescu," Catalin said.

She looked down, radiating a strange combination of shyness and privilege. Certainly she'd seen newsreels of Jackie Kennedy. When she lifted her chin in the air like dispossessed royalty and removed her sunglasses, purple circles around her eyes gave her a lost look. It couldn't be. Was this the daughter-in-law of the executed dictators of Romania? I took her coat and hung it in the hall closet. What on earth was she doing here? How had she found herself in Maine? A black swallowtail in the snow.

If there were a secret Gulag hidden above New York, maybe it was Maine, thrust into the dark Atlantic Ocean like an angry fist. Not only was this northeasternmost point of the United States a border state with Canada, it was the most obscure, its face turned into the wind. The beaches were savage and icy. Once it got so cold I saw a wave freeze solid in mid-crash.

Maybe not so bad a place to hide, or be hidden. I remembered a story I'd written about captured German soldiers imprisoned in Maine as lumber crews under armed guard. "Just try and escape," sentries said. "Look out there. Fir trees and wolves. Take your best shot. You might just make it."

"Did you bring her across the border from Canada?" I asked.

Catalin grinned. "Ask her. She's right here."

"May I address you in English?"

"I speak English, a little German, some Russian," Iordana said. I felt relief.

"I'm better at French, Hungarian, and, of course, Romanian. Even your Maine. It was 'wicked nice' of you to have invited me here." She smiled.

But, of course, I hadn't.

Catalin squeezed her wrist. They seemed close, like friendly cousins. He turned to leave. "Maybe you'll write a novel about her," he said. "I'm headed to my office."

The door clicked shut as he left. She tensed up at the low-grade rumble of a garbage truck going down the street.

"My library is upstairs," I said. "It's my favorite place in the house. There are fewer distractions there."

Her voice was so soft it seemed miles away. "Okay."

She followed me up to the well-lit library, taking in the green tile fireplace, oak wainscoting, and ancient grass wall coverings from India. I sat back at my desk. I turned my computer all the way off.

She perched on the edge of the inglenook bench with the worn velvet pad and studied the words carved into the mantel: *The Turning of the Worm.* "Shakespeare," she said. A twinkle. "'The smallest worm will turn being trodden on.' My parents would have enjoyed this. An English bard's subversive slogan carved into a Yank's fireplace."

"You were close to your parents, then."

Iordana shifted in her seat. I noticed a small moth hole at the knee of her cashmere slacks. She covered it with her hand. "Do you mind if I smoke?" she asked.

"If you need to relax." I hadn't meant to be so rude, but both my parents had died of lung cancer. Everyone I knew had given it up, but I knew full well this was still a European thing, and I instinctively understood the smoker's impulse to slow down and savor. "Sorry. Let me get you an ashtray."

Because I sensed she needed the ritual of lighting up in order to gather herself, I switched to a seat across from her and opened a spiral notebook. I waited a full minute while she exhaled. Or was it a sigh? The glowing fire was still warming the room.

"What's the first thing you'd like to tell me?" I asked.

"I can't think of anything."

"That's okay. We don't even need to talk if you don't want to." We sat quietly for a minute. Sometimes the most revealing remarks are those left unspoken.

"Why don't you ask me some more questions?" she said. Another tiny smile. "Like a therapist."

"I'm nobody's therapist! I'm a Scorpio, so I'm too defensively barbed. Too ready to take umbrage and sting. But how about we take turns until you become more comfortable?"

Iordana waved her cigarette around the room. "Interesting. Did you do the restoration yourself?"

Had I seen on the news, the "fugitive daughter-in-law is an expert in the decorative arts"? Perhaps her question was along the lines of, do you cut your own hair? "Partly. I worry sometimes it'll never be finished. My turn. Is it lonely being here in Maine alone?"

"I'm not alone."

There was no chance she was ready to elaborate. When I'd been restoring my house, a chandelier I'd failed to properly secure had crashed to the floor from a high ceiling while I slept. There was no prelude or postlude, only darkness and a jumble of shattered crystal fragments scattered across the floor. Over a series of months, I'd been able to salvage the treasure by carefully piecing together the prisms, trying each in this position and that until everything seemed to fit. Maybe this was the way I could give Iordana her voice back. I would be in the dark, trying to guess what her circumstances had looked like, imagine the click of her life's disengagement, the whoosh of its descent, the sound of it smashing on the palace floor.

That was it. I would be an investigator, a detective gently questioning the survivor of a head wound—or a heart wound. I'd make a Scheherazade of her yet.

Iordana jumped at the sound of the Porsche backfiring as Catalin pulled away. Had he been there all this time?

"Where were you just now?" I picked up my pen, ready to take notes.

"I was in a car, speeding in Bucharest. There was blood on the seat."

"That must have been hard."

"I can't stand to think of it."

"Maybe you could tell me about your earliest memories growing up."

She stared into the fire.

Chapter 1

Bucharest, Romania
Reading Coffee

Under a ragged coat lies wisdom

ONE OF MY earliest memories is of Lidia, our Bessarabian gardener, coming into our house to read my mother's fortune in a coffee cup.

First, Lidia directed, "drink it down and stir what's left, because it's your future." Once my mother finished, Lidia took her cup and turned it upside down on a napkin. The silt from the thick Turkish coffee spilled down on the insides of the cup and left patterns, like lace, like rivers. Then, Lidia cradled the cup in the palms of her hands, almost in a caress. She looked deep into it the way one might look at a storm across a lake. Or into firelight.

"If a white rivulet is interrupted by a black blotch, it means something is going to happen to you on a trip."

If a smudge matched a certain pattern as the silt descended, it might be a serpent, an enemy who'd sting you in a few days, embarrass you. A dog shape meant a friend was near.

In the early 1950s, we moved into our gray stone two-story house on Herastrau No. 12, and Lidia came with us. This was the house where I remember being happy. It had been "donated" by a dispossessed Armenian merchant after the war. Upon arrival my parents discarded everything, from the stained-glass windows to a Spanish suite upholstered in red Cordoba leather and Louis XV furniture, something they came to regret later.

Biri, my pet lamb and closest friend, liked to eat the ivy that crept up the walls, and I loved to make fantasies and stories out of the vines and clouds as they ran together at the top of my window. Lidia made a pen for Biri in our tulip garden, near my seesaw.

When *Tatuca* (Daddy) Stalin died in 1953, our country went into mourning with the rest of the Communist Bloc. Special music was played on the radio for months in honor of him. But before too long, whispers on the wind suggested not everyone was so sad. Things were changing. Lidia, sensing this, began to wear a clove of garlic inside a handkerchief with knots tied in all four corners. She told us she carried it around to reverse any curses.

Though she'd substituted Socialism for religion in her girlhood, my mother began to call on Lidia more and more. Having no gun, it was the only thing she could turn to in this land of "organized atheism". But my mother was not alone in this–before it was all over, Romanians everywhere sought answers frantically in coffee cups, tea leaves, tarot cards, even kernels of corn tossed furtively behind their desks.

Some of my mother's friends began to drop in for these early-morning coffees. They never discussed events or names, but everybody knew what it was all about. If the bottom of your cup was too white, you might be a boring person, but at least you were safe. Sometimes Lidia would stick one of her long, tapered fingers into the black goo at the bottom of a seeker's cup and say it meant her soul was in shadow, that she had problems. If a lot of black clung to the bottom for dear life, that someone might disappear. In the new Romania, a fallen one could suffer a mysterious reversal of health during her next hospital visit. Far worse would be to survive as one of the whispered half a million souls seized via internal deportation. You could wake up in a labor colony.

Lidia peered over the edge of the cup to see if there were a storm coming, an ill wind blowing against her cheek. She stared into my eyes, seeking some sort of recognition, some hint of confirmation.

I wanted to tease my mother about it, but when Lidia saw this on my face she asked if I wanted my coffee read, too.

I refused. Even then I was very secretive, very private, didn't want to share my life with anybody. I never wanted to believe that my fate was already written, because I was afraid it would be true.

Immersed in his government papers, my father, Iordan "Petre" Borila, would have nothing to do with this *prostii*, this nonsense, whatsoever. Soothsaying was frowned upon by the government. Whenever he saw Lidia in conference with my mother, he only shook his head.

As Ministru, he was a key member of the Socialist Republic of Romania's Central Committee. Half Bulgarian and half Romanian, he grew up with grenades around his waist but no shoes. During the Spanish Civil War he was shot in the upper left leg, the hunk of flesh cut from him the size of a soup can in order to include the bullet, without anesthesia. He'd then come back and fought alongside my mother in the Divizia Tudor Vladimirescu, a special Romanian unit formed in the Soviet

Union to overthrow Axis control of Romania and fascism in general. Finished with Romania, they'd swept the *fascisti* from Hungaria to Czechoslovakia.

Sometimes, he'd come to see me, his namesake daughter, after I was asleep during the many long nights he worked late at party meetings or returned halfway to morning from visiting factories as far off as Brasov. He'd bring me tiny treats–bon-bons; Romanian pearl-shaped candies in a small metal box; or, my favorite, Soviet "Mishka" chocolates rolled in pretty papers adorned with pictures of two or three bears. In Russia, my father whispered to me in his gruff, sweet voice, all bears were nicknamed "Mishka", "Mikey".

Other than these precious moments, I knew it would be wrong to expect my parents to have much more time for me. Ecaterina, my revolutionary journalist mother, was forever charging ahead with the surge of current events. Imprisoned at 16 in Tirgu Mures for distributing handbills, she rose to fame as a news correspondent covering the War to Reunify Korea.

One early morning she came and stood in my doorway before heading off to her job as editor in chief of *Elore* (Forward). When she looked around my room, it wasn't just a look. The shadows of our two bodyguards passed behind her. She leaned over, and I thought she was going to kiss me. Instead she said, "Be grateful someone will make your nice bed. The furniture in our old house was made by political prisoners."

I tried to picture our old house, but all I could see was Lidia's rainbow of coffee cups, white, green, pink, yellow, blue, with small matching saucers. I remembered Lidia's blonde hair and very large hands as she turned the cup in her powerful palm. I tried to see the figures she saw, but I couldn't.

Like the rest of Bucharest, we were "wide asleep", unsuspecting of the dangers of the mist that was slowly encircling us. Back then we hadn't yet seen the *scinteia*, the sparkle of the monster Nicolae Ceausescu was to become. Strike that. The monster *I* was to become.

Chapter 2

The fish rots first from the head

WHEN MY parents' status in the Party rose with my father being named Vice Premier, so did our fortunes. We moved across the street into the mansion formerly occupied by First Secretary Gheorghe Gheorghiu-Dej, our old ally. This house, directly fronting Herastrau Park, was resplendent with stone alleys, cherries, Japanese bushes with pink flowers, and Russian birch trees. Four individual suites with bedrooms and sitting rooms ran luxuriously through this structure, one for my parents, one for other family members, and one for me.

My mother loved flowers and was devoted to our large garden, where she grew everything from primroses to cyclamen. Among the treats this house afforded was a greenhouse where Lidia could still read our coffee cups as well as a private cinema in our basement for us to watch newsreels and the latest films.

We didn't "own" this house—my parents refused such a capitalist indulgence—but instead were issued it as housing. It was a fact—many of my friends lived in issued houses with gardens and villas seized from royalists and upper-middle-class families, mostly people with money before who were now unsuccessfully suing the government for restitution and occasionally walking slowly past the houses and looking up at them with shadowed eyes from the streets.

I can still hear the booming laugh of Gheorghiu-Dej drowning out the voices of the other grownups at parties my parents threw downstairs while I drifted off to sleep late at night. The scent of his tobacco etched my memory forever.

Our First Premier had developed a taste for Viceroy cigarettes. He was never without them, the clouds of smoke from his exotic Virginia imports floating up from his mouth as he held court recounting King Michael's abdication and negotiations with our comrades who became the People's Democratic Front and the Central Committee. It started a fashion, and for the longest time every good communist was nobody in Romania unless he had one of these cigarettes between his fingers.

Gheorghiu-Dej had sleepy eyes like a matinee idol, and he approached his challenges with intelligence and irony. He'd been in power either as premier or first secretary of the Romanian Workers' Party or president of the State Council since the revised constitution of September 24, 1952, the Soviet model that made us more like the USSR.

In any event, around 1958 it was suddenly decreed that foreign cigarettes were a bourgeois indulgence, so our scientists at the National Academy were invited to work night and day to make an exact copy of Gheorghiu-Dej's favorite, Viceroy cigarettes.

The exoticizing of such capitalist indulgences ushered in the snake of a new aristocracy in Romania. The *Garda Vechea*, the old-guard communist party members, were turning into those they'd fought so hard to bring down. Many of these people had spent much of the 1930s in prison in rags for their beliefs, *Ilegalist* communists who were now capitalizing on their prestige to make a better world for their children.

The families of these *Ilegalisti*, ours among them, were honored with special food privileges, cars, free hospitals appropriated for their use alone, and free medicine.

In time "everyone" had bodyguards, butlers, even crews for a fleet of inboard-engined Italian Riva speedboats carved from mahogany and teak which were made available for our exclusive use. We had only to make a telephone call and one of these long, low boats with white, green, and taupe cushions would appear with a reassuring hum along the shore of whichever *Ilegalist* villa we were staying at on Lake Snagov, attended by a young soldier in dark pants, a white shirt, and a uniform cap.

It was delicious, inevitable. Behind every imitation Viceroy cigarette, dubbed "Snagovs" after the lake, you'd find one of the first beautiful people in Romania.

BUCHAREST WAS IN the midst of a building boom when the red snow came. I was with my friend Ileana, one of the sophisticated ones. Her father ranked perhaps sixth or seventh in the Central Committee. Mine ranked ninth. Ileana inhaled Snagovs, wore heavy Czechoslovakian nylons, had her own hairdresser and an easy air of being too cool for school. But most wondrous of all, she wore high heels, strictly forbidden to me by my mother. They caught my eye as we were walking home from class. Then something else brushed my cheek.

I looked up. "This red snow is… beautiful." I watched the ash sift down to the rooftops of our capital city.

"You're strange," Ileana said. "Red snow? This is Western trash, fallout from an 'enlightened' democratic people." She grabbed my arm and started running. Elders had grumbled about rumors of red dust from the French Algerian nuclear experiments in the Sahara before, but in a Communist Bloc country, who'd listen? I'd never seen it until now. It was soft on my skin, and warm. I'd imagined it would be sandy, since it had come from a desert. It was all over my hair but didn't sting my eyes. Ileana pulled me under a canopy. "Get with it," she said. "Put your scarf on. You look terrible with that stuff in your hair. You remain forever in the back of things."

"I don't care, it's wonderful." I did a little dance. "The scirocco brings it from Africa."

"Spare me, Doe Eyes."

Paprika-red, it sprinkled to the flat roof of the Patria Cinema on Magheru Boulevard and skidded down the coffee-colored awnings fronting the new indoor grocery complex where party members and lucky others bought pineapple, shrimp, salads, and fruit cocktail. The red cloud wafted from the Calea Plevnei to the Piata Amzei along the Piata Victoriei. Residents thunked heavy wooden shutters against it in every window. Cars sped by with wipers on, mostly boxy black Soviet Zis and Zils, which we laughingly called "This" and "That".

Two older men dressed in black frowned at us. "This is deadly," one of them said. "You girls should not be out here. Get inside." He made little scurry motions with his dead white fish hand. "It's going to get worse." He squeezed his neck. "People can't breathe."

Older men were funny. I imagined teeth on the fish hand, and then the eye on its side, his ring. The evil eye, green.

Other people scurried, too. A grandmother spit three times delicately on her granddaughter's head for good luck and gasped, "I am *un*staring you to take away the evil of others from you." The red ribbon on the little girl's head sparkled with the moisture, looking even more vivid in the red powder swirling all around us. "There. Come on. Be careful to step out with your right foot for luck."

"Where can we go?" Ileana said, but she already knew. Though it was scandalous for two young girls to go in unescorted, we sailed through the doors of the Hotel Lido. Massive in its reinforced concrete with barely a flourish of gold around the huge arched door, the Lido made me feel as though we were stepping into an oyster, a few degrees cooler from the cave effect of the enormous lobby. On the right side wealthy Britons checked in with their baggage at the registration desk, and on the left tall green plants choked a dark, paneled room where young gentlemen slouched in chairs and drank amber fluids from glasses.

Ileana led me by the hand to a corner table for my first woman-to-woman talk.

We sat down, the feeling of the room spreading all around us like a dress. As Ileana began my education, I felt like I was pushing off in a canoe, into the dark part of the river where the rocks were.

"Will you tell your parents we've come in here?" Ileana said. She scanned a menu for punches and cocktails with the most mysterious names.

"This scares me."

"Are you afraid of the dark or the men?"

"You know we're too young."

"But can you believe it?" Ileana said, a little too loudly. A few of the men noticed her. This made her words more important.

I closed my eyes. *Yes, yes, yes.* "No." I felt the crinkle of my identification papers in my pocket. It had been just a year since I'd gone to the photographers and had my pictures taken. At fourteen, all good Romanians reported to the security station in their sector to have identification papers made, a sort of intra-Romanian passport that had to be carried at all times and could be demanded by the Securitate at any time. You needed them to enroll in school, enter a government building, travel on public transportation, register in a hotel, or even buy food. It was unthinkable to travel without them. If you lost your papers, you'd be suspected as subversive, a danger to the state. I knew we were different when my mother approved the photographs and sent one of our bodyguards to get the papers for me. I didn't have to wait in line at the police station like my other schoolmates.

"You don't feel comfortable here?"

"I'm worried, but I think... I like it a little."

"A little like that man over there?"

A young man in a rumpled shirt sat with a very new coat thrown over the arm of his chair. A single zippered kit bag crouched near his feet. His shoes shone properly, cautiously. He gave us a sly wink.

"What are you two doing in here?" the barkeep inquired.

"We're waiting for our parents. They'll be right down." Ileana raised her leg beneath the table so that her nylons made little cool zooms against each other beside my bare leg. She was beautiful-dangerous, catachresis like the red snow.

"Shall we be like little girls," she said. "Or shall we talk of men?"

"The man I'm thinking of is my father, who'll punish me when he comes back from his meeting. In actuality he'll watch my mother punish me, but he'll approve of it."

"How did they meet?"

"My parents?" Few of my friends had asked me about my parents before. Drinks arrived like strangers at the table. Light reflecting into my lemonade lit up our corner of the room. I peered into the glass. I stared down as the grain of the tabletop began to turn into human faces.

"Isn't she *Boanghen*?"

I frowned at the derisive term for Hungarians, but didn't look up. "My mother is proudly from a free Romania. Her family was Hungarian, by way of Transylvania. That's why she's been honored with her position at the Journal, where she promotes diversity by writing exclusively in Hungarian."

"Jews?"

"Why do you ask that?"

"My mother told me."

"She is. So what?"

My first taste of casual anti-Semitism. It was on Ileana's face.

"I'm not supposed to play with you."

"What?"

"If your mother is a Jewess, then you are a Jewess. It's like dipping your foot in water. If you're wet, you're wet. Stop looking at me. Look at your dark dress and sullen face. You look like Anne Frank."

I blinked at the comparison. Did Anne Frank have such privileges? Were *her* parents party members? Was she driven to school each day in a limousine?

I looked up and noticed how the light bathed Ileana's perfectly bronzed skin. I tried to change the subject. "Your tan is really something. Where'd you go on vacation?"

"My parents have a new place at Constanta. What a swinging seaport! You should see the place everyone's saying the Ceausescus are going to take. Don't tell me you guys are still stuck in Mamaia."

She studied me. Even though hot resorts were springing up at the Black Sea getaway where oversexed Ovid had been banished for writing *Ars amatoria*, my parents preferred the stately villas at Mamaia. "Now I know you're my friend," I said.

"Oh?"

"Only a friend would insult me so."

"Ah, I meant nothing. We're all from good old communist families." *That hair*, her narrowed eyes telegraphed to me.

I read her mind and smoothed my hair as she tried to dismiss everything Borila with a glance. *My father's hair.* He'd fought with Dolores Ibarruri, whom they called La Passionaria, and later made secretary of the communist party in Spain. He was in all books about the Spanish War. "Just so you know, my mother was in prison with Gypsies, by the way. She's taught me Gypsy curses, so watch out."

Ileana laughed. "I'm frankly worried about contamination from Jews. We had Jews in the government years ago–they got the hell out. So why do I like you?"

"Do you?"

"I don't know. Do boys like you?"

"I'm sure I don't know."

I hoped they did like me. I hoped they liked my long, straight hair and large eyes. And the way I looked down a lot, a popular mannerism for a girl in Romania.

"I mean, your father brings you chocolates in the night."

Had I actually told her that?

"The little girl of the chocolate nights. Wouldn't you like to be visited by a boy from school instead?"

"No."

"And so you like girls?"

"I didn't say that. I will love someone, later."

"And it'll be a big part of your life, won't it, Doe Eyes?"

I stretched. I didn't like Ileana tiptoeing into my thoughts like this. "Not a part," I said. "Everything. Love will be everything to me."

"And will this everything be with Petre Ionescu?"

"No. He's in my classes, nothing more."

"I think he's out of this world."

The man with the rumpled shirt smiled, hearing everything. Ileana tilted her head in his direction and whispered, "Is he a rapist? A swan butcher? A moral defective?" She began an intrigue about him. Then we saw a friend approach him and swing another piece of luggage against the wall and from out of nowhere Ileana said, "So what do you think about Valentin?"

"What? No. I have no interest in him."

"So you know who I meant."

"Yes. Valentin Ceausescu. There is nothing."

We returned to our discussions about parents and our tantalizing lack of an escort, the certain trouble when our parents found out.

"They'll find out," I said, not for the first time.

"How, will you tell them?"

"No, they'll just find out."

"And what then? Ha! Burned by the broth, you blow on everything before you try it. You're too cautious. *Cine se frige in ciorba sufla si in iaurt.* I'll bet you even blow on your yogurt."

Chapter 3

Take your heart in your teeth

O F COURSE MY PARENTS found out, and I was grounded. That summer, I became obsessed with movies. I watched everything I could get my hands on, approved or not (you could get anything you wanted if you had parents like mine with a private screening room): German movies; Italian movies; Soviet movies; British movies; even movies from Hollywood–*Lawrence of Arabia* and *To Kill a Mockingbird*. I watched *Jules et Jim* starring Jeanne Moreau and Oskar Werner, and *A Very Private Affair*. Occasionally I watched a Hungarian movie with my mother, but she ducked the darker ones like *Megszallottak, The Obsessed Ones*. Together, we'd stick to the sillier shows like *I'll Call the Minister*.

But my secret favorite movies were the cool ones, the New Wave French. I wanted to be Anna Karina. I bobbed my hair and imagined I was Jean-Luc Godard's muse. I watched each episode of *Vivre sa Vie* at least a dozen times and memorized all the lines. I imagined I'd be discovered as a star with my big dark eyes and my habit of looking down that Ileana had made such fun of. I did the "Café Scene" in front of my mirror. So immersed was I in films that I began to see everything as through the camera's eye…

FADE IN: The road through the Carpathian Mountain range goes beyond Predeal and Brasov and begins a spiral to the loftiest promontories, vistas that allow the viewer to half-imagine she is seeing all the way to the resorts of the Black Sea coast, named today for planets: Venus, Saturn, Jupiter, Neptune, as well as Techirghiol Lake to the east.

Screening the views of the coast are millions of black fir trees that greet travelers on all sides like a dark beard, the bare rocks jutting in stubs and fingers beyond the cars and wooden guard rails that separate the road from thin air.

These rocks and trees go on forever.

But before this forever was a dark red Buick passenger car driven by our chauffeur, Comrade Proscanu, on its way down from the highest observation point on the summit. Zoom in to a dark figure inside its oval green glass rear windshield–me, sitting sulkily with a newly short haircut and my hands on my skirt. Beside me, my mother. Father up front, trying to see. One of our two bodyguards, Comrade Mocano, behind in the rumble seat with his pistol. I liked Mocaneata, as I'd nicknamed him, so much. He was very small and dark, with olive skin. He couldn't stand to be tickled and would die of it if you just tickled him under his wrist, which I'd just realized I'd grown too old to do. Mocaneata was my favorite of our two bodyguards, so devoted to communism he'd named his son "Cincinel", Five-Year Plan. He was kind, with good intentions, but clumsy–like a jumpy squirrel in a gray and maroon suit forever messing up out of good will.

"I don't know why you cut your hair," my mother said. "Don't just sit there. Answer me."

I looked at the road spilling down the mountainside, the gravel edge fringing the road and beyond that, wild poppies. Then the savage drop.

"It's my life to live," I said. "I've done nothing wrong."

My father rolled his eyes.

"Nothing? First you go with her to the hotel alone like hookers and now you want to dress like one. And we suppose this is nothing?"

My father said nothing. Instead, through our front windshield, his eyes were glued to something at the very bottom of the hill. As I watched, that something became a very fancy car. His face was frozen.

My mother yammered on. "You thought you could hide everything from me. I know, I know, you said you had no choice, everyone was going into the hotel, you couldn't breathe, I wasn't here, I was in Czechoslovakia. So it's all my fault. I might as well have cut your hair myself."

"How could you know?" I smiled.

"Don't talk to me like that, young lady."

"Hey, isn't that a Pobeda Victory? What a car. Wouldn't that be Comrade Ceausescu?" Moceaneta was almost chirping. What could this mean?

The car got closer. My mother reached forward and pressed my father on the shoulder to let him know she also saw. Still, she wasn't finished with me.

"But why listen to Ileana? Is it not from her advice that you were jettisoned from school?"

"Kicked out, Mama. Nobody talks like you anymore."

"I have seen her, the way she disgraces her school uniform."

I had to admit that was true, even though I wasn't going to give my mother an inch. Even as schoolgirls in all our classes, where only Russian was spoken and where we'd all worn the very dark brown Soviet uniform with the black apron and big pleats compulsory for emerging communist nations, Ileana had hiked up her skirt by rolling it at the waistband and tightened her bodice with safety pins.

"She does *not*." I studied the approaching car and took in the shiny chrome and the little fluttering flags. It was much bigger than ours, and a newer model.

"Even worse, discarding the dark red *cravata* the administrators gave her, Ileana felt she was somebody because she wore instead a lighter red scarf in fine silk to indicate that her parents had participated in the Soviet convocation. Do you always have to follow her? This hair that makes your teacher say, 'Get out of my class. What is this curl that goes in toward your neck? Do you think you're Irena Petrescu or one of the French actresses with Jean Marais who's come to visit?'"

"No, Mama. I wouldn't be caught dead looking like a French actress."

"How dare you go into school dressed as a woman? You know my liver problems require me to go to the waters of Karlovy Vary in Czechoslovakia for a cure. And then I come back to hear from the whole world what you've been up to. Inmates have better hair-dos, cut from a pot. Oh, what have you done with your beautiful long hair?" She began to wring her hands, but I noticed her voice get lower as the strange car grew closer.

FADE TO BLACK: Maybe we could wrap this up if I blamed everything on Ileana.

But I didn't want to risk my friendship, because Ileana really was somebody. When our science teacher dared question her about her refusal to sweep all her hair behind her white hairband, Ileana drew herself up like the famous Bulandra and snarled, "Do you know who I am? Do you know who my father is?"

The teacher held her ground, at first. Then Ileana said she was coming into school the next day with a bodyguard and a pistol to shoot her for her malicious and politically induced comments. She fluffed her bangs *on the other side* of her headband and walked away. Ileana was the first to do this, like an arctic explorer. Now all of the other girls wore their hair that way.

But to actually threaten the teacher? Okay, that was going too far. Maybe Mama was right. Maybe Ileana could be a bully. I was surprised, but I felt a bit ashamed. I hoped my mother would never learn what Ileana had said about her in the hotel.

I looked at my mother. As a girl, she'd been a wild-eyed communist revolutionary. Even now she didn't wear so much as a wedding ring, presumably to keep herself austerely in fighting trim. What would she have cared back then about *hairbands*? So conservative were they in raising me, they were losing their edge.

The two cars were 100 yards apart now, with bodyguards from both sides solemnly concealing their pistols in greeting.

Gravel skidded under the tires, and the door opened, with my stony-faced father stepping out. We were on an intermediate promontory that opened up on trees that took on three shades of blue interrupted by flashes of red and orange. Up here, fall was just beginning to stir.

Maybe being a communist daddy wasn't so easy. I wasn't even sure of what he did at the Central Committee. "Minister of Something," I carelessly said once, and he'd overheard. "Such privilege you enjoy, Little One," he said. "One day this life will disappear around a corner."

Though I hadn't bothered to learn much about my father's business, everyone said that the thug Nicolae Ceausescu was next in line if something should happen to Gheorghiu-Dej.

I watched my father's square back advance to the superior car while Mocaneata bounced unsteadily out to the running board, looking around. This was going to be bad.

"*Salut*, Comrade," my father said.

"*Salut*."

I was surprised to see to see my father's rival was so short, with the smirk of a salesman. Nicolae Ceausescu advanced from his car and beat his breast–this shaggy-dog put-on of a walk. His two bodyguards followed his every step as he leaned into my father. I'd overheard my parents commenting that he'd made a career out of claiming to be the youngest communist ever sent to prison for his beliefs, but hadn't my mother also been sixteen when she was sent to prison for the same? He was a talker, this one, I'd heard my father say, quite the orator who managed to take credit for everyone's work. The two men stood there and shook hands vigorously up and down in the *tovaraseste* style familiar to comrades, where Nicolae made sure to encircle my father's hand more boldly with his greater grip. There were some gruff laughs and a quick sidestep as if they were wrestling.

"So you've been up there?"

"Without a doubt, Nicolae. The old world is still up there."

Mocaneata shifted. Way below the car three white birds flapped their wings as they landed on a black-tipped fir.

Nicolae took two steps back, like a nineteenth-century actor who'd been stabbed in a melodrama. His face darkened; his smile disappeared. "You speak to me of the old world as if there are problems with the new? How do you come to me like that? Whence issues your equivocal s-syntax?" Because of his theatrical umbrage, Nicolae was losing for the moment the long-waged battle against his stutter. He stared with *ochii ca mure*, eyes like blackberries, trying to flatten out his Oltenian farmer's accent.

A more perceptive man than Nicolae might have noticed my father's bushy eyebrows rise imperceptibly. He forced a big smile. "I meant nothing except to tell you about the beauty at the summit. I recommend it to you as the purest view."

Nicolae's face turned violet at this. The cars, the roadside, even the mountains seemed to grow quiet in anticipation of his rage. "You see fit to recommend something to me? Should I consider this an order, that only you know how to appreciate the beauty of Romania as a true patriot of the old ways, this purity, eh? You dare say something like this to me?"

Nicolae looked over at our car, as if to make sure his audience was paying attention.

I sensed my father listen for the snap of Nicolae's chauffeur's Tokarev 7.62 semi-automatic and the messy echo of Mocaneata following suit, but it didn't come. Sun slammed down on the hoods of the two cars while beyond the rail was all this cool and green, this recommended beauty that was so infuriating to Nicolae.

"Would not anyone want to see the mountaintop? If I made a recommendation, Comrade, it was out of respect for your sentiments for the beauty of this country, and nothing more."

"What? What?" Nicolae was in a frenzy now, staggering to his automobile and slamming both hands down on the hood. His forehead was vermilion. "What do you say to me now, old fox? You are so feeble you do not know your place?"

"Get down," my mother said to me. "Below the seat."

Mocaneata pounded softly on the windshield, quick like his heart. He too motioned for us to get to the floor. Instead, my mother got out of the car. Both men turned astonished to her for a moment, full of respect.

In contrast, Nicolae's wife Elena Ceausescu stayed inside, a well-coifed silhouette behind the glass. Another head bobbed beside her: Valentin.

My father looked much older than Nicolae. His war wounds had stiffened his gait, and chronic pain lined his face. But he didn't look afraid. He set his jaw firmly and crossed his arms, but his eyes took on a faraway look as he seemed to remember something else, from his childhood.

He was just thirteen when his mother was dying, with snow two feet deep around his native village. In high fever and delirium, she'd called him to her bedside and mouthed, "If only I could have some grapes. Couldn't you bring me some grapes now?"

He agreed, but deep drifts muffled the doorway as he ran out in tears. He went everywhere looking for them, impossible in wintertime, coughing and falling with brimming eyes only to have a policeman detain him in the street and ask him endless questions. He was finally allowed to return home, only to find his mother gone. He hadn't been able to give her those grapes. We alone knew about this recurring nightmare that crept into his thoughts when he least desired it.

He looked down at his empty hands and then up at Nicolae, who took this moment to rush toward him in hopes of making him flinch. Nicolae put his face millimeters from my father's and said, "From you and your relative place in the Central Committee I will not take instructions. I will not forget this outrage. You neither understand nor appreciate Romania better than I. Would you like your caviar seasoned with glass?" He motioned to his chauffeur and bodyguard. "You are out of your depth."

My father's expression changed. He was comfortable with this killing talk. He smiled coolly, having found the grapes.

"And then, with me out of the way, you would be free to continue to the top of the mountain where I have recommended you to go, would you not? Up along that trail, where I have been, to the left, comrade. I tell you the view is fantastic."

Silence. Nicolae scowled. A bead of sweat trickled down my father's brow. Ceausescu's skin was now ruddy but dry as leather. So it was true, what I'd heard my parents say. Nicolae was unable to perspire. Old ladies and Gypsies marked this about him constantly, this old-world sign of dishonesty, just as they shook their heads at the lack of hair on his forearms, another unlucky trait.

And then came a flap of wings that reverberated over the mountaintops and cracked the blue ether that hung over the peaks that were so large their distance away was unclear. It sounded so much like a gunshot that we all jumped. How could one bird have made so much noise? Mocaneata, *ververita*, squirrel that he was, nearly dropped his pistol.

Then two more birds lifted off slowly, egrets probably.

Nicolae began to laugh generously, without reserve, at Mocaneata. "We know how to live, Comrade Borila, do we not?"

Slowly a more natural color returned to his face. He clapped my father on the back and trudged toward the Pobeda, shaking his head. But when he turned around for a departing glance, his face was purple. His eyebrows dropped so low in a deadly squint they almost touched his cheekbones. With a roar of gravel the state cars started up. For a moment the cars drew closer, and in the flash of the glass I looked at the passengers, the young man in back.

Valentin, his son.

We passed, and to my surprise Valentin looked directly at me, his unusually long face and green-tinted eyes coming within five feet of us. I held the look as his face disappeared up the hill, looking down at me now from the center of the green oval glass in the rear of the Pobeda. I watched the young man vanish in the smoke above us, shifting myself around to eye him further, my parents oblivious to my posture. I stretched to see the gray dot of the car as its windshield flashed for the last time turning to the left on an ascent as vertical as the top of a pencil.

My father touched my mother's shoulder. He took a deep breath. "Well, that went well."

Chapter 4

Defend me from chickens;
I'm not afraid of dogs

WE WERE HONORED by an invitation to join Gheorghe Gheorghiu-Dej and his family at their Timis mountain retreat. It relieved my parents to feel safe as part of his sphere, almost able to forget Nicolae Ceausescu and the immediate dangers of marginalization he threatened. On the way there, my father caught me off guard to ask me the only favor he asked of me in his life:

"You don't have to say Lica is a great actress," he said as our Buick sped westward along Soseaua Kiseleff beyond Tineretului Stadium, "but just say something nice about her movie–it'll make them both feel good." Gheorghiu-Dej's eldest daughter had just wrapped shooting *Tudor*, Film Studio Bucuresti's lush-costume documentary about the life of nineteenth-century Wallachian leader Tudor Vladimirescu. It was filled with scenes from a battle my parents were very familiar with, so we were given an early copy and would obviously be invited to comment as an appreciative audience.

My bad luck was, I'd seen the film. In my newfound, acutely perceptive "critical eye", Lica's performance was two hours, eighteen minutes of hell. So turgid, so pathetic. How was I to compliment this and still keep my 18-year-old's "artistic integrity"? She was plump like the American Liz Taylor with big dark brown eyes, really *e data dracului*, striking in a frightening sort of way.

When the door opened, there was the imposing Gheorghiu-Dej; the younger sister, Tanta; and the voluptuous Lica. Our Premier had no wife, and I hadn't wondered until now about whether she'd died or been discarded, the fate of so many of my mother's friends. Lica, who stood in as First Lady for many state occasions, gave me a warm smile.

Before I could protest, Gheorghiu-Dej swept me up into his big hug, lifted me in the air, and laughed. "Uff! One more year, and I won't be able to do this!"

Long seconds after he set me down, he was still struggling to catch his breath. He certainly didn't look so good this evening.

Despite their welcoming manner, I was not able to congratulate Lica at dinner. Over the din of silverware and crystal, I offered nothing, trying too hard to craft the "perfect incisive commentary" that would make them all see how mature in my tastes I'd become. This infuriated my mother, who rasped the word *impietrit*, "stony", into my ears. My parents hadn't brought me here to flatter our hosts but rather to be kind, and I'd done neither.

Gheorghiu-Dej's sad wave at the door was the last time I ever saw him.

FATE TOOK revenge on me for my rude treatment of Lica. Barely a week later, in early November, some cinematographers wishing to court favor with the Nomenclatura, the privileged ones, "impulsively" flattered my family by offering to give me a screen test for a role they said I'd be "perfect for". Why not? I'd considered careers in medicine, biology, and law the week before–a young girl's thoughts. Romania's Hollywood was packed with wives and daughters of the Central Committee, and their involvement was alternately frowned upon and cheered.

By then I'd decided unreasonably that since I couldn't sing, couldn't paint, and didn't lead my form in science, perhaps now, during the dawn of Romanian film, I must surely be able to act. This fascination took up a week of my life; I'd been encouraged about it a number of times by friends who considered me "dramatic".

Besides, in frustration with my teenage misbehavior, my mother set it up.

So I showed up to audition for the role of Ileana Cosanzeana, the fairy-tale princess who is always rescued by Fat-Frumos, or Prince Charming, the "beautiful youth", at the private home of Beate Fredanof, one of our best actresses. Over tea and cakes, we talked about a painting she had on the wall by Victor Brauner, who'd barely escaped Paris during the Nazi occupation. Then I began to recite a poem by Mihai Eminescu that I'd been given to study overnight. Listening to myself with growing humiliation, I made it through only two lines before stopping myself. "I can't do this," I said for the first time with conviction. I started giggling uncontrollably, which just made it worse. "I'm terrible."

Oh, was I terrible.

"Oh, thank you so much, Madame Fredanof, goodbye."

I laughed in my tears as I departed from her living room with no one chasing after me, begging me to reconsider. In the car

home, I consoled myself that I was making my biggest contribu-
tion to Romanian theater–by getting *off* the stage. Strangely, my
thoughts turned to Valentin Ceausescu, son of my father's mortal
enemy. Where did that come from?

IN LATE FEBRUARY 1965, my chain-smoking buddy Nora suggested
we meet up with some of our friends at Ionel Dalea's house, one of
many gray stone mansions on the Primaverii. Going to Ionel's was
just something a few of us *Uticesti*, or members of the UTC youth
group, did. Ionel's father was somewhere in the Central Committee, and Nora liked to spy on Ionel's older sister because of the
way she walked, her hot pink couture, the way she glided down a
flight of stairs to an adoring audience. She was "very ladylike and
feminine. And very sexy," Nora said.

She looked me straight in the eyes through the smog of her
lipstick-stained Snagov. "Tinu will be there."

Hadn't she heard? "Tinu and I are over."

Tinu was the son of Leontin Salajan, head of the Army Ministry
and the only person I ever saw Nicolae Ceausescu treat as a close
personal friend. The Salajan and Ceausescu estates were in the same
Nomenclatura neighborhood, separated by a single ivy-covered
wall. I'd seen them attend soccer games together: malevolent
"twins" with stocky builds, white shirts, gray trousers, and curly hair
under matching black curly lamb hats. They leaned in and laughed
together even as my parents steered us to the other side of the field.

But Tinu was a beautiful boy. Tall and athletic, he starred
in basketball and soccer, and was certainly the handsomest in
school, with a brush haircut the color of chestnuts. He was my
first love. I was discovering, though, that Tinu was almost too

happy-go-lucky. He was always having these little accidents. (Years later, as a military officer, he stepped out of a long silver Soviet TU-95 Bear aircraft into pure air with a grin. Breaking both legs in the thirty-foot fall, he remained in good spirits.) I was bored.

"Well, there'll be plenty of other guys there," Nora said. She thrust her open pack of Snagovs toward me. "This is going to be a real party."

I lit one and took a puff. We'd been promised all Snagovs would be the same, but this one was black and bitter.

"Sure, I'll come."

Nora leaned toward the foyer mirror and refreshed her thick eyeliner, expertly smudging the corners with her little finger. She pushed me out the door with a purposeful look on her face—like a gymnast about to make a run toward the pommel horse.

Walking along the manicured lawns of our Nomenclatura enclave, Nora regaled me with news of her recent trip to Stuttgart in Germany's lazy south, where she'd enjoyed midnight theater with a pack of hipsters making the scene in the Schillerplatz.

I followed. Before long we arrived, checked out the with-it sister, and made it downstairs to Ionel's parents' lounge, where Ionel was fussing with drinks, Russian and Communist Chinese tea in dark red cylindrical tin boxes.

"*Buna*," Tinu and I greeted each other.

I took Nora by the elbow. She rolled her eyes. "So it's down to 'hey' now between the two of you? Aren't you even going to talk to him?" She pushed my hand away.

We headed to the opposite side of the room, where on the TV images of American violence flashed across the screen. "*Buna* is all Tinu and I ever have to say to each other, even when we're alone."

Nora shushed me and pointed to the screen. The state commentator was giving us a carefully guided tour of the United States: guns for all, violent demonstrations, the assassination of Kennedy, the execution of southern blacks in Selma. No surprise, since this was all we ever heard about the West.

"Enough." Ionel turned off the TV. "The US must be hell on earth." With a Texas drawl he said, "I heard tell in America you can up and shoot a communist, no trial or nothin'!"

"Yes, it's so much better here in our great Socialist Republic." Nora was nobody's *lingau*, licking toad. "Political dissidents–degenerates all, of course–are slammed into prisons and work camps for re-education. Opponents just disappear. Only Americans practice hiding under their desks during air raids and build bomb shelters. We Romanians are so much more intellectual and fatalistic." She raised her voice. "In the event of a nuclear emergency…" She swept her hand out, inviting us to finish the old joke.

We chimed in: "…Form a single line and walk in an orderly fashion directly to the cemetery."

Ionel clicked the TV off. He turned to me, his fellow movie buff. "Dana, can you believe that Liviu Ciulei has just been nominated for Best Director at Cannes for *Forest of the Hanged*? Do you think there's any chance it'll happen this time?"

"Get serious," Nora said. "No Romanian has ever won anything at Cannes."

The mahogany-paneled room was filling up quickly. Ileana came in with a crowd that included lovely Anca Brucan, daughter of our Ambassador to America. I leaned toward Nora and dropped to a whisper. "Nora, Tinu's coming over here. I don't want to get into it in front of everyone." I started helping Ionel sort through some albums. "Pretend we're deep in a private conversion."

Ionel fiddled with the hi-fi, something Italian, and soon it shimmered with the jazzy beat of the Swingle Singers and their modern interpretations of Bach and Handel. The lights were turned down by sly, conspirational Nora. Today there would be kissing.

I plopped down on the couch angrily, without a boyfriend, listening to the warped dissonance of the Swingle Singers. Someone I took to be Tinu climbed over the back of the studio couch and sat close to me. I was so annoyed I pretended not to notice. Determined to stare ahead, I looked across the room only to see Tinu getting a drink. So the boy beside me was someone different! And then against the crisply ironed pleats of my woolen skirt I felt a hand slide into mine. A stranger whispered, "You star in the movie of my dreams." It was so cheesy a line, but I was thrilled. The record changed with a click. Just at that very moment a warm breath kissed my ear. A stirring voice started singing along with the Beatles' pulsing "I Want to Hold Your Hand". To me, and to me only. I froze.

I neither withdrew my hand nor returned the grip, but instead pretended not to feel the increasing waves of warmth the stranger was sending to me. I was thrilled to the bone. Somehow I didn't have to open my eyes to know I was going to see the spectacularly irregular features, the big green eyes and scrawny muscularity of Valentin Ceausescu. I dared a quick look. Up close his irises had a disturbing motion, like sand at the bottom of a river.

In terror I froze as I felt my back slowly grow cold. Oh, no. How could I take my hand back? I'd never allowed myself to think of this boy. He was in a younger section at school. He seemed two feet taller than the last time I saw him, though he'd never been far away, always on the other side of the room. But he was communicating a lot with the way he was holding my hand, as if he were sending a signal of delicious trouble up through my arm.

And he was not *ugly* ugly. I stole another glance and took in his very strange forehead and the three-quarter-length brown wool-and-leather jacket he was wearing with the collars flipped up, very much in style, eccentric. Gold cufflinks sparkled at the end of the pale blue shirtsleeves that outreached his jacket, an unusual touch. I felt his big presence beside my narrow shoulders and was amazed by my own curiosity, my changing feelings, my excitement at being smaller, and weaker, than this man. Long after the music shifted to a new song, I allowed him to continue to hold my hand, though neither of us said anything. Wasn't this impossible, to sit with Valentin beside me, stronger than me and yet wanting to be near me? Who would speak next?

Valentin had earned the enviable title of goalie for the school soccer team, though that seemed barely important in my little sphere. What he had now, in this semi-darkness, was this hand. Others were dancing the artless slow dancing that entailed draping body parts over one another and shuffling about as if asleep, but Ionel, Ileana, and Anca—Valentin's former girlfriend who'd been so reviled by his mother that she'd commanded school officials to "Drag her by her tits out of his class"—were staring at Valentin and me now. I smiled, looked down, and shook my head back and forth as my temples warmed. This was nothing. There was no need to make anything of it.

But it was the way he had *taken* my hand, and by taking it seemed so convinced he now possessed it, that made my breath draw short. Everything was wrong about this. I was giving up a much more handsome and popular boyfriend, but for this? This forbidden boy was becoming... interesting. I dared a sidelong glance at him and saw Valentin in a new light, his dark hair and eyes now glossy with intelligence, and found him jaguar-handsome.

Knowing that others were surprised by our wordless union sent a shiver of excitement through me, too.

Near the record player was Tinu, already talking to another girl... Nora! Yes, he was obviously accident-prone.

How could I have feelings for Valentin, who'd had such presumption to take my hand and to be so warm? I'd never felt so much odd passion. I was fighting that same strange repulsion-fascination that would draw me closer and closer to Valentin, in spite of our parents' wishes, in spite of, strangely, my own.

One song, "Big Girls Don't Cry", ran its course as I stared through the dim light at the top row of a bookcase and focused on the shiny binding of Ian Fleming's *Goldfinger*.

Still another song. Four more. The Beatles, Elvis Presley, Gilbert Bécaud, Charles Aznavour. Valentin didn't say a word but simply held my hand, something so oddly *de pe vremea bunicii*, from my grandmother's time, that I felt myself growing faint. Well over an hour had passed with "us" together. For we had indeed become an "us". Valentin put his face close to my neck and said, "I have loved you for a long time."

Later that night, Valentin walked me home, singing *"Nata per me*, you were born for me; I love you and will always love you,"* something by Adriano Celentano, the Italian singer-movie star.

Across the street from my house, in the old Park of Stalin (a park of many names renamed Herastrau by Gheorghiu-Dej), we shared our first embrace, tentatively, *sa incerci marea cu degetul*, "to try the sea with your finger".

Valentin's kiss was very different from Tinu's. He had very small rodent teeth like his mother's, and I felt them. I was very surprised at his kiss. It was a real kiss, but childish, inexperienced because he was so eager. I admit I liked it partly because he seemed overwhelmed to be near me. It tasted like sawdust and olives, a very young smoker's kiss, but also very fresh. What would my mother say about my letting him kiss me, when we hadn't even had a first date? And this would be before she found out who he was!

A FEW WEEKS LATER we were in the park together, necking on a bench, when a policeman recognized us. To my surprise, the man spoke only to me.

"How dare you do this? Don't you know who you are so that you can set an example? I didn't expect to see this from you."

I wore a sleeveless dress with big red *bujor*, peonies, on a white background, my hair now shoulder length. I felt luxuriant and loved. I wore no makeup and no stockings, my legs still stinging from the peroxide bleach I used because one of my girlfriends saw me dressing before gym class and teased me, calling me gorilla instead of Borila. Everyone forgot it a moment later, except, of course, me–shy as I was on this unaccountably humid night in late April, confronting a policeman in front of my house at the dawn of the sexual revolution.

People, from maids to officials to priests, speaking in whispers, soon called us "The Romeo and Juliet of Romania". We knew the axe was about to fall, but somehow that made it even more alluring.

My mother caught me off guard as I came home. "Do you know who you're getting involved with? Don't we have enough worries with your father's poor health?" Her slap knocked me against the side of the door. My father was in his study, books piled to the ceiling, reading. Mama knew he was so near he could hear everything. She hyperventilated. Then she finally drew a deep breath. "*Usuratica*. Slut. Kissing in public. How could you do this to us?"

I knew Mocaneata wouldn't have betrayed me to her. It must have been our other bodyguard. He was so different, big, tall, and *bradul*, like a fir tree. It was hard to talk to him. I suspected it was he who'd told my parents about my going to the hotel with Ileana, too.

I summoned my strength to stare directly at her. "Do you want to know what happened? I don't know if we spoke any word. *He took my hand*. There was some music." I looked down. "We saw each other again, tonight."

Mama dropped her voice to a whisper, showing her teeth. "He's a hood. They're gangsters. Do you know who you're getting involved with? Don't you get it? The Ceausescus want us dead. Don't you know?" She'd touched me in anger only once before in my life, so I was truly alarmed when she now shook me by the shoulders.

The first time was many years earlier, when I'd called one of our cooks a whore. I was so young I didn't know what the word meant, but I'd heard it earlier that week in school. The cook was still crying when Mama got back from a late night of work at the newspaper, and, too tired to sort out the niceties of my innocence and justifiably certain of my rudeness, she slapped me in the face. Learning a few days later that I hadn't known the meaning, she was so sorry, but she didn't seem so sorry tonight.

"Oh, and you are very grown up now, with these heels," she said. She looked down at the white pumps I'd picked out myself. "Stand up when I'm talking to you."

I *was* standing.

I stood straight in the doorway and looked defiantly at my inquisitor. What she said next I couldn't believe. Gheorghiu-Dej had just died of cancer, and Valentin's father had seized control of the Central Committee! This was what she was telling me! Why hadn't Valentin mentioned it? I knew only that I'd have to tell her about the kissed look I had on my face. In truth I was glad to have told her.

"Stand up." My mother's chest heaved. "Oh, but you are bad." In the library my father audibly turned a page. I felt disheveled, victorious, tears coming down my face. I stood up but leaned against my right heel. Suddenly–POP. The heel snapped off and I fell against the door frame and gathered myself up.

"You, you…" My mother screamed and raised both fists to hit me just as she passed out and crumpled to our foyer carpet. I watched her left leg disappear under a mahogany table as a calm expression settled onto her features. Her chest rose and fell in shallow little breaths. Papa called a doctor, who came during this lull and said that even though she'd been unconscious for over a half-hour, one in a series of high blood pressure spells, she'd be all right. My father sent me to my room after carrying her, finally roused and screaming again, to her bed.

"I didn't know," I shouted through the walls of my bedroom. "I have done nothing wrong." Why hadn't Valentin told me? I knew he and I shared a disinterest in politics, but wouldn't anyone have casually let slip that his father had been elected First Secretary that day? No. Valentin and I even felt a little awkward that our parents were of high rank. This was already established between us. Maybe it was exactly like him not to mention it.

BUT GHEORGHIU-DEJ dead and replaced by Nicolae!

The rumor mill went into overdrive. Lica and Tanta's furs and jewelry would surely be confiscated! Was it really cancer? Had the KGB "helped" Gheorghiu-Dej to the grave because of his cutting ties with the Soviet Union? Or was Nicolae involved? In the weeks that followed, my mother criticized Valentin only with the television on and water running so that the Securitate–Nicolae's maniacal security force–couldn't hear us.

My father improved on this by never mentioning it at all.

I became a complex person in their eyes, evil-beautiful with a secret. To ensure that Valentin and I stayed apart, they took me away to Neptune for the entire summer, a very long summer, but, oh, for nascent love *degeaba*, did that prove a mistake.

The summer of 1965 was the summer that everybody who was anybody moved to Neptune.

Chapter 5

1965

Waves sound like breaking china

NEPTUNE, on the Black Sea, was made out of nothing. Everything smelled brand new. There were half-finished hotels, red-tile-roofed villas, wonderfully built terraces, wood and concrete gardens, trees, flowers, and beaches with colorful tents where an uninhabited swamp had existed for millions of years. Our comrade architects had been given, for once, a free hand. They'd been told, to their sunken-eyed stupefaction, "Make two dozen villas for senior party members. Make sumptuous hotels for their guests. Make them beautiful."

Here, and nowhere else, Nicolae demanded unbridled creativity, and to a great degree, the architects succeeded. Each private villa had a long portion of sand, doled out like sugar to members of the Central Committee. Every villa had stairs that descended through the gardens to the water. The most important ten or fifteen families had our own villas, with others reserved for visiting foreign guests.

There were theaters, night clubs, swimming pools, and health clubs where you could watch movies, play slot machines. Only

Valentin's family remained ten miles to the north, at Agigea, an old palace that was Gheorghiu-Dej's summer residence on the Black Sea. There were iron bars on his gate, a red roof, and lots of trees. This palace was closer to Techirghiol Lake and its creepy black sapropelic mud, renowned for its curative properties. This summer villa was forever disappearing into the trees.

Some people sunbathed topless at "2 Mai", the Bohemian beach just to the south of us, but I was hotly forbidden this practice before I ever considered doing it. I was the good teenage girl, missing Valentin but in awe of this resort city growing all around me.

Having sulkily acquiesced to my parents' plan, I enjoyed the gardens around our villa, reading, swimming, and taking in sights in moderation with my contented but boring parents, who were, as I liked to say, "not dead, but at rest". There was no way I could see Valentin, nor he me. Or so I thought.

THERE WAS a knock on the door, and Comrade Mocano answered.

I went as well, to see who it was. Valentin!

"What are you doing here?" I whispered.

"I've brought something for your parents." He raised his eyebrows. He looked over Comrade Mocano's shoulder toward the interior of the cabana, past the bar and into the living room, where my parents sat in the half-light like statues hewn from stone.

The shapes moved, and Valentin stepped forward and handed a letter to my father, though it was my mother somehow who opened it.

Valentin shook his bangs out of his eyes and beamed at me while my parents read.

Suddenly my mother hopped up and down as if scalding water had been poured down her back. My father expanded his arms to a great length, like a bird, and then brought his hands together in a thunderous clap.

"What is it?" I said. My heart was pounding. Was it going to be joy, or was it the end of everything?

My mother shook her head furiously. If flames could have flashed from her eyes, they would have. She dove for the telephone.

"*What is it?*" I shouted now as Comrade Mocano melted away.

Mother must have memorized the phone number, because before I even saw her dial she was yelling. She sharply shucked off three or four of the administrators who guarded the First Secretary's line. My father shook his head.

"Is this He?" my mother said coldly, now in control of her anger. "Have you written this? *Your daughter may date my son with the express understanding that your family may expect no additional privileges as a result of their... now or in the future...*"

"Tell me." Nicolae's tinny, unmistakable voice vibrated across the room. "What is the problem? What do you want to say? You need something more to live, or what?"

"We want nothing from you," my mother said. "We're one of the first families, just as you are. There's nothing more we could have. How dare you–"

"Sign the letter and have him return it to me."

My father got out of his chair slowly and started over. I could tell the old pain was back.

"You know what I'll do?" my mother said. "I'll rip up my party card and send your son back with that. He can bring *that* back to you."

Papa caught the telephone receiver as she was slamming it down. He turned from us, spoke a few words to Nicolae, and closed the call. He turned back to Valentin, the muscles in his face relaxed. "You have nothing to do with this," he said.

Valentin seemed unnerved by his warmth, the *crispat*, the movable tension to his mouth. My father could paralyze with this kind of smile.

"When you're with her, you're responsible to me," my father said. "If you hurt her, I'll kill you with my own hands."

He made no further comment and went into the living room to console my mother, leaving us alone.

"How did you walk here?" I was irresponsibly delighted, no matter what the circumstances, to have my boyfriend with me now.

"It's not far."

"It's twenty kilometers at least. You didn't walk along the shore."

"No. I walked along the roads."

"There'll be more trouble, now."

"Won't your parents consent to this, so that we can be together?"

"Would you, the way it's written? It's insulting."

He picked up the letter and scanned it with a handsome but immobile face. Finally, he said, "I'm sorry about this. I didn't know..."

"If you love me, why didn't you think of this?"

"I love you," he said, "and now we can see each other forever." I showed him around the garden, and we walked down into the streets of Neptune until twilight, taking in the sights and watching a movie in an unmarked cinema reserved for the Nomenclatura. Then, on a lark, we went dancing in a club reserved for foreigners only. There, on the dance floor, Securitate members, not recognizing Valentin, dragged us out, ripping the shoulder of my dress.

"We heard you speaking in Romanian. Are you trying to pretend you're Greek?" they said, "or Italian?"

Too proud to show his identification, Valentin glowered at them as they hustled us with four members of the secret police into a Mercedes with a fake Austrian license plate. When they finally realized who we were, they apologized profusely to Valentin and dropped me off. As they drove away, I knew I wouldn't see Valentin again that summer, and I worried that I'd never see him again.

I walked over to the top of the stairs that began the descent to the sea, curled up at the edge, and watched the black waves turn lavender and green as they rose out of the gloaming. The moon for a moment lit up the stairs where I was. Here among the flowers, where no one could see me, either from the beach or from the house, I felt my eyes get salty and large, an ache forming in the center of my chest, caught in the ambiguities of *degeaba*, a concept peculiar to Romania that falls somewhere between "in vain" and "in spite of",

The water of the Black Sea rose up black as oil, glowing with purple and green but never blue, reaching Alpine dizziness before crashing into our beach and draining back with a snaky hiss. Waves were so heavy in Neptune they "broke china". The word to describe them, *sparg*, was the same we used for "smashed dishes". Some night freighters glowed and rose with the swells out beyond me, dark as dolphins. Just the freighters and me now. What if they never let me see him again, ever? I closed my eyes.

BUT I DID see Valentin again, in secret.

Back in Bucharest, our romance continued until one spring afternoon in 1966, when my father was working quietly in his office in the Central Committee. All of a sudden he was surprised to see his telephone flash, indicating a national emergency. Then and there he was worried about us, he told Mama and me that evening, and he was just about to call us when another telephone echoed with a nightmare jangle and an immediate summons to the inner sanctum of Nicolae. He entered Nicolae's office believing the country to be under attack.

Ever the Party loyalist, my father said, "How can I help?"

Chapter 6

Abundance, like want, ruins many

"WE DON'T want your daughter," Nicolae said, staring up at the ceiling and leaning back in his customary fashion, without offering pleasantries or tea. My dad told us the Great *Conducator* had a faraway look and seemed lost in his problems, a glass full of extra-thick red, green, and yellow pencils and a Mont Blanc pen set at the sheer front edge of his desk, his own red-bound volumes of political ideology conspicuously displayed in a bookcase behind him.

Beyond these were many books of Romanian party literature and poems that he could declaim at a moment's notice, whether or not it was appropriate, with heart and passion. Foremost among these favored poets was George Cosbuc. Glinting in front of him was a single glass of Borsec mineral water in a favorite tumbler of Czech crystal placed just ahead of the half-liter bottle itself. Nicolae would only use these tiny bottles with the red and white labels. "Otherwise the gases go out too quickly."

"We don't want your son," my father said. "Especially."

The old enemies agreed on only one thing: Valentin and I must be kept apart. At one point in Nicolae's tirades I was to be sent away to college at state expense, but then he interrupted himself and said, "Why should we send *your* daughter? We should give these privileges to my son, who is charged with greater learning." By fiat it was decided that Valentin would be sent to Imperial College in London to study nuclear physics the next fall. I would stay home and study here at Nicolae Grigorescu College of Fine Arts because I was a simple Bucharest girl. I'd undoubtedly be married and pregnant or dead by the time Valentin finished school, in any case no longer a threat, certainly not his intellectual or social equal. We were officially separated and began a double life where I had to pretend I didn't like him and didn't want to see him. Of course, the more they tried to keep us apart—particularly his mother—the more fascinating he became to me.

WHEN VALENTIN first went away to college in London, She, aglow in fox and mink, accompanied him with a retinue of cooks and aides to ensure a stable transition. ("She's even cutting my toenails," he said to me by telephone deep into the night.) Entering the university at the same time were two other Romanian boys, one the son of a famous scientist, and the other a rising party member himself, both of whom were attending on scholarships from our government in exchange for their watching out for Valentin.

There, in his suite at the Embassy—where he stayed until he was able to find a dormitory—Valentin argued furiously with his mother on my behalf.

"We accept her," Elena lied. "And she'll be in no danger while you're gone. Don't you believe me? I'll call her and meet with her to tell her all of this, the minute I get back. If she behaves and you love her we'll swallow her. As long as you keep up with your studies, we'll be proud of you, son."

This soothed Valentin for a while, but month after month passed without a word arriving from his mother.

Instead, Elena, through her network of Central Committee wives, began a disinformation campaign filled with rumor and innuendo about me that flashed all over the city. Ileana came to me with the astonishing details: *You go out with a lot of boys. You seduced Tinu. You're a disturbed, ill person. You're five years older than Valentin. You even have a slight limp...*

I didn't say anything. Ileana, beautiful as ever, cracked a smile. Then we burst out laughing.

"You sound like Richard III!" she said.

These rumors would have been funnier if they hadn't hurt my mother so much.

I didn't know what would happen to my family, or me, but I knew I was going to see Valentin again, whatever the risk, in spite of Elena's deceptions.

OUR HOUSE in Bucharest had six or seven large telephones which my parents—as did all members of our strata—employed ceaselessly during holidays. Though these observances held no religious significance, they were indispensable as pretexts for periodically touching base with allies. With all the political intrigue and undercurrents, it was important to know who would still take your call.

I learned the trick of imperceptibly leaving all but one of the phones off the hook when I expected a call from Valentin. I always felt a thrill upon hearing his quiet: "It's me." This was done late at night, which was all the more comic because my father, a light sleeper since the *Ilegalitate*–the decade when he and the other communist theorists were persecuted–often woke up without warning due to new medicine and insomnia brought on by his blood condition. Once he even wandered into another room and fell asleep on a couch beside one of these open phones. How delicate it was–it took hours–to ease the connectors back in place.

In any case, these delights were set up in advance in the tiny letters from Valentin that his sister Zoia would bring to me, mostly at one of two places: either under a linden tree across the street from my house, or beside the great green doors at the entrance to our state-maintained garage. The tree location seemed most portentous, as its *tei* flower had a sweet aroma not as strong as jasmine but excellent in tea for coughs, chest problems, rattled nerves. I thought of it as my "calm" tree, where I could have news of Valentin.

Standing there late at night at these rendezvous, Zoia seemed entertained, my friend, alive with the conspiracy. "Buna." She winked. "For you," she said each time, handing me the white squares and patting me on the shoulder. I knew I should destroy them after reading them, but instead I hid the letters in an astronomy book my father had given me when I was twelve. "When I was with the partisans, the stars were always there to guide me through the woods," Papa said. Since I couldn't ask for his advice about Valentin now, I hoped the stars would help me find my way down this treacherous path.

Zoia and Valentin were very close, but they weren't so close to their brother Nicu. He was an intruder in their life, three years younger, while Valentin and his sister were virtual twins–Elena claimed she was still breastfeeding him when Zoia was born. Zoia favored her father in appearance, especially in her nose and in the intensity of her eyes. Even Valentin's lighter eyes had that unnerving power to them, a stare that could chill you in its intensity. It was an unmistakable family trait.

Zoia was quite the collector. She had hundreds of dolls and stuffed animals; she collected old books and paintings. Her mother said, "You collect these things. You buy these from rich doctors, yes? Then if you bring these things here, the sickness from their offices is still in them. They're unhealthy!"

Zoia fell in love with a young man who secreted her away to elope in the mountains, an act of defiance that so enraged Elena she detached a squadron of military helicopters to find them.

The *Hormones* beat the fir trees around their chalet, their infrared sensors peering down chimneys and into picture windows. The airmen considered the information on their digitized heads-up displays: the two warm smudges on the infrared repeaters were Zoia and her boyfriend, the perfect circles in their hands, coffee cups.

There was nothing in the newspapers about this. But talk flashing through secret channels in Bucharest was, "Who is this boy? Exactly who are the many loves of Zoia?"

The truth is, Nicolae and Elena, the very parents who professed so much love for their children, systematically denied them the chance to establish a relationship with anyone.

One of Zoia's boyfriends, a *lingau* who'd gone through our neighborhood inquiring about which daughters of senior officials hadn't yet been engaged, had hit the jackpot and dated her for a while; I didn't know if it was he who'd holed her up in the mountains, where they were hunted down like teenage criminals at huge State expense.

Was it Petre Roman, who certainly dated Zoia and who would grow up to be the first Prime Minister of post-revolutionary Romania? All I knew was that when he dated her, his parents pleaded with him, "Do you want us to end up like Petre Borila's family?"

Her first fiancé, Dan Vinti, simply disappeared.

Her first husband, Dinu, was badly beaten at Bucharest's tramway station and thrown on the rail by the Securitate in an effort to dampen his spirits. Was it he?

AT THESE rendezvous under my "calm" tree, Zoia and I didn't prolong the conversation.

"Pa," she'd say. "Bye."

"Pa," I'd answer and then watch her disappear down Armindenului Street.

And how Valentin spoke to me in these letters! How we loved each other through three years of separation!

"Everywhere it's rain, everywhere it's fear," one letter began. "I am jealous of the sweat drops on your forehead," he wrote, extrapolating our situation into scenes from *Dr Zhivago*, which we'd seen together that first summer in Neptune. He told me what he was doing, what he was learning, what he was thinking about me. And I was thrilled because Valentin kept writing about returning from London to see me during vacations like Christmas 1967, when he and I used decoy escorts in order to see each other at a concert.

I arranged my arrival with an older boy whom I admired but simply used in order to see Valentin. I just walked over to this boy one day and said, "I have tickets to a Rubinstein concert. Do you want to go?" He misunderstood instantly. But then I explained, and we went up the stairs through the fluted granite and marble columns of the enormous new Sala Palatului Concert Hall, sitting under the vaulting shadow of the first balcony so that Valentin and I could be together.

I looked down at the long aisles of people flouncing into dark mustard seats, their scarves and coats settling onto the backs of chairs. Heavy, burnt-orange velvet curtains matched the color of the walls, with brown stairs disappearing on either side of the proscenium. This theater played host to performers from Dalida to Zubin Mehta and was a modern, much larger echo of the earlier architecture of the Palace of the King, which faced another street behind us. There was no presidential box here, so the hall was obviously constructed during the relaxed early days of Gheorghiu-Dej.

I'd never seen the Ceausescus at a cultural event that didn't steam with political undertones, so I didn't worry about seeing them here tonight. Whenever I saw Nicolae and Elena attend any sort of show, their party sat in a restricted area free of microorganisms because they so feared germs from the crowd or performers. They also feared that their clothes were being poisoned during cleaning, the way their friend Fidel Castro swore his were by the CIA. The circle of cleanliness had begun to get smaller and smaller, until only Nicolae and Elena seemed clean. Looking around, I took in the murmur of so many thousands of people. A new building really did make us feel as if we were going somewhere...

"Hello, Dana," Valentin said. I felt a thrill hearing him use my nickname.

"Hello." Instead of letting him bring flowers to me, I brought him tiny bouquets from my mother's garden–tulips this time, one of them dark red, nearly black, along with clippings from a Japanese bush. I couldn't stop myself. He was embarrassed–a man receiving flowers–and didn't know what to do with them. He swung them heads-down at the floor and then scrunched them into his inside lapel pocket.

His clothes were considerably different, as was his newly adopted London manner. Whereas formerly he'd worn only sharply pointed black shoes like the other boys, he now wore round-toed boots in tan suede, a closely cut suit, and had much longer hair, something his father had outlawed in Bucharest for everyone but his own son. My God, he was handsome.

"Dana," he said.

"Yes?"

"Try not to let your gorgeous lips move, though they're all I can think about. My mother would kill us if she knew we were talking together."

It was disconcerting that he brought mothers into the conversation. "My mother would kill us first," I said.

People around us were chatting, though, and pointing to someone they thought was Rubinstein's wife, Aniela Mlynarski, sitting twenty rows ahead of us and wearing a simple black cape. A man beside us criticized the pianist, but Valentin said he was a genius, that his reputation as a cosmopolitan socialite was undeserved. "He served as a military interpreter in World War I," he said, mixing some sophisticated English idioms into his speech. Valentin went on to talk about the sensation Rubinstein created in Spain in 1916 and his support of the Soviet regime just as the virtuoso began with Chopin's Étude Opus 10, No. 11. Next, Rubinstein played works by Manuel de Falla and Enrique Granados. In the hush that fell over the crowd, we did indeed feel as if we were in the "Paris of the East".

At *pauza*, intermission, we walked in the hubbub past the refreshment table on the second floor while other members of the audience purchased sandwiches from the white-linen buffet featuring a red caviar named Icre de Manciuria and snowy white bread. If you ate black bread in Romania you were considered *déclassé*. I craved it.

There were also little ham sandwiches enlivened by our famous Sibiu salami, but Valentin and I skipped these, disappeared into one of the Sala Palatului's many inviting recesses, and fell into a whisper.

"Can you see me tonight?"

"I'm afraid."

"It's only you and your mind and your family's mind," he said. He wouldn't acknowledge we were being followed and monitored by the Securitate. In front of us the attendant was expressing carbonated water into syrups of different color to produce soda pop.

"I love you."

"I love you."

We sat down together, unrecognized by the crowds of people splashing applause as the Romanian Symphony Orchestra launched into something quite ambitious by Albeniz.

But still he didn't dare touch me.

It was delicious, prohibited. What could have been more exciting than doing something forbidden by all of Romania–me and this "little prince" who in London could possibly learn how to make our first nuclear bomb? With the gilded curtains of the concert hall as a backdrop, I dreamed of this strange boy putting his mouth on mine. Folding half of his raincoat over me, he smothered me with a deeper kiss, my face nearly covered from view. But, returning the kisses, I couldn't help but feel anxious, for weren't we in great danger from the disapproval of the Central Committee and their wives?

Recovered from my reverie, I considered my love sitting beside me, our hands not even touching. Could Valentin ever understand what I was going through to be with him?

We were able to steal a few more precious rendezvous before he returned to London. My loneliness made the winter days seem extra cold and bleak.

"YOU are destroying your family," my mother screamed at me whenever rumors reached her of my secret ways of keeping close to Valentin. She did this for weeks, for months, until one time, with my face hot, I said, "Mother, I don't love him anymore. I'm seeing someone else."

"Who is this?"

"Vasilescu, Gheorghe."

"Honestly? You wouldn't lie to your loving mother, would you?" The greatest smile of relief spread over her face. Now, with this assurance, she knew it was all over, this fear, this hiding. "Finally!" she said. "No more Ceausescus! Word will get out about this new love." She kissed me. "I'm sorry about how difficult I've been," she said. "With your proper conduct and Papa's irregular heartbeat settling down, he will flourish and we'll be safe and sound again."

THAT SPRING, all I could think about was Valentin's promised summer return. Just as I hoped, it was everything he'd described in his letters; we managed to steal some secret moments every day.

We rode separately in friends' cars, ostensibly on dates with them, and then got together, shifting to the small saffron-colored Romanian-built Dacia that Valentin had waiting. In the stultifying July heat, our destination turned out to be Lake Snagov.

Without registering anywhere, we picnicked out of the car, and then, with much conversation about our love, entered the lake.

I was so dull, wearing an old-fashioned bathing suit of cream and faded green cotton with a pleated skirt, while Valentin wore something brighter from London, very tight and revealing. With the warm lake water up to our necks, we saw the poplars and oaks along the shore, along with the *stuf*, long reeds and cattails, and wonderful Asian water lilies that state botanists had imported for the lake—water lilies with bright pink flowers the size of ripe avocados.

It was here that Valentin came nearer me. In the water.

He came nearer and nearer and folded me into his arms.

It was silly of me, but in spite of my joy I found myself crying at this nearness, shivering. I held him so hard with my legs and arms that he seemed very moved and closed his eyes, too. We dressed quickly with shame and exultation and spoke very little on the way to the outskirts of the city, where I took a taxi to the other side of the park, then walked alone with my wet hair to the green gate of our front garden.

"You lied to me. You're seeing him again," my mother said in the doorway.

I still thought of the summer water lilies as she continued her tirade.

"You act like two dogs in heat. How dare you kiss where anyone can see?" she said at dinner that night. "What are you doing to us? This is something that must be very private—and not with him."

How could this old anarchist be surprised? Didn't she have her own sexual revolution when she was young? I'd heard the story of one of my parents' friends, a young man who'd had sexual problems with his young wife during the *Ilegalitate*, and all his friends gave him their wives for a night, with everyone consenting, to help restore his potency.

That was barbarous, immoral, perhaps a step beyond our young love, though I was too jarred by my mother's attack to tell her of this inconsistency in her logic.

VALENTIN returned to London and I continued with my studies. Then, ironically, I was sent to London with my father when he became seriously ill with heart trouble and needed treatment by world-renowned English specialists, just as Valentin was returning from school for another vacation. I barely had time to let him know about it on the telephone.

Our planes must have passed in the air.

Glum but excited about my father's prospects for a recovery, I joined him in a taxi from Heathrow Airport to the Romanian Embassy, where my father was entitled to the VIP guest suites.

The Embassy was a landmark building in London, close to Harrods department store in the center of the shopping district. Very old chestnut trees and webs of ivy crawled over this venerable Victorian town house, its great bay windows opening onto busy London streets alive with cabs and dark-suited members of the diplomatic corps grasping umbrellas and attaches.

Even more than Romanians, with our superstitions and traditional dress, the English behaved like costumed extras in a period movie. This tickled me because English people I'd met always made fun of us for being so "melodramatic". Wherever we went, once they found out where we were from, all anyone wanted to talk about was "Count Dracula", as they called him, and his Castle Bran in the mountains of Transylvania.

Castle Bran was actually the home of the one we knew as Vlad Dracula the Impaler, who warded off the Turks in the summer of 1462 during battles in Targoviste and Poienari. Yes, Dracula terrorized the hordes led by invading sultans by creating a wall made of 20,000 of their skulls. Yes, he skinned promiscuous maidens alive as a warning. He was a beastly madman, but blood sucking was a Western fantasy. We were all sure it took the repressed sexuality of British readers to set Irish writer Bram Stoker's pen in motion.

Late that night, we settled into the Embassy, with its great palms and lobby and Chippendale antiques, its too many serious clocks and teletype machines and enormous computers processing second-hand satellite information bounced off the Soviet troposphere. Dining-room pipe smoke mushroomed above the blue Wedgwood Embassy plate, and Romanian foreign service executives scurried around my father as we planned our itinerary.

The next morning, my father checked into the hospital as an out-patient while I telephoned home on an international Telex net. I could take lunch at the Embassy, hit the stripes and polka dots of Carnaby Street, and then put some finishing touches on my art history thesis, "Still Life in Romanian Painting", in the stacks of the Tate Gallery all afternoon before returning to pick up my father in an Embassy limousine.

During the following weeks there were blood tests and consultations, some of them linked up with Romanian specialists who'd be administering the follow-up treatment.

Though this sounded grand, this was nothing. Everyone in the Nomenclatura used foreign medicine almost exclusively. Among other things, it was the number one pretext for travel.

Aides-de-camp at the Embassy kept my father in touch with departmental happenings that came in on the wire, as well as sensitive national events.

Everything went according to plan until the 21st of August. It was 2am, and my father was sleeping soundly in his adjoining bedroom at the Embassy VIP Quarters when Ambassador Vasile Pungan woke us up with a yellow teletype sheet in his hands, marked Secret.

"Come back immediately," it instructed my father. "There is a national emergency."

"What could this mean?" I asked. Three more officials crowded upon the Turkish carpet and told us. Prague was flooded with tanks, students were dying, Nicolae was flying to Belgrade to confer with Tito. This, from our unlikely post in London, was our window on the Soviet Incursion of Czechoslovakia in 1968.

People flew around the office.

An aide took the liberty of packing our bags and briefed my father on his itinerary. Everywhere there were screens filled with Czech first secretary Alexander Dubček's face amid a crowd of sycophantic apparatchiks and young party intellectuals. He'd faced down Brezhnev and the Soviet Politburo. Now tanks were in the streets and Dubček, Cernik, and Smrkovsky had been kidnapped from their country and taken to Moscow.

Czechoslovakia was, for the moment, a decapitated nation disintegrating almost instantly back into the ancient cultural lines of Bohemia and Moravia, but an interim government was taking over and would continue with the 14th Communist Party Congress that the Soviets so feared. Women and children removed road signs everywhere so the Soviet troops would get lost, while men and boys threw themselves in front of the tanks directly, individual acts of resistance that culminated in the gripping suicide of the student Jan Palach, who burned himself alive in front of the cameras to protest all obstacles to Czech independence.

This young boy on fire, who looked quite a bit like Valentin with his dark long hair and long black coat, the flames audibly crackling in the jostle of cameras, was the shot heard round the Eastern Bloc. I didn't know what freedom had to do with fire, but seeing this boy, it changed all of my friends. It created our generation. I knew, seeing this, we'd never be the same.

So where did this leave my father?

It was true that, like all the other old-guard communists, he disapproved of the "crafty" way Dubček rose through his party apparat nearly to overthrow Antonín Novotný in a *coup de palais*. Acquaintances of my father in Czechoslovakia's Central Committee committed suicide because of the pressure Dubček brought to bear on them, humiliating them publicly because of their stance against "socialism with a human face".

But my father was a thoughtful man, respectful of pure party organization but not hostile to reform. He'd told me on the plane to London there was some merit to the "Two Thousand Words" which had started so much unrest the month before, a widely republished essay from Prague's *Literární Listy* that insisted upon a rapid departure to a form of near-democracy. But he was that unthinkable being–a "sentimental communist", an ideas person who'd never been quite comfortable when barefoot communism left the woods and came into the cities.

Like a lot of us, I think, he hadn't quite made up his mind except to say, very strongly, that, "You should never send tanks to resolve such a problem."

My heart broke when I looked at him now.

"He can't move!" I said. He was still in his bed, his face ashen. He hadn't had a good night. With two envoys standing over him, he read the dispatch.

"You are not to make comment to the world press. You are to proceed immediately to the Central Committee and report to the First Secretary's Office."

Papa's eyebrows rose. Was Nicolae suggesting that because he'd been schooled in Moscow on the pre-war brand of communism that was the fount of inspiration for international revolutionaries such as Ho Chi Minh, because he'd known Stalin as well as Novotný and Tito and served as a partisan for the Soviet Union, my father was now capable of denouncing Bucharest's strong reaction against the Soviets' invading Czechoslovakia?

Nothing could have been further from the truth.

But this was a masterstroke of bureaucratic maneuvering, to imply he was so pro-Soviet that he posed a danger to the state in this foreign capital of London, and by the looks these young officials were giving him, Nicolae's deception had worked.

Yes, Nicolae had taken the time to hurt him by suggesting he'd deliberately gone to London to put himself out of reach at a critical time, even though Nicolae had "bigger fish to fry".

For how could my father go back? How could he not go back? If he didn't, he was a traitor. If he did, his health would be jeopardized.

He struggled to his feet and began getting his things together. In the lobby and in the covert operations rooms, black and white televisions showed crowds of dark-coated students, guns, tanks wheeling and stopped by thousands of shouting people alternately threatening and running.

I telephoned my mother, and upon hearing of our premature return, she said, "This will kill him, Dana." The line crackled with static. "They're stopping his treatment."

Before 7am on August 23, 1968, we were in a Romanian civil Tarom jet aircraft with the Alps in view below us. I could trace the Rhine for a while, and then I absently paged through a newspaper.

My father was asleep, a bag of medicines beside him. His attending physicians were learning just now that their patient had disappeared. I imagined their shrugging shoulders.

Upon landing, we found the city thronged with people, mostly students shouting support for Nicolae and Tito, who'd by then issued their denunciation of the Soviet action. This was the best thing Nicolae ever did, maybe one of the bravest things ever done against the shadow of the Soviet Regime by a single person, and it rekindled the pride of our nation. It set our sights, for the moment, on freedom.

Now, with this show of bravery against the Soviets, even I was proud to be from the same country as Nicolae, though this pride was tempered by my hatred for what he was doing to my father.

The black sedan was waiting for us, to take Papa home like a political prisoner. I kept my head beside his the whole drive through Herastrau. His breath had a funny rattle to it, and I attended to his every syllable in case he lost consciousness, wanting to be able to report on his last words to my mother, who was already fielding telephone calls when we walked in the door.

"What was he doing in London when we needed him most?" her "friends" asked her.

"What sort of Romanian is he, to run to the critical ears of the foreign press?"

"Lies. He was there only for medical treatment!" she said.

In the silence that followed, my mother heard the unspoken words, "Will he now go to the Soviet Union? Your life is about to change, Ecaterina."

A FEW days into this barrage of questions, my father pulled himself out of bed and tried to confront Nicolae directly at work. Later that evening he came home, and in answer to our questions said quietly, "There's no problem. It's a misunderstanding. It will all be cleared up later."

His eyes lied. He hadn't been admitted to see Nicolae, though he'd visited a number of senior party members supporting his innocence. Though he was very ill, he forced himself to seem unusually alive and with glowing words told us he still retained enough influence to make his peers see the truth.

My mother hyperventilated, gripping the back of a chair. "You *will* see Nicolae."

She directed my father's answers with her stare.

"Yes."

Because of this promise to my mother, Papa would have his showdown with Nicolae, who wouldn't even bother pretending to listen. What kind of quixotic bout could it have been by now, anyway? No ruler in the world was hotter than Ceausescu. Spontaneous crowds assembled in the squares and along the paths of Nicolae's motorcades to cheer him. News outlets around the world were taking notice.

"Everything is wonderful," Papa kept saying.

But I couldn't think of politics. Where was Valentin? Was I bedazzled with the new world that was making my parents obsolete?

Students were on fire, my parents were being "disappeared", and I was in love.

With crowds outside our house, cheering, I reached Valentin by phone.

We had our own codes by now. Just as the Securitate called Nicolae's house "the old oak tree" and his presidential helicopters "the hawk" or "the eagle" in their private communications, so had we encrypted our favorite meeting places.

If I told a friend I wanted to meet my friend Gheorghe at the Art Museum, it meant I'd be waiting for Valentin at the base of some thousand-year-old trees near Baneasa on the outskirts of Bucharest at noon. I'd watch him drive up amid the towering, cathedral-like trees and run to him.

It was as if we rode in two separate trains headed for the same destination. And that destination now, according to Valentin, was marriage.

He returned to London to complete his studies.

I waited for him, writing him, loving him in secret all through 1969. In fact, my mother became totally convinced Valentin and I had broken it off when—just before he was to return after graduating in the summer of 1970–some of her friends told her about a cover story in *Paris Match* linking Valentin with one of the daughters of King Michael. The story went that they'd met in Africa on safari and fallen in love. "Look," the women said, "here are pictures of the two of them barefoot, with Valentin sporting a daisy between his toes." People were forever speculating about liaisons between communists and disaffected royalty and celebrities throughout Europe; *Paris Match* fanned the flames.

Dating non-communists was ideologically forbidden to us, but it was often overlooked because it was so glamorous. I just knew it couldn't have happened in Valentin's case. Our wedding was just two weeks away, and he laughed when I asked him about the *Match* article. I didn't believe this intrigue with King Michael's daughter ever happened. Talking to my beloved, I could hear the authentic intonations of passion in his voice–inexperienced as I was, there were some things I knew. On the eve of our wedding, barely a few days after Valentin had come home from London, I summoned the courage to tell my mother the truth.

"WHAT? What? You're destroying yourself and destroying your family!" My mother strode back and forth between two windows. The way she walked with so much stateliness, people called her "captain". She made two fists and pulled tiny spindles of hair from her scalp. It was beautiful silver-white hair, very straight. For the first time in my life I saw her cry. My father, on the other side of the wall, said nothing. Mama stopped short. She raised her hand as if to hit me but instead hissed right in my face. "How can you do this? How can you be so cruel? You are leaving this family to become Lucifer's daughter."

"I love him, Mama."

"You were always the trusted one. When you were young, grandmother let you, and you alone, cut carrots on the parquet floor. You were so beautiful, my only daughter. Don't you see this?"

She pointed to a bust of me in my early teens. A patriotic young sculptress had stopped my mother and me during a concert and asked if I could pose. This took weeks and was the scandal of the school, with other girls calling me "tramp" and asking who did I think I was. But it was chaste, showing my long braid descending down my back and my eyes set upon an idealized romantic future, the perfect young comrade.

After the exhibition, a cast of it was given to my mother, and she treasured it because it would never meet boys and defy her. It showed what I should have been, glinting in the half-light of her study. How I despised it!

When I was a good girl, she put it on the mantelpiece, and when I was naughty, I'd find it outdoors on the terrace or in the basement. "And now," my mother said, warming up, "you deceive us in the guise of love. Do you know what love is? How do you intend to make a living? Do you intend to cross over to his family, to become a Ceausescu?"

"His family doesn't want me. Please be happy for us, Mama."

WE told a few close friends we were getting married, and they were delighted—and afraid. "Are you sure?" they said. "Do you know what you're doing? Aren't you dreaming of green horses on the wall—impossible things?"

"We love each other."

"But do you know what's going to happen to you?"

Whatever it was, it happened all of a sudden. When we went to Elias Hospital for a blood test, the officials were afraid to do anything.

"Do you have permission?" they asked, trembling at the ID card Valentin gave them.

"What permission would I need? *Sint major si vaccinat.* We're twenty-one. We've had our shots." He fixed his eyes into the stare.

They gave us the little white card certifying our health.

VALENTIN'S youngest uncle, Ion Ceausescu, came to our wedding, as did his grandmother, Mama Mare. Nicu and his girlfriend Donca came too, along with Ileana and a few others. Our wedding rings were made from some gold chains I'd bought in Venice while staying at a *pensione* during a vacation with my parents—chains we'd had a friend melt down and recast in order to avoid a jeweler's questions. The resulting rings bore the intertwined symbols I&V on them, for Iordana and Valentin.

Getting married was more a civic function than a romantic transformation. We weren't married in a church because we were still good comrades; the state ceremony was conducted by a magistrate. I had no wedding dress but instead wore something turquoise with white dots while Zoia came in a state of nervous excitement, all in white, as if it were her wedding.

"Why are you afraid?" Valentin asked me.

"I don't know." I took his hand.

The absence of our parents cast a cold shadow over the ceremony. We drove off in Valentin's new mallard-green Triumph sports coupe, but upon checking area hotels for rooms found there was nowhere we could stay. Hotel manager after hotel manager looked at Valentin and shook his head.

Valentin shrugged it off, but I was nonplussed.

Didn't I feel an occult excitement at being "that" woman? I had dark glasses, my hair was shoulder-length and modern, and my husband was handsome and newly bearded.

I wanted to feel like Princess Grace, but, considering my prospective "mother of all mother-in-laws", I was beginning to feel a bit more like Anna Karenina. Most of all, in spite of my adult decision to marry, the little girl with the long braid was there with me, too. I loved this boy.

"We have nothing to worry about, Dana," Valentin said. "We are young and we have the music."

In the end we drove into the far reaches of kilometer-square Herastrau Park and fell asleep in the car, my head in his arms, the lights of our parents' homes visible with those of the other senior officials, flickering through the trees at the opposite side.

Chapter 7

*You are walking around
with the painted crow*

B ECOMING a Ceausescu was like stepping through an invisible membrane of fear, though in my happiness I was barely conscious of it. Like my country, I tried to ignore the evidence of trouble all around me.

Everyone had some advice.

My English teacher said, "If they ever invite you and give you a glass of wine, please try not to drink it. You'll never know what it contains."

"You should go to Elena, get down on your knees, beg for the safety of your family, and never dare to cross her again," a party official told my mother.

Our marriage occurred without any mention in any newspapers, according to the long-standing practice of not allowing information about the lives of the Nomenclatura into the hands of the public.

Instead, following Elena's instructions, officials of the Gospodaria-de-Partid, which handled billeting for the inner circle of senior officials and their families, presented us with a Faustian choice between two places to live—one cooled by the immediate proximity of his mother near the Primaverii, in a better building approved for young couples and pensioners of the Nomenclatura to stay, a place where one could court favor, and another on the far outskirts of the city in a shabby apartment building where clerks and scriveners and tradesmen lived.

It was one of those modern Romanian blocks, the bare apartments so small one couldn't move in them, filled with gloomy lives, clanky plumbing, and reduced prospects—Bucharest's Siberia.

Full of love for each other and a desire for freedom from his parents, we decided together to choose this last place, hoping it would mean a fresh start for us.

Shortly after we were married, Valentin went to see his mother while I went to see my father, to check on his health. "Now that you've done it, you're still my daughter," he said with a warm smile. "I wish you every happiness. Nothing's changed. And he's our son now."

My mother wasn't so friendly and refused to look me in the eyes. The minutes dripped by until Valentin arrived outside to pick me up. Here in the tiny cockpit of his Triumph, he held a box toward me in the darkness.

"What's this?"

"Want a chocolate?"

I kissed him intimately. "You bought these for me?" I said, thinking of my father's souvenirs.

"When I was leaving, my mother told me, 'take them with you.'"

"Did she ask about me?" I flirted with him. "Did she tell you to give them to me?"

"No."

I looked out the window at three speckled pigeons being fed on a bench by an old man. One of them flew away. "Then you shouldn't have taken them," I said. "I don't want anything from her unless she really accepts us."

"Come on, try it." He held out a little piece of Belgian chocolate. I was already a little put out that Valentin had seen his parents twice now in the first week of our marriage. With my forehead getting hot, I glared at him.

"What is this? Am I from Biafra? She gives me these things while she's so busy destroying my father?"

He shrugged. "We might as well accept a wedding present, if it's good chocolate."

I shook my hair.

"Why can't you understand she's just a mother doing what mothers do, giving her son a box of chocolate?" Valentin said.

I wanted to send the chocolates back, but wouldn't they explode into more trouble if I dared to do that? It seemed so subtle—with this tiny "present", I could no longer be myself. I kept absolutely silent as my beautiful, easygoing husband drove me across town. Maybe I'd overreacted, maybe he was naive. Was I cornered already? Whatever I decided, it might hurt somebody. Still, how could a box of chocolates possibly hurt me? After all, wasn't everything a matter of degree? Calm yourself. Laugh.

The worst thing would be to act neurotic about things. Enemies of the state were always portrayed as "insane" before they were locked up.

Sure, it was nothing.

Running up to the seventh floor of our eleven-story building, we rejoiced upon returning to our tiny, unfurnished flat. There was no bed even in the bedroom, but that was all right, because it didn't look as if there were room for one.

I hugged Valentin as he unlocked the door. But upon seeing it swing open, we were shocked to find the apartment was now fully furnished. Oh, it wasn't much, a bed, nightstand, a chest of drawers, and a refrigerator of the simplest kind, but "What kind of a present is it when the giver breaks into your house to give it to you?" I asked Valentin.

He shrugged and told me of a loving mother. "She used to chase me around with her bedroom slippers, slapping me if I didn't get the highest grades. She loves Zoia, me, Nicu. She's just a *mother*."

"It's just that few mothers in history have had their every wish granted."

"Can't you be happy with the way she is? These are nothing, just gifts. It could be much worse. What is just a wave will pass like a wave."

BUT the waves didn't pass. From that time onward I never felt there was such a thing as a locked door. It was certain that Elena was telling us, with these gifts, that we could make no movement without her approval, even here, and now I began to agree with my friends that we were being monitored day and night and insisted that we walk into the little park at the foot of our building whenever we wished to talk about something in private.

Elena had given us those two choices in apartments–a clearly outlined dilemma–while my mother offered no suggestions, advice, or help for the she-devil of a daughter who'd put her family in danger. Having survived the Stalinist experience, she knew she and my father could be banished easily enough, or simply "disappeared".

She cried whenever she saw me, and I couldn't comfort her, even when I tried to tell her I loved her.

For many years she'd collected things in an old fruitwood hope chest for her good daughter, delicate fabrics and laces of great sentiment for my family, and she made a point now of declining to offer them to me. "They will be given to you one day when you are eventually married to your true husband."

"I don't want anything from you if you can't acknowledge me as a married woman," I said, though in all things my mother had been my best friend until now, and I had no intention of abandoning her.

In the end, my wedding presents were nothing from my parents; two pots, two plates, two soup bowls, and two white coffee cups with pink roses on them from my old Nanny; six dessert plates from a friend, Ana; and two old pillows, a coffee service for six, and a garbage can from an aunt–stones from which to make a soup out of our new life.

Valentin laughed it off and immediately secured a position as a physicist at the Institutul de Fizica Atomica for a monthly salary of 1,400 lei, where he would work and simultaneously train for his doctorate. The Wrangler blue jeans we liked to wear were worth 1,000 lei apiece at an exchange rate of just over six lei per US dollar on the black market, so we had to be careful with our money.

Actually, I was excited about the idea of thrift. The only way to be free of the Nomenclatura was to escape their influence, and that meant going without money. Or so I thought.

Having graduated third in my class, I managed, with my art history degree and a swap with another girl who'd coveted my draw of a position offered in Constanta, to get a job for 900 lei a month as a guide at the *Muzeul de Arta Al Republicii Socialiste Romania*, our national museum of art showcased in King Carol's old brownstone palace. I remember how proud I felt when security issued me my entrance passes for the museum as well as a lecture on how important it was to keep these new papers ready for presentation at all times. Securitate officials reminded me that our national art collection was housed in the same palace where members of the Central Committee met to discuss state secrets, so our location was very sensitive. I was to lecture to groups of travelers and children about the Romanian Collection. I would visit museums in other cities as well as make presentations to factories and deputations from other towns. Otherwise, I was to mind my own business.

EACH night, I came back to our little apartment and clacked around with my old china, waiting for my nuclear physicist to come back, kiss me gently on the forehead, change into tennis clothes, and, perhaps a little too often, disappear out the door.

This was nothing. He was an exciting, tender, and attentive lover and devoted to me in his own way, but he loved his many friends and never thought to ask if it were all right to see them at any given time.

Besides, once he got caught up in the mysteries of his studies, which he conducted in a restricted building in a wooded enclave called Magurele on the outskirts of Bucharest, he spent more time at work than with his friends, returning late at night with a mushroom pallor to his face and tired eyes.

"I can't tell you about it," he said, but then he told me about it anyway. We were never so close as when we talked about nuclear physics.

One dark evening, when he saw me furrow my brow and quickly light up a Snagov from his glowing Pall Mall, he laughed. "There is no radiation. We work with ideas. The plutonium is three buildings away, and the gaseous diffusion plant where it's purified is miles away from us. Besides," he waved his hand, "it takes over 100 years for just a gram of radium to make enough heat to boil a cup of water for tea. Look!" He held aloft one of my Nanny's very plain teacups and threw me a dazzling grin.

I looked down and felt happy I was married to this reassuring man. Turning back to our gas stove, I gave a stir to our soup of sour cream and breadcrumbs, a few vivacious chunks of beef and cabbage thickening the mixture.

Blacklisted from Nomenclatura privileges, we sometimes had to wait for an hour at the little *Alimentara* grocery store across the street for delights like these, sometimes just five minutes. Romania was rich now in the early 1970s, so with a little patience, anyone could get simple meats without food coupons, as well as soft Chinese toilet paper in any color, condoms in boxes with three butterflies on them, quail eggs, and chocolate truffles.

My husband loved expensive food but enjoyed our simple dishes just as well: potatoes, eggs, consommé, perhaps a tube of pork. For lunches I made us ham and bologna sandwiches, and then we'd disappear down the stairs of our flat together for our separate destinations. I went by bus to work and back, enjoying traveling with my neighborhood friends.

On other nights Valentin practiced speeches, and he asked me to make suggestions as he bolstered his talks with scientific and humanistic insights. He quoted everyone from Sir JJ Thompson, who discovered the electron, and Lord Rutherford, who discovered the proton, to Fermi and Oppenheimer, even Bob Dylan for comic relief. One week he was playing around with Einstein's 1934 line, "It's like trying to shoot birds in the dark in a country where there are not many birds in the sky," aptly applying it to his own work and Romania's efforts at this time.

Valentin was the kind of genius who made hard work fun. He was often sent abroad for research, and every summer physicists from all over the world came for a conference he helped host in Brasov. His father allowed these conferences but in actuality felt they were a waste of time. Like all good communists, he believed in his heart that the only true way to one's knowledge of nuclear physics was through good old-fashioned espionage.

Where could we have gotten our uranium and plutonium isotopes? Where did the Soviet Union and the US get theirs? At one time the chief source for such materials, even for the US, was ostensibly neutral Canada, from the Eldorado pitchblende excavations at the bottom of the polar cap.

That's not to say that we got them there, for we have mines of our own. The Soviets took mountains of uranium from us after World War II by claiming that the richest of our uranium-rich regions were still pro-Nazi. Requisitioning the land and ore from entire Transylvanian villages, they made prisoners of the mountain people living there and forced them to transport it from our northwest regions to their Caucasus. Oh, we were such bad people, working with the Axis powers and then switching to the Allies when it was politically expedient—or so the myth went.

We had a great supply of uranium in a very crude form right here at home. The problem was, with the exception of the CANDU plant in Canada, all the existing international plants needed a much more refined form of uranium. Ceausescu's greatest dream was for his engineers to design plants using stolen Canadian technology that would refine Romania's naturally cruder form of uranium which could then be marketed all over the world. Nicolae himself cared nothing for nuclear power, especially since we had all the oil we could ever use. He desired instead to be an exporter, the envy of all communist countries, but this was not to be a dream fulfilled.

In the meantime, there were ways to acquire the refined uranium we lacked through a number of sinuous paths. In some cases Middle Easterners and Pakistanis were the intermediaries for such materials, at other times Americans. I didn't exactly know where our terrible materials came from, just simply that they were here in a secret laboratory in Bucharest and registered, as were China's, India's, and Israel's, with the World Institute of Plutonium Control in Vienna.

In fact, it was a bit more difficult getting the boron steel or cadmium needed to make control rods to reduce the speed of the neutrons than it was to get these radioactive base materials. Impurities were a problem as well, though Valentin once frowned and asked me, "What form of energy isn't dirty? Besides, only forty percent of our work is for the military. I'm a theorist only."

I laughed. "I worry about you."

Later that evening, looking up from my book, I realized Valentin was so excited about his research he was talking to himself. "You and your atoms," I said.

"What do you mean? This isn't just a description of subatomic particles," he said with a spangle of perspiration on his brow that made me love him. "It's a description of physical reality. There are moments when time, energy, and motion become almost the same thing. Dana, can you believe this?"

These were fascinating ideas to be pouring coffee in the background to.

"Do you feel the Soviets should have the only bomb?" one of Valentin's friends said in the apartment another time. "Look how they treat our Navy. They authorize us only the use of their outmoded diesel-electric Romeo-class submarines, and only two at that. Diesel-electric, when we have some of the finest minds in Europe. Does it make you feel safe when you're treated with this condescension? They're still laughing at us for sinking the *Krab*."

It was one of our national embarrassments that in the 1930s, the Soviet Union gave our Romanian sailors an experimental mine-countermeasures submarine, the *Krab*, which we promptly sank in the Black Sea, the entire crew drowning. In negotiations with Moscow for more technology, this tragedy, this old "joke", regularly came up. Our military men since the *Krab* had to overcome the belief that our science, even our culture, was second-rate. I think the motivating strength behind Valentin's studies was more national pride than national defense.

He and his friends were an elite cadre of young men and women who went about their duties like Robin Hood and his Merry Men, long-haired, smoking, and good-natured, joking with the innocence and naiveté that intellectuals have the arrogance to foist upon their loved ones. The big block at that time was the lack of a perfect vacuum. There was a lot of talk about the vacuums needed for their pressurized isolation experiments–vacuums that they were unsuccessful in getting above 45 million inches of mercury, another embarrassment.

The pursuit of these vacuums was sexy to them, more interesting sometimes than their young spouses. But I understood. For the moment, I was a contented Maid Marian, though there was no roentgen identification badge to check on the nightstand every once in a while to make me happy to find his levels well within normal limits. He never worried. He was popular for having disdain for the political life, and he was known in Bucharest as a maverick who'd had the integrity to stand up to his parents when he needed to. Moreover, it was widely known in Bucharest that, in spite of his many published papers, he refused the ridiculous promotions his superiors begged him to accept so that they could please his parents and therefore earn more funding for research from the Central Committee, a decision I supported with relief.

His parents dismissed him as a dreamer and turned to his younger brother, Nicu, as a more malleable subject. Nicu, it seemed, could be groomed to step up to govern the next generation of communist royalty. Nicu was attending the right university as well, the one here in Romania designed for statesmen, diplomats, soldiers, and plunderers, the Academia De Stiinte Economice Si Sociale Stefan Gheorghiu.

IN SPITE OF this, my happiness began to be complicated by anxiety. When did it start?

Perhaps the fear crystallized with a telephone call.

"Mrs Ceausescu?"

"Hello?" Valentin was in a corner chair, reading. Our telephone number was a new, unlisted one, so I was surprised, as I hadn't anticipated any calls from the few who knew it.

A strange voice hissed into my ear:

"You monitor me through the window with a laser. You want to read my mind," a woman said.

I just hung up.

Then she called back and said, "Why do you want to hurt me? What have I done to you?"

I didn't know what to say.

She called again a few days later, ranting. Her voice was sharp, urbane, her language not a country tongue. When you tell a lie, you're speaking *iordane*. She called me *Iordane*, a pun on my name, and suggested I was married to Nicu. "You Ceausescus rape through windows with lasers, you daughter of a dirty shoemaker."

The calls continued for weeks, even though I complained to the phone center, so finally Valentin called the Securitate at the Primaverii.

"It's going to take months to trace her because we think she works at the phone division. The calls were coming from within the system. But don't take her seriously," the Securitate representative said, using the usual refrain—we had no dissidents or criminals in Nicolae's Romania, only "crazy people".

The caller began to come to our apartment and bang on the door, making a lot of noise, so they finally caught her. Her threats and hatred of the Ceausescus and our having to turn to the Securitate for help symbolized to me the impossibility of a quiet and anonymous life.

I saw the Securitate at my work as well.

Agents supervised our museum. They just appeared and discussed "problems" with the director. They passed through our offices and tried to be friendly, but somehow their very friendliness made us feel as if we'd done something vaguely traitorous. I don't even know how we knew they were from the Securitate, we just knew.

"How is work?" asked a tall, sophisticated, devastatingly handsome man in his thirties one dreary Wednesday. All the women stopped what they were doing.

I just smiled and nodded. He kept walking, which strangely disappointed me. Wasn't I in charge of the office?

"Do you have a minute?" He turned to Doina, who was sitting behind me.

The rest of us looked at each other, then hurried on with our work. Doina followed him into the hall, where we first heard laughter, then low voices through our open door.

We heard the click of another door shutting as the movie-star-like Securitate leader entered another office, leaving my friend standing alone.

"What did he say?" we asked when she returned to her desk.

Doina shrugged her shoulders and tried to smile. "To be on alert, for people like you."

"Come on, tell us every word he said."

"He asked about the exhibition, that's all... and not to forget to make our reports after the Italian delegation leaves."

"Okay, sure," we said. Case closed. Whenever foreigners came to the museum, we were required to write reports on what they asked to see, what they'd said, and what we talked to them about. We weren't allowed to collaborate on these reports, supposedly so they could be cross-checked for accuracy, but we knew it was really to see if they agreed.

Doina coughed. "And... not to rent my house to foreigners anymore." I saw color rise to her cheeks. She settled into her chair and leaned her head on her Olympia manual typewriter.

No one said anything. Psychological terror is the sword of Damocles. It just stays up there, never falling, held up by the scaffolding of a national paranoia.

"WHERE'S DOINA?" I said the next day to the museum director when I saw her desk had been cleared.

"She's transferred," he said, "downstairs to Archives." He turned to walk back to his office.

I swallowed. "Why?"

"She's been under a lot of stress lately."

Transferred. Demoted, he meant. Archives was nothing more than a dark cell in the basement. Not another person! This was too much. I returned to my desk and tried to work. By afternoon I got up the nerve to go to my supervisor.

"But her work has been excellent."

"Look, it's none of your business. It wasn't my decision."

"She's never missed a day of work."

"What would you like me to say, Comrade? Someone reported she was acting strangely."

"But she knows more about the Thracian period than anyone in Bucharest. She studied twelve years for this job."

"I'm sorry, Comrade."

"But it's not true. I know it's not true, and you know it's not true."

"If you want to help her, *Tovarasa*, don't make waves. The more you say, the worse it will be for her. At least she's still in the building." He got up and shuffled papers in the file cabinet behind him.

I bit my tongue. Silence was nothing new. Ever since the Turkish occupation, we Romanians had earned a reputation for being able to submit to authority without losing our temper. There was even an adage about us that went, *Capul ce se pleca, sabia nu–l taie*, "the head that bends, the sword doesn't cut."

We were afraid of the informer branch of the Securitate because it was rumored that there were more than 100,000 members, recruited at every workplace. You never knew if your co-workers were being rewarded for reporting any irregularities or on your every comment. The Securitate made us feel we were all guilty–*we just hadn't been discovered yet.*

We feared, for example, if we had relatives abroad, no matter how long they'd been there. All of a sudden your job vanished, and many times we'd hear on Radio Free Europe that people who'd emigrated had terrible car accidents at their new homes.

The cult of fear spread to the streets. I was walking with a friend from the museum when I heard a screech and a patrol car stopped short beside a young guy.

"Present your identity card." The policeman's voice was sharp.

I was thirty feet away, but my heart pounded in my ears.

The policeman snatched the card from the boy's hands, glanced at it. "When was your last haircut?"

The boy, whose hair was roughly half as long as Valentin's, looked up, surprised.

"Are you certain this is your card?"

The boy started to run.

Another policeman tripped him. "*Hai!* Here, with me!" Both officers laughed. "Who does he fucking think he is, John Lennon? We'll put a stop to that."

"Where are they taking him?" I asked my friend.

"Where do you think? To be shaved, at the police station. Goodbye to his beard, and most of his hair."

Food lines formed as Nicolae began to exert control over the markets via the Securitate, diverting goods to other countries for a building boom in his honor.

There was a joke running around that went, "Have you heard of Romanian Roulette? Just criticize the government to your five most intimate friends. One of them is surely a member of the Securitate."

We also joked and called ourselves "The Polenta People", *Mamaligari*. Polenta was a national staple that went all the way back to Dacian times, a sort of ground cornmeal that you could only cut with a "magic" string. The joke about polenta was that when you cooked it, it would *boil in water but never explode...*

But how much boiling could my beautiful country take?

BECAUSE of my actions, my parents were to feel the heavy hand of the Ceausescus' control before the rest of the Nomenclatura, though everyone would feel it in the end. The oppression happened little by little, so that no one could point a finger.

First, they were seated further toward the back during party meetings and conferences at the Central Committee and at the Sala Palatului.

Next, my mother wasn't invited to a party meeting and reception that she'd attended for the past fifteen years. It was just an administrative error, wasn't it, but we knew, oh, we knew, that this was not an oversight, and my mother cried on her bed for most of the night. I cried, too, as I held her. For the first time I felt deep guilt for being so selfish. We were falling. Not knowing where the bottom was felt worse than the security of knowing we'd already found it.

Now my father sat on a bench at Lake Snagov and looked across at the villa he was no longer allowed to use.

"I'm sorry, Papa." I put my arms around his rough old head.

"The view's just as good from this side." He reached up to hold my hand. "Maybe even clearer."

Now groceries were no longer delivered to our door by a party van. The cook all but evaporated. So did our gardeners—even Lidia, who'd become such an important part of our family. The staff of live-in maids who used to surround my mother turned into one woman who came once or twice a week. My parents' access to commissaries for the Nomenclatura was taken away. "You have no place here," they were told by petty bureaucrats sitting behind ledgers.

Towels were no longer available at the Club at Neptune. "You are not allowed." Towels. Now somebody else enjoyed them.

My mother got a nasty little call from a steward at the government pool: "Since your husband has been in declining health, and we're so sorry to learn about this, he won't need a state car every day now. No, *Tovarasa*, you're not losing anything—you have only to call when he's attending a state function, and you'll be driven there in comfort. There, do you see? We'll take care of everything. And instead of burdening you with the presence of the chauffeur and the extra bodyguard, you'll have the able simplicity of Comrade Mocano with you until your husband returns to health and increased activity. As a matter of fact, why bother with Comrade Mocano? Long live the state."

"Long live the state." My mother called me at my office. "See what you've done?"

Now, I saw.

My mother was no longer welcomed where Romanian seamstresses made custom copies of French- and Italian-designed dresses for the Nomenclatura out of imported cashmere and silk. She was not vain and cared little for the fancy clothes, but all her peers went there; she was hurt.

"I have no time," her former seamstress said, looking away. "Come back in a few months."

Next, they lost the privilege of staying in suites at Romanian Embassies; in fact, their travel stopped. I was restricted from leaving the country, even on business. When my co-workers went to Paris, Milan, and Florence, Germany, Poland, I was *verboten*.

Valentin tried to intercede, but in the middle of 1971 his mother herself refused to allow me a passport to accompany him to Germany. Finally, when I wasn't even allowed to go on a work junket to the Soviet Union, I borrowed Valentin's car, drove to the Central Committee, and asked Cornel Burtica, our former ambassador to Rome who knew Valentin well and now dealt with matters of culture, "I'm not allowed even to go to another *communist* country?"

"I'll look into this," he said. He shrugged his shoulders as if to say, 'Don't you know I can't help you?' He'd been a friend of ours who'd even joked with Valentin and me about our situation before, but now he was chilly.

I left his office, went home, and waited for an answer that never came.

Now my parents lost hospital privileges and weren't allowed to see the top Romanian and European specialists who treated senior state officials. At least they could still go to Elias Hospital, one of the few hospitals in Romania that didn't have to keep cats in its operating rooms to fend off the rats, but my father was no longer allowed to see his personal physician, who, soon after complaining of his reassignment, died falling from an eighth-story window.

"He grew wings," the Securitate said. "He was crazy."

Because their pensions didn't entitle them to live in the Gheorghi-Dej house anymore, my parents had to move to a smaller house.

On the 23rd of August, 1971, the 27th anniversary of our liberation from the fascists, my mother was scheduled to receive a *decoratie*. No invitation came, nor did the award. Finally, a week after the ceremony, she was astonished to be presented with the award only in the third degree, receiving it at home while others of the Nomenclatura were invited to get theirs with public acclamation.

Her ten-year pension increase didn't come as she'd expected, and still more awards were refused her.

"You've worked a lifetime for the party," my father said to her. He went to Ceausescu.

"Why is this happening to Ecaterina? Why is her pension less than her peers'?"

"What are you trying to tell me, that you haven't enough money to live on?"

"It's not that it's not enough; it's that it isn't fair. A law's a law, and the same retirement benefits should apply to everyone in her strata. I want to know the reason."

The pension wasn't increased. And then, one at a time, all tasks were diverted from my father's office.

He said nothing to us.

Finally he went to Nicolae again. "I want to work. No more assignments have been coming. It's a fiction that I'm working. I've got a chair and a desk and this office in the Central Committee, and I want to work for the Romanian people, Comrade. Please let me help."

"You've been ill," Nicolae said. "There's no problem at all. Don't worry about yourself; it's a worldwide proletarian revolution against the capitalist hydra, not simply a forum for your personal ambitions. Go back to your office; you're wasting my time when there's no reason. We've got other problems. Your problem is nothing."

Nothing happened.

My father went into overdrive, exploding with memos and propping up departments adjacent to his. Everyone noticed his industry and apparent return to health. He came home happy during these few weeks, working in his study late into the night. Nicolae even gave him a few tasks.

Then, on the eve of a major party congress, my father was summoned into Nicolae's office.

"Tomorrow we make the announcement that you will be retiring for health reasons," he said.

My father gripped the edge of a chair.

"I can still work. I can still be of use to the Party."

He was still a partisan in the woods, even in civil life at sixty-five, sweetly and absurdly keeping his *nom de guerre* (Iordan Rusev was his real name–Petre Borila was only his fighting name) like his old friends did and jealously guarding increasingly moldering state secrets. He never told anyone anything that reflected poorly on party leadership. He was a true Romanian patriot, who was also so revered in Bulgaria that the house where he spent his early years bore a plaque in commemoration of him.

"He's a Soviet spy," Elena sniffed to her friends on the Central Committee.

Meanwhile, he was on his way down with dreadful, wordless speed.

Books from the National Academy were no longer brought to my parents upon request, even for my father's industrial research, for he continued heartbreakingly to send in reports from home which were invariably returned unread or lost on arrival.

Now my parents could no longer shop at the places where the best food was. Before, meats and groceries had simply been delivered from the best farms, prepared by and of the finest quality from the kitchens of the most renowned caterers in Bucharest. Caviar, imported beverages, cigarettes, coffee, things that were not on the market abounded around us. Growing up, I realized this was an extraordinary privilege, but I didn't appreciate it. Now we had to wait in lines five hours long just for a few strips of bacon.

My mother couldn't do it, so I did it for her.

Often they went without. My father became ill again, and from his hospital bed, he asked her if everything were all right.

"Yes," she said. "There's no problem." But she spent her evenings swearing in Hungarian. "Not even a match catches fire in this country," she said. "Everything goes wrong."

"Tell me what to do," she said to my father's doctors during the weeks he was allowed to stay at home. "He's ill. He needs to follow a strict medical diet, but I can't get him the food he needs."

"I'll get it, Mama," I said.

"But you're the last person on earth they'd give food to."

My father finally realized the extent to which privileges were being taken away, but he was beyond caring. "I don't want anything," he said in his hospital. "I just want some of my old comrades to come in and say hello."

We begged his friends to visit him, many of them people who'd fought with him in the war, but they refused. They wouldn't say it, but they were afraid of being associated with him. We were abandoned. My father had begun to step away from the hard line and show the first signs of disillusionment, and now it hurt him that the early promises of the communists were not being kept. He still dreamed that socialism could provide the purest democracy.

When he took a turn for the worse in 1972, he was shunted over to a paupers' ward. The last time I spoke to him was during a visit where my mother screamed at me in front of him. He raised himself on his bed and held my hand. "Let our daughter be," he said to Mama. "I hope she'll never do anything that will make her ashamed."

Then, a few nights later, saying he was having a heart attack, the attending physicians gave him an injection.

"Don't do it," my mother said, superstition and fear combined with insider's knowledge overcoming her. "Not with that needle!"

Even at Elias they still boiled their needles instead of discarding them after each patient. Once they were boiled hundreds of times, they got very dull–our doctors often apologized to us while searching through boxes of dead needles for one sharp enough to puncture our skin.

By this time my mother didn't know if the staff were there to help or hurt my father.

"Look. It makes him feel bad. He's not tolerating this medicine."

My mother was with him until the end, but though I'd seen him almost every day for six months, I couldn't get in to see him during his final days because the hospital was in quarantine. Even my mother couldn't leave the hospital if she wanted to. There was uncontrollable influenza in Romania, epidemic in Bucharest. I waited until nine or ten on New Year's Eve to see my father before an orderly walked up to me.

"What is his condition?" I asked. "My husband wants me to go to the mountains, but if I can see Papa, I won't go. I'll stay here and wait instead."

"No one's allowed to go into this hospital. Your father is sick, but not about to die. Go on," he said.

By now I couldn't argue with Valentin, who'd been pushing for this vacation. I just wanted to sleep, but I couldn't, because it was New Year's Eve and Valentin had planned a big celebration. I was so tired of all this fighting, tired of watching my father weaken day after day... I had weakened. "Okay," I said finally. "We need the rest."

I rode while Valentin drove and talked excitedly about the party. He'd secured permission from his parents to stay at their Predael villa while they were away.

"There are forty different palaces for my family's use, at least one in each province. Predael's deserted, but it's one of the best. I've got the keys. It'll be great," he said.

Arriving just before midnight, we drove past two armed sentries, who recognized Valentin immediately, and then zoomed along a narrow road lined with high fir trees.

We celebrated with the friends at a villa a few miles away. Afterward, bleary-eyed, we returned to the Predael lodge to hear the telephone ringing.

"I am sorry to inform you your father is dead," a voice on the phone said.

I felt dizzy. A strange politeness overcame me. "Thank you." I couldn't think of anything else to say.

"Now it's okay for you to see him. The quarantine's over."

Papa was gone. I could feel my throat contracting and getting salty. I threw myself on a bed upstairs. Valentin stroked my hair and talked with me softly. "We have to try to get in," I said.

We were on our way downstairs when we were shocked to see Nicolae and Elena entering the foyer.

I looked at Valentin quickly, but he seemed as surprised as I was; in fact, far more.

She was wearing a bulky copy of a Christian Dior suit and stood with her legs apart.

"Condolences," she said. "Right, Nicule?"

Nicolae nodded slowly.

"We're going to see him," I said, stunned that they already knew, and then looked at my husband. It was raining now, and Valentin was in no condition to drive. The house and grounds were swarming with staff. Valentin slapped himself in the head.

"How could you possibly be here?" he asked his parents again. They grew impatient with him.

"Do we need your permission?" Elena said as an aide brought her some Turkish coffee and juice.

I had to see Papa. I had to see him. Perhaps he wasn't dead.

I steeled myself to ask, "Valentin seems so upset. Is there anyone who could drive us to the hospital so we could see my father?"

Elena regarded me shrewdly. All I could think of was Papa on his deathbed–irrationally, I half-believed I could revive him. I had to get there. What if they were too lazy to check and see if he had a pulse? Could there possibly have been a mistake? He was not in the best part of the hospital. What if they were refusing to medicate him, or worse, overmedicating him? But he was dead, wasn't he? Thank you, yes, your father is dead.

"How dare you ask this of us?" Elena said. "Exactly what do you want from us?"

"I'm sorry. It's just that Valentin seems so tired, and I thought–"

"How dare you! Did your mother bring you up to be like this? Why are you making such a big fuss now? Valentin is perfectly capable of driving you, aren't you, Valentin?" Like an animal who just bites, Elena was instinctively twisting things around so that she was the maligned one.

"Yes. I can drive us there, Dana."

"Are you sure you don't want helicopters to take you there at state expense?" I thought I heard her shout after me, the green and varnished wood paneling flying past us as we bumped and crashed out the door into the rain. "Is there no way in which we could make you more comfortable in your grief? Did you hear her? What nerve!" Elena said to Nicolae. "Did you hear her?"

We raced there, and the same orderly let me into the hospital. Papa was still on his bed. I felt him, and he was cold all over, but—to my astonishment–he became really warm for a moment when I embraced him, as if he'd been waiting for me before departing. Then the fire went out and he became cold.

My father was buried with honors at the top of a hill in the Park of Liberty, where Gheorghiu-Dej was also buried. Ceausescu didn't send even one flower, an omission that sparked whispers among all the funeral-goers, as Nicolae always sent large arrangements on the death of old party members. My mother didn't want her husband buried there. "I don't like the company," she said. She felt she wouldn't be allowed to visit him as time wore on, and in the end, she was right. It was guarded by soldiers, and we had to identify ourselves every time we tried to get in. A gas flame burned in the middle, and there was Gheorghiu-Dej in dark red marble. Above this, the park sloped upward in a semicircle like a Greek outdoor theater. There were more red columns and flat black tombstones in black marble. This was where people disappeared. It was a very cold place up in the stars. You couldn't feel anything, and you couldn't plant the flowers you wanted.

It was cold up here, and even I could feel the chill, a chill that began to grip the rest of the country.

Chapter 8

You're getting drunk with
cold water

NINETEEN SEVENTY-ONE was the same year my in-laws took an eye-opening state visit to China and North Korea. They were enthralled by the power of these two countries which had virtually declared their independence from the Soviet Union.

Of course, the Ceausescus only saw what they were supposed to see: millions cheering and honoring their leaders in mass demonstrations; apparently thriving manufacturing economies; fearsome internal security forces; and boundless personal wealth beyond Elena's wildest imagination.

What a show it was. Upon their return the Ceausescus, including Zoia and Nicu, were determined to reinvent Romania in this dazzling image, and suddenly awe-striking 200-foot banners of our leaders' faces appeared in cities and villages everywhere, from the mountains to the Black Sea. When anyone in our country said "He" or "She", no one had to ask who he or she was.

Nicolae, who'd come to power promising the closing of work camps and the release of political prisoners, now began readopting

Gheorghiu-Dej's practice of selling passports to American and Israeli organizations helping desperate Jews and Germans to emigrate in order to finance the building of factories and the purchase of modern machinery he'd coveted.

You know the story with Snow White and her mother, who says, "Tell me who's the most beautiful"? Well, maybe that was Nicolae Ceausescu, only the mirror here was the nodding heads of the Central Committee. "Isn't it terrible when we're forced to execute traitors?" "Isn't it too bad we have to sweep away one-fifth of Bucharest's historic district to create the world's largest building?" "What could be more wonderful than our triumphant return from Iran?" If an unsmiling face appeared in the mirror, it was wiped clean.

In 1975, Nicolae Ceausescu asked, "Could it be true? Am I this good?" "Yes," said the sycophants. An old man rose with everyone looking. The Central Committee strained to hear. "*You make a mistake,*" Constantin Pirvulescu said. "*You have become a cult of personality, a dictator. Dracu!*"

So close to Transylvania, the word for Satan is still Dracula.

Nicolae, "The Danube of Thought", just stared. In no time at all the old man was evicted from his villa, and we were never allowed to speak his name again.

THE resulting chill that crept over Romania was subtle enough that at times I could almost forget it. We began to visit the Pesca-rusul, the Seagull restaurant, the closest thing we had to a regular getaway. It was located right in Herastrau Park near the Alley of Roses, lovely bushes that were part of the national collection. The interior and exterior of the building, built before the war, were painted bright white, and beyond the garden paths, ivy, and benches was a pretty view of Herastrau Lake, where rowboats and sailboats danced on the waves.

Diners from government agencies were visible on the outdoor terraces, as well as on two floors inside and in the stone basement's rathskeller bar.

A few yards away from the restaurant was its namesake statue of seagulls by the same artist who'd made such an idyllic sculpture of me when I was a girl.

At the Pescarusul we often ordered crayfish or *mititei*, a spicy meat snack–not hamburger, not sausage, but something in between. And we did enjoy the Romanian Dunarea cognac and champagne we could get there, named for the Danube river.

From the grounds outside we could see a lot of lights across the lake, and to the right were the lights of the modern government buildings and what we called the *Casa Scinteii*, or house of sparkles, the skyscraper that housed the headquarters of our national newspapers, principally the *Scinteia*, the largest, on the top floors. This was where my mother had worked every day during the length of my childhood, where she'd spent so many long nights writing. I often looked at the building and found the cluster of lights that had been her office. In front of the building was a forty-foot bronze statue of Lenin. And always the lake, the lake, breathing in its sleep beside the restaurant like a living thing.

There were other restaurants, for example the Chivu Brothers, where you could get good fish, and nightclubs such as the Melody, where the martinis were icy and where you could see lovely girls dancing sometimes nearly naked–paid like we all were, with state salaries–but there was only one Seagull, one Pescarusul, one place like this in Herastrau.

IT was during these days that I came home late one afternoon to find Valentin sharing some Azuga beer, named for a little town in the mountains, with the tennis star Ilie Nastase.

This very large man with very long arms looked up in a most friendly manner when I approached him. He had the self-possession of a crow, one of those big blue crows or ravens in the works of Carlos Castaneda or spiraling over the castle of Vlad Tepes.

Valentin was obviously overjoyed with his new friend but not fawning. Valentin was a dedicated tennis fan. I was lukewarm, but seeing Nastase up close was an entirely different experience.

"*Buna*," I said, walking around Nastase's long, long leg that reached halfway across the tiny kitchen and ended with a size-twelve lump of white Adidas kangaroo leather with black stripes.

"The man of the hour," Valentin said. "Can you believe what a fight our sorcerer here gave to Stan Smith?"

"Congratulations," I said. "What did you do?" Whatever this lanky, clean-shaven hunk with the sharp beak had done to a Stan Smith, the Yank must have deserved it.

Nastase put his hand on his heart. "Everything I do is in service to the glory of Romania."

"That's where I was last night," Valentin said. "Nasty here broke serve six times against Smith in the exhibition match."

Nastase turned back to me with the same magnetic smile and shook his head. "So this is Juliet," he said softly. He wore a dark blue warm-up suit of the newest double-knit fabric that I supposed he'd been issued while playing in the *US Open, Forest Hills,*

New York. Or at least that's what the embroidered logo on his breast pocket broadcast. The kit bag at his feet sported the legend DAVIS CUP–with swagger came swag.

"Will you be at tomorrow's match?" Nastase said without raising his voice at the end, making it not a question but a statement of fact. I was embarrassed to notice his smell in the room. It was a good, strong smell that was clean but that of a fighting animal.

Valentin poured three more glasses of the yellow beer.

We talked.

I went into the kitchen to make coffee while Valentin and Ilie became engrossed in a plan about playing tennis together by the lights of the Arcul de Triumf at the nearby Stadionul Tineretului, the only outdoor night courts in Bucharest. Valentin had learned to play there, as had Nicu. Ion Tiriac had risen to fame there as well, under the tutelage of Tache Caralulis.

"Tiriac is the brain and Ilie is the magic," was the phrase of the month in Bucharest's restaurants and nightclubs. These tennis players were the toast of the town.

It was deep into the night when I looked over at my husband and Ilie, still laughing and talking. Nastase was a big star, but I learned he was taking care of his mother, his sister's sons, all of his relatives. He always liked to share what he had. Just as he instinctively played tennis so well, so was he instinctively a caring person.

A third pot of thick, Turkish coffee steamed happily on our stove as I joined them again. You could see this little kitchen of ours glowing all the way to the Carpathian mountains.

"Stop it, you two." Valentin enjoyed his role as host. He grinned. "And why are you both perspiring?"

It was warm in the room. Anyone but a Ceausescu would have had a glow on. Nastase clasped Valentin on the shoulders and took a long look at him.

"I am emotional, so I sweat a lot," Ilie said. "When I see others who don't, I seize on this. People are not aware of this. But you can see me all in water. If I tell a lie, you see. If I am nervous, you see. So it makes me wonder what makes others so cool."

I jumped in, a little too quickly. "Oh, Valentin perspires."

"Yes, of course." Nastase studied me.

THE next night, we all watched him play another match against Stan Smith at the Progresu Courts. Night tennis was becoming the new cinema for our city of 2.3 million, with a new set of national stars.

The two players were twin towers, perfectly matched by their contrasts. Dark-locked Nastase was mongoose-guileful in his signature moves. Sandy-haired, mustached Smith, with his engineer's precision, was as exotic to us as all of America. Nastase won that night in three sets, using spins and tricks Smith himself might have conjured, people snickered, in, say, a million years.

After the second set, Ilie walked over to our seat and talked to Valentin. Without addressing me once, he mopped his wet hair and brow and folded the white towel lengthwise before absent-mindedly tossing it over the rail, where it was quickly snapped up by girls in the front row.

WE saw Ilie a lot, off and on. Florica Popescu, a girlfriend at work, asked me at lunch one day, "Are you in love with him?"

"Oh, yes. It's wonderful."

When she said, "What does Valentin think of this?" I realized she was asking me about Nastase.

"He's a friend of ours, nothing more. Who said this to you?" I was capable now of giving her a puncturing stare of my own.

"Everybody who hears you talking about him with such admiration says it..."

I assured Florica that I wasn't in love with Nastase, though I loved him as much as did anyone who came into contact with him, including Valentin. "It's just that a lot of us are friends who meet at the Pescarusul." There was Nastase and Catalin Tutunaru, the race car driver whose wife, Ludmila, I'd known since kindergarten. "This one falls off the sides of mountains in cars he's racing, but he always lands on his feet." Catalin was descended from landed gentry who'd been able to keep their property after the liberation. If even half of the stories I'd heard about "the Cat" were true, he had no fear of death.

"I know Catalin," Florica said. "Wasn't his father the Dean of the College of Engineering for Motor—"

"Yes," I said, "but what we like about him is his sense of humor. He knows Peter Revson and..." I told her about the rest of our friends at the Seagull. "Come on and see us there."

"Does Zoia go there?"

"Sometimes."

"What about Nicu and Donca?"

"A lot."

"What do you talk about?"

"Ilie almost never talks about himself. He just becomes so fascinated with what you're saying that you feel you're describing your life better than ever before. Others listening to you crowd in to hear what you're going to say because Ilie projects so much animation into whatever's happening."

Of course we all knew that some people were paid to listen to the goings-on at this café, but we loved the Pescarusul in spite of its double identity as, like the Athenee Palace Hotel, an intelligence nest where a good half of the waiters were Securitate.

AFTER an exhibition match in 1974, we met up with Nastase in Herestrau Park, accompanied by the gorgeous, very tall Belgian princess Dominique.

Ilie said, "Oh, we're all too young here. Where are the old people? If you don't have an old one near you, you'll have to invent one."

But who'd have wanted to invent Nicolae and Elena?

We started walking across the gardens to the Pescarusul, Nastase's long hair shining rough and blue at the nape of his neck, all six feet of Dominique gliding along with her big brown eyes and sensual mouth. She didn't look tall near him; walking as she did with an animal's grace, she looked like a young Sophia Loren. Both Valentin and Nastase walked with an athletic crouch, nearly identical in their big strides.

On the way, we saw no interesting old people.

But we did see groups of young girls in the park, walking without their mothers now. They noticed Nastase in particular, and he acknowledged them in the grand manner, with a different quip for each.

"YOU like Nastase too much," Valentin teased me after we watched him at another match.

"All of Romania's in love with him. But I'm your wife," I said. "I'm in love with you. Everything he has in tennis, you have in physics. You two are exactly alike, except you're the more mysterious, never thinking of being jealous of me. Didn't you see the carful of girls waiting to pick him up after he left the restaurant? He has that yellow Lancia, but people just take him from place to place."

"I didn't see it." Valentin grinned. "Who cares?"

"I care," I said. "About you."

He slipped his warm arm around my back while lighting a cigarette with his other hand.

"After a night with Nastase, everybody makes love. He has an aphrodisiac effect on people. He's doubling the population of Romania." He embraced me very gently.

"So you do love me?" I asked him again, just to make sure.

He knocked a chair down, and laughing, picked me up in his arms.

I LOVED Valentin's endearing eccentricities, such as his habit of always taking his watch on and off while talking.

"What do you want?" I laughed each time he did this. "Do you need to know what time it is?"

"No, I don't. I don't know why I'm doing this!"

He'd so patiently waited for me to be myself again after my father's death, and went many times to Papa's grave with me.

He brought music alive for me, surprising me with banned records and books such as *Catch-22* that we'd read aloud together. I loved everything that touched him, from the ordinary black straight razor he used all the time to his Equipage aftershave.

He was the most exciting, considerate man I ever met. Strangers came to Valentin, ringing at our door or at his working place, and they wouldn't be thrown out. Any of our friends would come to him with their problems, whether they were personal, professional, or medical; even my dog fell in love with him, and, to my amusement, did everything she could to sleep by his side.

"I love you," I said, looking up into his eyes.

In our spartan apartment I showed Valentin and the listening ears of the Securitate, the tape recorders built below our floors, that I loved him with my whole heart. But our happiness in this little apartment was not to last.

Chapter 9

Do not put your spoon into the pot which does not boil for you

THREE weeks later, Valentin received orders for the compulsory army service all young men owed their country.

Because he was a college graduate, the orders were only for six months, but I was sad when they came. My husband approached the upcoming separation with his customary buoyancy.

He'd only been deployed for a few months when word reached me that he was ill with influenza in an army dispensary north of the center of Bucharest, halfway up a ridge.

Leaving work early, I raced there in my car and passed the statues of Romanian heroes that guarded a small park not far from the front gate.

Soviet trucks buzzed everywhere under the steaming camp lights. Showing my identification papers, I got past the first sentry and, leaning out my car window, asked for directions to the clinic from a soldier passing by.

"It's up that street, but no one's allowed there because the First Secretary's wife, Comrade Elena, is there visiting her son."

I disregarded him and headed down the street anyway. I could see a cluster of parti-colored Mercedes blocking the entrance to a drab two-story concrete building. I parked several feet away from this tableau and hurried up the stairs. As I reached for the door, a guard stepped directly in my path and shook his head.

"No visitors today."

"I'm here to see my husband, Valentin Ceausescu."

"No visitors today by order of Comrade Elena."

"You don't understand. I'm his wife. I am Iordana Ceausescu."

A funny look came over his face. "I have explicit orders to let no one who is not on the family list enter the hospital."

"What are you talking about? I *am* his family!"

Suddenly down the corridor I saw a rigid profile, unmistakably Elena. She came within thirty feet of me, attended by a ridiculous coterie of senior officers, but I knew she'd seen me.

"Comrade Elena!"

She pointedly did not turn, and the guard said, "Obviously your family connection is not close enough. You must move your car—you can't park there."

I refused to argue with him, turned, and left.

AFTER several weeks, Valentin was sent home to convalesce. When I told him what had happened, he said, "It was overzealous security. It happens anywhere. They have to protect her, and they didn't know who you were. I can't believe my mother! I feel terrible, but what could I have done?"

"You say 'what could I have done', and what could your mother have done, but a lot gets done when you two are doing nothing. She wouldn't let me see my own husband."

"They were protecting her. They didn't know."

"I told them who I was, but they wouldn't discuss it with me. I was told to go home. I couldn't even wait outside."

"Let's drop this." Valentin darkened, then smiled and put a big arm around me.

He soon forgot about this incident, but it left me with the feeling that I didn't fit in anywhere.

In early 1975, Nicolae, Elena, Zoia, and Nicu visited King Hussein of Jordan and were invited to dinner aboard his boat in the Gulf of Aqaba.

Elena fell in love with the yacht and crudely hinted about how grateful Romania would be for such a gift until Hussein felt compelled to present her with an exact replica of it, made in the United States. The yacht was named the *Friendship*, symbolizing "the friendship between our two countries". This was the apotheosis of a Ceausescu pattern—Elena had a charming way of "admiring" a lot of things during her travels in every corner of the world. From jewelry to minks, hosts were made to feel it was rude and would be to their detriment and dishonor if they didn't fulfill her whims.

Once acquired, the yacht was docked in a secret place on the Black Sea like a Christmas toy discarded, never to be used again.

Nineteen seventy-six was the year many people in the world heard of Romania for the first time. A beautiful, tiny, fourteen-year-old gymnast, Nadia Comaneci, from the poorest section of our country, astonished the world by winning a cluster of gold medals at the Montreal Olympic Games. Not only did she win, she scored perfect tens in her events, which had never been done before, and suddenly the world had an instant heroine. It was impossible to turn on Radio Free Europe without hearing "Nadia's Song" played again and again.

First Nicolae and Elena were happy to be photographed with the young star, then furious when "that child" eclipsed them in the international headlines. Worse still, her coaches, the best in the world, were Hungarian, which the wire services did not fail to mention, so they were replaced with Romanian-born understudies. As irritated as the Ceausescus were by her growing fame, they were conscious of Nadia's usefulness as a political pawn.

As RELATIONS BEGAN to thaw between Valentin and his parents, our fortunes began to rise. Valentin surprised me with the lure of an apartment hunt. Together, we found a three-room flat with a nice terrace and gardens on a street named after a bird, Strada Brancutei. We were only two or three minutes from the Arcul de Triumf, built for the coronation of King Ferdinand and Queen Maria in 1922 (though you couldn't tell it, because their faces had been rubbed off the structure by enthusiastic communists in the 1960s). I resolved to celebrate this period of tranquility every day. I plunged into domestic chores with a relish I didn't know I possessed.

We'd just gotten settled in when a wave rolled under my feet. "It's *cutremur*," I said, flying through the air as I hit the opposite wall. "An earthquake!" More waves vibrated under me, like a massage.

Valentin and our red cocker spaniel, Olsa, were still on our bed, he reading a newspaper and she dozing. Our black-and-white TV slid from the table and crashed. I stumbled backwards. Free of my grasp, the electric iron I was using to press Valentin's slacks now wickedly burned the trouser leg. I lunged for the cord. Above us the low thunder of our neighbors' library shelves rumbled to our ceiling amid the tinkle of breaking windows. Struggling to my feet, I saw Valentin and my spaniel continuing on as before, oblivious to everything. I actually saw Valentin turn a page. "You two!" I laughed. "What kind of a dog would not be howling at a time like this? What kind of a husband? It's an earthquake! Brace yourself!"

"Come on."

"No, really!" Cracks raced through our plaster, and people shouted everywhere, flinging open doors and running down the corridors.

Now we had his attention. Outside on our landing, old ones were crying. I ran out to see if anyone was hurt. Luckily they were just frightened. "It's worse, it's worse than 1940. We have to leave. Watch out for the aftershock!"

We ran down to our car, Valentin sockless. Immediately I was shocked at the damage I saw all along the way as we raced to check on my mother. Whole buildings had collapsed. Ambulances screamed. A bridge, riven in two, seemed to have spilled cars onto the street. We found Mama cleaning up shards from my copy of the statue made of me as a girl. It had fallen over and broken off its nose.

"You should have taken it."

"I won't keep myself in the house." I laughed, then noticed a shadow cross Valentin's face.

"Mama Mare!" He tore at his hair with his right hand. "Grandmother's all alone."

"In the Primaverii?" I asked. "What about your parents?"

"They're in Africa. We've got to get over there."

We started out.

I'd been in the main palace a few times, but never like this, unescorted. As we approached, I could see policemen and soldiers swarming the grounds.

One of them stopped us, glanced at Valentin, and nodded. "Comrade Valentin is coming in a yellow Dacia," he said into a radio as we were waved ahead through the solid green wall of the electric gate.

This gate was heavy, with a small arch in it. The driveway that appeared when it swung open was porous and bright white, possibly coral from the Caribbean.

Immediately inside the gate was a stone monitoring post, where a man screened messages and talked quickly to us. I could see the small pistol under his coat.

"Is Mama Mare all right? Where is she?" Valentin asked him.

"We've moved her into your parents' house. We thought it was safer."

A circular driveway curved around a fountain surrounded by rosebushes and immaculately clipped grass. Skidding to a stop, we ran to the main entrance and climbed the gold-carpeted stairs through two Corinthian columns that ascended in stone. After we hit the platform, we entered the foyer sealed by glass double-doors. Despite columns and big rooms and mirrors and chandeliers, this modern stone palace was a bleak stuccoed rectangle.

"Mama Mare!"

Standing on the Persian carpet, we immediately saw Valentin's grandmother crumpled onto a couch covered with gray, beige, and pale green silk brocade, and ran to help her.

"I'm tired," Mama Mare, Elena's mother, said.

"Don't worry," Valentin said. He kissed her and stroked her hair. "We'll take care of you." Her nurse appeared with some lemonade for the old lady to drink, and I looked around at the black concert grand piano in the reception room. A black-and-white photograph of Nicolae, its glass cracked, lay on the top.

A small fountain gurgled to the left of Mama Mare. Behind it were the shards of two three-foot turquoise Sevres vases worth at least $30,000 each. Paintings everywhere were askew; one of a peasant woman by Grigorescu swung from its side. Some crystal was broken, but the famous garbage-truck-sized chandeliers Elena had fallen in love with during visits to Versailles were intact and ugly as ever. Matching gold and crystal sconces lined the walls. The floor spreading before us was of overdone marquetry. The rooms ahead looked as if Elena had sneezed gold everywhere, on the chandeliers, in the bathrooms and on the fixtures—*everywhere,* even woven into the upholstery of chairs, which were covered so thoroughly you couldn't recognize their style beyond the fact that they were poorly wrought state copies of furniture from Venice to the Taj Mahal.

We went into Valentin's old room, where one window was cracked. The decor was frightening, everything Florentine-esque with a lot of wood carving. Silk wall coverings changed color from room to room, but listlessly, artlessly matching the same brocade pattern of upholstery and lead-heavy drapes festooned with thick gold tassels and fringe.

"Dana, over here."

In Valentin's study was a statue of a small boy playing a violin. Gold brocade armchairs blazed from the two corners around chests of drawers with carved acanthus pulls. A French or Dutch tapestry hung on the wall behind his desk; a silver water pitcher with a plate beneath it sat on it.

His bathroom was pink with polished gold. "I don't know why," he said.

The other bathrooms had gold cleaning utensils, fixtures, and tiles. One had two gold toilet brushes. Why two?

It was deadly quiet. We moved along.

As I walked through the corridor, I saw perhaps thirty family pictures and oil paintings showing the Ceausescus with Valentin, Nicu, and Zoia but no husbands or wives. We walked past the kitchens where the taste testers worked, and where the Ceausescus' food was electromagnetically scanned each day. What would the long lines of people waiting for food say if they saw this? How could anyone sleep here amid this plunder? Every object in the house had a sticker with an inventory number scrawled on it.

"Let's go," I said. "We can take Mama Mare with us."

"No, she's better off here with her nurse. We should check the rest for damage."

We walked into the natatorium, where Italian mosaics of fish and godlike human figures shimmered on the walls. The recreational pavilion continued through a door to a shower, sauna, and weight room, but I couldn't take my eyes off the swimming pool, lit from beneath and glowing now, the umbilicus of the pool-cleaner moving like a snake inside it.

In a room off to the side was an infirmary where Nicolae and Elena had the only state-of-the-art medical equipment and disposable needles in the country, as well as a private dental office, just as there were in all their other villas.

There were also quarters for the Ceausescus' black Labradors' private veterinarian, who had to attend to the dogs twenty-four hours a day. These dogs traveled in their own separate limousines to all official functions and slept on divans with the sheets changed daily. Poor Dr Tudoran–his every movement was recorded by the guards. He took to drinking, developed an ulcer, and slowly lost his mind.

We went down to the basement past the bar and looked into the plush, fawn-colored movie theater covered in brocade.

In a storage room built like a bunker, we saw stacks of leopard skins and tusks from Idi Amin; gold and silver presentation platters, pitchers, tea sets, loving cups; priceless marble statuary; Turkish and Persian carpets; Ottoman chalices encrusted with jewels; Chinese lacquered furniture and antique porcelain; crystal; Delft pottery; and paintings from all over the world.

It had taken an earthquake for me to see Ceausescu greed as it really was, and I knew how bad these excesses would look to my countrymen. I felt ashamed even to be looking at them. How could this staggering greed not infect my husband?

"This isn't you," I said.

"What?"

"This... place. This isn't you."

We took an elevator to the top floor. There we found a green-house and an aviary flashing with finches and canaries. A few of them had gotten free and were flying over some broken glass. One of them flew directly in front of us in a gold blur.

Down the hall, Elena had a large closet off her bedroom that was stacked with paintings. "Well, we might as well pick up my birthday painting now," Valentin said.

Your birthday what?

"My mother told me to choose one, for my birthday. Come and look."

I saw work by Pallady, Tonitza, and other great Romanian artists, all politically correct.

"No." I didn't want to take anything from the palace. I didn't even want to see any more. If you join this *hora*, you must dance, the old saying went.

"You pick it." I ran out of the room.

Next door, Zoia's suite was blinding–white carpet, white walls, virginal white freesias, white draperies, white bedspread, white pillows, white Galle vases, one of which was shattered.

Hearing footsteps, I turned and caught my breath. A small dark man with black-rimmed glasses and military posture was six inches away from me. Though he was dressed in civilian clothes, I recognized immediately that this was General Ion Pacepa, the country's top intelligence officer. With all his monitoring devices, there was no need for an introduction.

He spoke in a pleasant, soft voice. "Are you looking for Zoia?" He looked like the violin player he was, not the nation's preeminent spy. He'd monitored Zoia's love affairs for so many years now that he'd developed a paternal affection for her. He'd even convinced East German diplomats to present Zoia with her Mercedes 450SL.

Valentin chatted with him for a few minutes about family matters. Pacepa seemed so gentle, but I'd heard people in our circle whisper about his agents' diabolical use of radioactive substances known as "Radu". Rumors went you'd be directed alone through a certain prison cell or corridor contaminated with radioactivity and you'd soon become ill and then die of "natural causes"—various kinds of cancer. Pacepa himself was to report, "Service K added radioactive substances supplied by the KGB to its deadly arsenal. Ceausescu himself gave the procedure the code name 'Radu' and he would issue the order, 'Give Radu to Popescu.'"

I stood nearby, unable to think of a thing to say, as my husband and the general talked.

Valentin looked absolutely at home.

NEARLY one thousand people perished in that earthquake, a time when many of my cherished beliefs began to crumble into dust as well. Two more years passed, and I felt us slowly drifting apart. Valentin found more and more reasons to see his parents and siblings, while Nicu Ceausescu was developing a reputation as a drunk and a bully. During these years, the only times I remember enjoying spending time with any of my in-laws was when we dined as a foursome at the Pescarusul with Nicu and his girlfriend, Donca. Nicu was at least decent when he was with Donca, who seemed to have a calming influence on him. I liked her, too. She looked and acted like the American actress Ali MacGraw—fearless and confident.

On one of these evenings, whispers from the tables around us gave me chill bumps up my arm. Nicolae's shadow had disappeared. General Pacepa was out—gone. Moreover, he'd walked off with all of our country's national security secrets. "No one does this!" "There's a bounty on his head! He's debriefing in America with the CIA!" I felt strange because I was glad that Nicolae had lost such a strong ally but frightened about what he'd do without him. Naturally, the patriot in me was stung by the loss of our national secrets, but what would happen now that Nicolae was enraged *and* unchecked? In the backlash that was sure to come, how far would the Securitate go?

The next day, some of my colleagues from the museum were dispatched to Pacepa's house to recover any rare artworks he'd "stolen from our people". I was glad I wasn't included on the mission, but on the other hand, did it mean no one trusted me to be there? It was almost a ritual activity to inspect the homes of anyone who'd disappeared.

In late 1980, Valentin and I were summoned to the Primaverii.

"I don't want to go."

"Will you stop worrying! We have to break the ice sometime," Valentin said. He knew he was dragging me to the place I loathed more than any other in the world.

When we entered, some attendants were polishing silver, vacuuming carpets, and washing windows. Elena motioned to a series of oversized charts scattered over a table.

"This," she said, "is your father's plan for the Palace of the People, a testimony to his greatness in honor of the party and the people of Romania. It's going to be completely marble, the eighth wonder of the world, larger even than the American Pentagon."

The architectural drawings depicted a monstrous structure almost arctic in its size, with a lobby more than a hundred meters long, four underground levels and a nuclear bunker to house the ministries, and twelve stories above ground where pretty Spirei Hill once looked down upon the city. These raw, blue cliffs of marble looked like a design for the gates of Hell. Over Valentin's shoulder I could also see plans for a new presidential palace and a larger Ceausescu tomb.

"Eleven thousand chandeliers? How can we afford this, mother?" Valentin said, his dark, rough hair well over his collar and his hands in his pockets.

"We're the richest nation in the world. Now that the hydro-electric dams of Iron Gate II have finally been finished by the Hungarians, your father's true Ceausescu Epoch has begun with the canal connecting the Danube to Constanta, completing Charlemagne's dream. Our dark, rich soil gives forth the sweetest berries and fruits known to man, and–"

"Save it, mother. Where's the money coming from?"

Elena made a quick little frown and spat out "Nixon."

"Really? He's long out of office."

"While he was in office he made the loans possible from the United States. He wanted to be a part of our cultural revolution. We let him believe he understood us, as we did for Ford and Carter, who gave us most favored nation status once we set up an office in Atlanta to buy peanuts from his imbecile farm. Peanut-head didn't want the kind of revolution they had in China, when the United States lost its shot at trade with Asia."

"But mother, isn't this another China?"

"Of course not."

As usual, she changed the subject as soon as she was challenged by her son. She threw him a hideous smile and spun around. "Come along down the hall, Vale, and see the report on the revolutionary new farming techniques we've introduced. Our tractor firm in Brasov is already setting new records of human production, thanks to designs we've developed, as is our new tire plant in Copsa Mica. What a triumph."

"I've heard of the Carbosin tire products factory," Valentin said, his tone alone describing the black lungs of the Transylvanians who worked there as virtual slave labor, the black chemical byproducts covering all buildings, fir trees, streets, and windows with a sticky substance that would never wash off. "Everyone talks about it. Father told me about it when he returned from hunting at Cabana Capra."

Cabana Capra was Nicolae's secret retreat near the top of the Fagaras Mountains. The front door was hidden behind a waterfall, and it was used for state summits because it was so well protected and the crashing walls of water provided natural sound attenuation. It was also a hunting lodge where bears, deer, and wild boars were fed and then chased by guards right in front of Nicolae's gun, a dangerous duty since he was a terrible shot. On national television, the whole country was shown footage of the same poor boar being killed over and over again.

Elena said nothing to me during this visit, and I thought I was off the hook until we got home and Valentin said, "Oh, by the way, Mother wants to see you alone tomorrow."

Chapter 10

The knife has reached my bone

ALONE? How could she know? How could she have found out? Maybe she'd noticed I'd quit smoking. Valentin and I hadn't told anyone I was pregnant except my own mother, had we? A baby was something I'd wanted for so long—a baby! Even then I knew it was foolish, but I still clung to the impossible dream of a simple, uncomplicated life, with children and laughter in a modest house surrounded by greenery, out of the public eye. I hoped beyond reason that somehow a child would bring Valentin and me closer together.

Maybe the three of us could be a real family. Valentin had been so happy when I told him. He'd been so tender and protective that we seemed like new lovers. Maybe we had a chance.

With great trepidation I went to the Primaverii and was directed by a maid past the anteroom where guests left their umbrellas, coats, and gloves and where Elena gave instructions to the house staff. I continued past the pantry and finally past the marble hall that led to Valentin's boyhood room, kept in perpetual readiness for his return through all the years of our marriage, into a third space, where Elena sat and considered me now. Looking into her eyes, I felt a pang of sorrow that I'd been summoned to *her* to talk about my unborn child instead of being able to share the joyous news with my dead father.

Here she was, so powerful that she and her husband had sucked the life out of all legendary characters in Romania and become the only ones people remembered. She looked up at me disagreeably and vigorously bid me come closer. Then, without rising, she coolly extended her hand.

I might have greeted her by calling her "Comrade Academician Doctor Engineer Madame Ceausescu, Outstanding Activist of Party and State, Eminent Personage of Romanian and International Science," the way others did, but I opted for a simpler "Good morning."

"You may sit down."

I looked around at the rooms Valentin moved so easily about. After a silence Elena transformed into something almost friendly as she began to speak.

"Valentin tells me you're going to have a child."

"Yes." I relaxed for the first time into a smile.

"No." It was that simple, her mouth a tight line as she shook her head once. "This is not right for you. It is not right for Valentin, and it is not right for us." She looked directly at my belly, her lips curled in a sneer. I moved my hand to block her stare.

"It's in your *burta* now?" she said. Her voice took on a vulgar, metallic quality.

"Yes." I was disappointed that my reply sounded so small. My face felt hot. I gathered some courage. "We love each other. Wouldn't you like your first grandchild?"

"Certainly not at a time like this," Elena said. "Do you think you're ready to have a family?"

"We've been married ten years."

"You're not mature enough," she said.

"But isn't every woman supposed to have five children for our nation?" I asked.

Romania's laws against abortion and birth control had come to us in 1966, when Nicolae and Elena learned to their embarrassment that Poland had a higher birth rate than Romania–twenty-eight births per thousand to our fourteen. The Ceausescus wouldn't stand for it. As a result, our hospitals were crammed with new mothers and babies we couldn't possibly care for. This crop of children was called the *Generatia Decreteilor*, the generation of the decreed ones. There were so many pregnancies that the death rate for women in delivery more than doubled in one year.

By the mid-1970s, condoms and birth-control pills were banned in Romania, so we learned more stealthy ways to prevent childbirth. We smuggled in pills, condoms, diaphragms, copper coils, and Sterilette inserts after traveling to other European countries. For fear of discovery, some left intra-uterine devices in too long and didn't have them adjusted or checked, resulting in an epidemic of ruptures and infections. Doctors who came to our aid were arrested along with their patients.

While birth control was outlawed, abortion was considered even worse–a form of treason–a criminal act against the state. The underground response was that some doctors administered abortions and claimed there were emergency conditions. If caught, these doctors were jailed. A few of my friends took injections to induce abortions in France. At home, illegal abortions were performed on dining room tables or by Gypsies who inserted red plants called *muscata*, "the one who bites".

Our birth rate went down *again*, and Elena became furious. As a result, she instituted forced examinations. It didn't matter if we washed floors or were daughters of the Nomenclatura working at the art museum, we were shouted into lines and herded to dispensaries in every factory or office for surprise medical checks. At first, the tests involved collecting body fluids that were injected into frogs, but soon this was deemed too expensive and time-consuming, so actual surprise physical examinations began. During these mass tests, which occurred as often as every three months nationwide, examination gloves weren't thrown away. They were put in metal chemical disinfectant boxes and reused.

Anyone who'd had a miscarriage was interrogated by the Securitate on suspicion of having induced it. One of my friends committed suicide after such a session. She hadn't had the courage to tell her family she was having an out-of-wedlock pregnancy, so she used a modest home remedy–a razor.

Perversely, those unable to have children were severely taxed for this–we actually had to pay money for the children we didn't bear.

With the whole country forced to give birth, was Elena saying she wouldn't accept a grandchild, my child?

"Now let me get this straight," I said. "Everyone's supposed to have children–but just not your own family?"

"How dare you say this to me?" She spat at me. "We're building a workforce greater than the world has ever seen. What applies to others does not apply to you. What's your problem? Look at you, drenched in Chanel. We already gave you the plum job working in the museum, surrounded by beautiful things. Isn't Valentin enough of a family for you? Our son is too young to be a father." She gave me the evil eye.

You mean you're too young to be a grandmother. "But we want this child, and we're going to have this child," I said. "Since you've asked me here, I've come to tell you I want to have my baby in safety. We love each other and have thought for a long time about this. It's time to start a family. I'm thirty-four."

"How could I forget you're much older than Valentin?" The Genius of Science was, as ever, perfecting her Genius for Getting in the Dig. "There will be no baby with my approval."

I stood. "Good news or bad news, we'll have this child."

Elena tried another tack. "You're too skinny to have a child."

"Many women much smaller than I don't have problems. Valentin and I love each other. It is time. How could you not approve of our child?"

She stared at me with the words Jewess and intruder reflected in her eyes. I knew the old look well enough by now. She deflected my returned stare. "Your mother doesn't approve of this child. Why should I? Perhaps here we finally agree."

It was true. I hadn't spoken to my mother since she'd hung up on me upon hearing I was pregnant. How did Elena already know this?

"That's something different," I said. "You've talked with my mother?"

Elena grandly waved her hand no, as if my mother were someone on the other side of a desert–a *miraj*, no doubt, if not completely a ghost–oddly amused that she was still alive. Years ago, they'd gone together to baths and health spas in cities all over Europe–she, my mother, and about twenty other wives of the *Garda Vechea*. But now my mother was too powerless even to be an embarrassment to her.

"Forget about your mother. She's old and retired, a load on the State." Elena smiled and warmed her voice. "But you, if you do not have this child yet–if you *wait*–life could improve dramatically for you. If not, you've forgotten the privileges you already have. Heat is a privilege, and food. You will learn what it's like not to accept favors."

"Then I will learn it." I turned away.

"That's fine. This is something I understand. *O faci pe piela ta.* You do it, you'll feel it on your skin. Do you know what the Comrade will say about this?" she said as I left. "He will be very displeased."

I RETURNED to our apartment in frustration at Elena's control over our lives.

"Don't worry," Valentin kept saying all night after I told him what happened.

"I'm not worrying. She can't mean such a thing. What woman wouldn't want her own grandchild?"

"You don't understand her, I don't understand her. Even now she thinks she's doing the best thing. She just doesn't think we're ready, perhaps."

"You love her," I said, "and I admire you for that. But she's just told us not to have our baby. What should I do? Should I run away and bear my baby in the woods, and give him to a woodcutter and his family?"

"I love you, Dana, and we'll have this baby. He has a right to live. I'll be the proudest father. My mother wants to pretend we're still children, like any mother, but she'll get over it."

Like any mother? I didn't need her to get over it. I just needed her to leave us alone.

Valentin didn't talk for a long time. He spent the evening reading. I couldn't sleep, so I spent the night in a chair in the living room. Around 3am, Valentin woke up and found me there.

"Why are you up so early?" he said. When I didn't answer, he said, "All you do is worry. I love you, but you have to be more fun."

"I'm trying, with all my hope and breath, to be fun."

"That's what I mean. Forget the hope and breath. Just get to the fun. Relax. You've become more and more like your mother, the tsuris vacuum-cleaner."

"I'll leave the hope and breath to our child." I laughed. "I promise, Valentin. There'll be lots of fun." I walked to our bleak window and looked at the night trees asleep in what small corner of Herastrau I could see, the leaves sleeping easily and unseen on the eyes of my own child, my own magic child so much like a faraway song on the wind.

Everything would be all right. My company tonight was the hum of the refrigerator, the sound of running water in other apartments, the rare swish of a privileged car heading toward an early meeting. She thought I was nothing. I lit a Kent to my memory of Elena and prepared myself for an all-out battle with my in-laws. In her mind, I really wasn't much of a human being.

But my son was, yes. I was sure it was a boy.

My beautiful son.

I went to Valentin now, full of hope. To make room in bed he slowly rolled over, turning his shoulders away from me.

As New Year's Eve approached, I continued with work, preparations for the baby, and plans for a small party we'd be attending with some friends at a borrowed villa on Lake Snagov to welcome the arrival of 1981. I knew my friend Donca had been pregnant for some time with Nicu's child and might have a festive maternity dress I could borrow for the party, so on a whim I called her up one afternoon to ask if she'd lend me one.

I looked forward to talking with her, because it had been several weeks since we'd spoken. How lucky Nicu was to have her. She'd suffered through his many scandals and refused to ridicule him for sucking his thumb at age thirty. She dared to argue back with him when he addressed her with "Fa," an informal, degrading form of "you" that people used in the mountains. "Ba," she'd answer, using the masculine form.

I called Donca, but no one was there.

I tried again.

Then, on the third day, I called and her sister answered. "How dare you call here?"

"What? What's wrong?" I said. "I was just calling Donca to borrow some maternity clothes."

"How dare you! Don't you know?"

The silence hung for an eternity before I said, "You must tell me what's wrong."

More silence.

Then I heard the receiver click.

I rang her up again. "All I want to do is speak to Donca."

"My sister isn't able to come to the phone, as you well know."

"What's wrong?"

"You're calling to borrow some maternity clothes, right?"

"Nothing more."

"And who's asked you to do this, witch? Just exactly who?" She was sobbing, and her voice was quivering.

"I'm coming over there."

"Oh, don't!" she cried. "It isn't possible that you don't know."

"I know nothing. Is Donca all right? Was it Nicu?"

She moaned. "Oh, not Nicu, the weakling. They took her, strapped her onto a table, and took the baby out of her belly. We all tried to stop them. She's still in the hospital. The baby was more than five months along."

"Who did this?"

"State doctors at the clinic. They said she had an emergency condition that threatened her life. And in a way, she did. She was bearing a Ceausescu child!"

"Doctors came and picked her up?"

"No, idiot, Securitate. So now we have some clothes for you and your Jewish baby. We wish you all the luck for your fine scion of the Ceausescu clan. Do come and select your clothes. And give your family our best regards."

"I'm sorry," I said into the telephone. My words froze. "I knew nothing of this." I thought of Donca lying on a bed, a big X on her abdomen, a void in her life that would haunt her forever, like living beside a lake with the water drained out.

"We thank you so much for your sorrow and solicitude." Her sister hung up.

I spent another automatic day at the museum, making an inventory of pieces of precious metal for the national collection, thinking about Donca and feeling the life inside me. I tasted the metal in my mouth. Nicu had seemed so tender, waiting for his son to be born. I felt sick, sorry for Donca and afraid for myself. During the walks I'd taken with Donca the last few months, she'd seemed so happy at the prospect of having a child. Later she'd been disturbed by the avalanche of letters and threats she was receiving about the baby penned by "concerned citizens" worried about her trapping Nicu in marriage. But this?

This intrigue had Elena written all over it.

"I DIDN'T KNOW about this!" Valentin said when I came back from work and confronted him. "How could Nicu have agreed to this?" He began to sing a song by Leonard Cohen. "Oh, father, father, please change my name; the one that I am using now is covered up with cowardice and shame."

I looked up at Valentin. Was he the same man I'd married? Promising to help Donca, he kissed me with the mouth I loved so much, and it still tasted good. I felt weak and comforted by his strength. Perhaps this excitement was due to my condition, he said. I should go to my doctor the next day, have a complete checkup, and seek his recommendations about how I should take care of myself. I should calm down.

I looked up into his unusual eyes and fell in love with him all over again. I hugged him so hard I hoped all my worry would drop away. I didn't want to lose this man. If he spent too much time away from me, he'd never come back. I blinked away the tears in my eyes and tried to look sexy.

"I haven't told you the good news." He stroked my hair.

"Your office isn't moving, is it?" Many offices had been moved three times in recent months, all in the attempt to fool the US satellites that monitored the Institutul de Fizica Atomica.

"No, Dana. I'm going to Dubna for research."

"Why do you have to go now?" It seemed impossible that he was going away to the Soviet Union.

"It's important." He affectionately fluffed my hair. "Take care of our baby." He ran his hand smoothly over my belly.

"I do worry too much, because I love you," I said.

"I love you, too." He kissed me. "And I love our baby."

"When will you be home?"

"In a week, no more. Go back to sleep."

I stirred when he kissed me goodbye and woke when he closed the door.

Chapter 11

One man's death makes another's breath

INSTEAD OF one week, Valentin was gone for three. By the time he returned, things were getting noticeably worse for everyone. Nicolae, in an attempt to gain international prestige, had decided to pay off the $10 billion in foreign debt he'd incurred industrializing our nation all at once.

That meant everything we grew or made was for exportation only. State workers were assigned to work six, then seven, days a week. Our beautiful vegetables disappeared from the shelves. Dairy products were all but gone, and sweet cakes were barely made with an atom of eggs or butter. Instead of being able to buy ten kinds of cheese, we could buy one if we were lucky enough to find any.

To celebrate Valentin's return, I went to the back door of the Arcul de Triumf restaurant to buy a morsel of meat and legumes. The clerk in the kitchen, a friend who'd been slipping food to us for months, said, "It's no longer possible. I'm sorry."

A waitress we knew who happened to be back there picking up an order looked at me with tears in her eyes. "*Tovarasa* Dana," she said. "We were instructed not to serve you anymore." By now I was showing my pregnancy. She was ashamed.

When Valentin tried at that restaurant and three others, the answer was the same. We didn't have to ask why.

In desperation, Valentin turned to his uncle, the one who'd attended our wedding, and Nicolae's youngest brother made it possible for us to buy food directly from a farm once a week near Bucharest. I opened the door the first week to three luxurious bags of green spinach. I took as little as I dared and gave the rest to my childhood Nanny, who still lived nearby and was very dear to me. In fact, she and I had been discussing her caring for our future newborn when I returned to work.

WITH oil rationed, everyone in our apartment block felt the same bone-numbing cold. "Can you believe they expect people to live like this?" Valentin gasped cheerfully, dancing on the balls of his feet on the tingling floors. He made us each a cup of imitation instant coffee. Families all over the city were exploding–if they weren't asphyxiated first–because they often used their faulty gas cook stoves for heat.

The newspapers reported everything was fine and we had more than enough, but we all had to wear coats night and day, even in bed. Then the electricity was rationed. Valentin didn't seem to care. In fact, the cold weather brought out the best in him. He was courageous, and these were some of the happiest weeks of my life.

"Your mother is trying awfully hard to be good now," I laughed when I hadn't heard from her in a month, and Valentin, to his credit, laughed back.

Now our soup had little or no meat in it, and like our neighbors we added herbs to the water to a brain-snapping peak. This was how we all paid for the Palace of the People, the Canal, and the modern living centers we were "giving" to each village.

"ARE YOU sure?" Valentin asked me only once, and not without kindness. "Are you sure you want this child?"

"Would you flavor your soup with your own son for meat?" Whenever I was hungry, I'd think of this. It was the phrase I rebuked myself with. Then I felt cold and small and said, "Valentin, you know that sooner or later the end is coming. Your parents will no longer be in power, and we'll take the blame along with them. Maybe we'll deserve it, too, but not a child. Should we bring a child into the world to face this along with us?"

Valentin was suddenly serious. "I am aware of this. No matter what, when the trouble comes, the three of us will be together. I will always be there to protect you."

NASTASE glumly returned for a visit. Dominique had just won a large divorce settlement from him, and after an ugly court battle, he'd also lost custody of his baby daughter. He was staying with his parents in his villa on Andrei Muresan, about five or ten minutes from our house.

Though I knew it pained him to bring it up, he mustered a smile and asked us what we'd name our baby.

"That's easy–Dani Valentin," Valentin said before I could answer. "His mother's Dana, and her father's Iordan. And it was Daniel who fought against the lions without fear."

"Daniel, eh?" Ilie turned to me.

I'd really wanted to name him Iordan, after my father, but my in-laws would have hit the roof.

"Yes," I said. "We've thought about it a long time. In early Hebrew it means, 'God gives it, God judges it.' We thought about Julian for a while, but how pompous Julian Ceausescu would sound, like Julius Caesar. Imagine the children at school."

"And what if he's a girl?"

"We've always known Dani is a boy. If he's a girl, he'll be Valdana, but that's impossible. I feel he's already here with us now."

Ilie turned to Valentin and said, "So what's up with your brother? I hear he's been busy."

"He's not really my brother. We're all orphans," Valentin said.

Nastase looked hard at Valentin and laughed. "You could make twice as much trouble as Nicu if you weren't so lazy. Nicu wakes up at 6am every day to begin his full day of shaping youth in his own precious image at the Central Committee of Holy Assholes. 'Who will I oppress today?' But he works at it. Get off your can."

"Nicu's not so happy," Valentin said.

Catalin had just told us about a party he'd attended with Nicu, an orgy of food and drink for some officials and sons of the Nomenclatura, including Mihail Bujor, later a diplomat to the US. The proceedings were warming up, and Nicu'd been drinking a lot. Everyone laughed, and he laughed harder. Suddenly he leaped up on the table. "Do you see how they laugh at me? Do you see these sycophants? There's nothing I can do that they won't like, because they're so afraid of my father. Isn't that right, sycophants? Watch this."

Nicu pulled down his trousers, walked up to each black-suited guest, and urinated into one water glass after another while the room erupted in laughter. His aim wasn't very good. "Look!" he said. "Do you see how funny I can be? They're shitting their pants in fright, but they don't dare to stop me."

As the weeks passed, I felt a glow because of "the child who should never be born", but Elena's doctors had some bad news for me. They threatened me with horror stories about monstrous deformities and pain during delivery. "Your first two trimesters didn't go very well at all," they said. "You must terminate now, while it's still possible."

Only one doctor, tall with curly blond hair and a prominent nose, disagreed. "I've even been asked to put you to sleep during your next checkup and abort the baby," he said after the others left. "Make sure all your future appointments are with me."

When I tried to do exactly that, the others came to me and said, "Your mother-in-law has ordered that in your best interest we should advise her of each step of your condition. She's told us that, like her–and all other Romanian women–you're to have a natural childbirth and you're not to be issued any sick-day releases, no matter how you feel."

My one advocate, the tall doctor, smiled and came a good deal closer as if to kiss my cheek but really to whisper in my ear, "I've told her I've already determined that a cesarean delivery is the only safe course to take because of the position of the baby in the uterus. Don't give it a thought. I'll convince her to change her mind."

"How?" Will you walk up the marble dock at Lake Snagov and tell her at a reception for senior officials? You're a sweet obstetrician who cares for his patients, and they need you. It's best to stay out of this. "Has she come here herself?"

"No, she's only spoken to us by telephone."

"Is it possible for me to have a natural childbirth? I'd like that myself."

"We don't need to decide right now," he said. "Because of your age, we need to keep all of our options open."

"Should I keep coming here?" Elias was a party hospital, and my father had already died here. I had to know.

"Of course."

But when I left him I could see a worried look in his blue eyes.

In my ninth month, when my due date came and went without labor pains, Valentin took me to the hospital, but my doctor wasn't on duty. Instead, his superior, a senior physician, looked in on me and said, "No, there's no concern at all. I've already talked to your mother-in-law, and we're going to have a perfectly wonderful natural childbirth."

"Who'll perform the delivery?" Valentin said.

"I will."

"But doctor, I don't think I'm in labor. I felt some stomachaches before, but I haven't felt one for several hours. Should I come back later?"

He frowned. "You feel nothing at all?"

"Nothing."

We checked in, and I spent a week there, with Valentin visiting me daily. Finally, on the eighth day at sunrise, the tall doctor came in and whispered to me, "We've waited for a week for permission to deliver this child. I can't wait anymore. It's a crime to wait one more hour. Stop reading that book. You have pains. You can't act like that. Scream."

"What?"

"Scream." He gave me medicine to induce contractions and rushed out of the room. "Scream!"

While I began to call out, I thought of the airplane crash my parents had been in while they were young revolutionaries. They'd been sent by Stalin from Moscow to join a pro-Soviet partisan group and follow it west with the front, fighting the Germans all the way. Instead of leading the group of Romanian and Transylvanian revolutionaries, they were shot down in their plane by the *fascisti*, plunging into the darkest forests of the Soviet border.

My mother broke her ribs, but she loved to tell me about the "real moss" on the ground where their plane crashed, "beautiful, like in a fairy tale." They were days of forest travel away from civilization and now in danger of execution from Stalin, who was annoyed they'd failed to carry out their mission on time. They were among the only survivors who incorporated themselves into the dark of the woods and were nursed back to health by partisan families, the men in long beards "like big elves", my mother told me.

My parents ended up fighting with a band of people in the woods for months over territory disputes totally below the purview of global politics, and they were so happy they almost remained in that world. Even when they were older, my father used to point out any moss he might find on a mountain or near the lake, and my mother would smile without saying a word. This moss from their youth made them young again, and I imagined myself lying on a bed of its emerald green, young myself with my father stroking my hair. I opened my mouth and began to make the loudest noise I'd ever made in my life. With a wave of relief I recognized the face of the tall doctor regarding me anxiously as I looked up from my bed of moss.

He bent over and said one word to me.

"Scream."

"What?"

"Your water has broken."

Is that what he said?

I let out another little yell—yes, that was it.

But the tall doctor seemed irritated with me. "Help yourself! Scream!" he said. "Pretend. Haven't I told you? Make more noise than anyone in this hospital. Now. Now!"

I let out a shriek, then another, and then I thought of Elena watching the baby die underneath my smooth belly, and I screamed a deep blue hell of a scream. I screamed thinking of the baby cut dead out of the womb of Donca, a husk discarded like I was about to be discarded. They moved me now into a very small operatory where I was quickly connected to a monitor and felt my baby stop moving inside me while I screamed. "Oh, he is dying!" I cried and screamed more. He is dying.

"There's no dilation," the tall doctor shouted as I yelled, and several nurses filled the room. Was this an operatory or a broom closet? Where was I? A nurse rolled me on my side and injected something into my spine. So this was the last light I'd see, me and my poor child. This small place.

Chapter 12

Crooked logs make straight fires

THE KIND DOCTOR was cutting me, but I couldn't feel the lower half of my body. He was sawing me open and letting light come into that dark place.

Blood was everywhere. Why was I conscious? Should I be seeing this? I looked down and saw it was black blood. The nurses looked at each other.

The doctor plunged his hands into me, and more blood spilled on the white sheets. He pulled out a tiny thing dark with blood and wiped it down.

"Long, wide, and fair." They whisked him away as I held out my arms. A nurse gave me an injection. Warm amnesia flooded over my body, and I fell asleep in spite of my struggle to stay awake.

"Where's my baby?" I asked when I woke. "Where's my husband?"

"Your husband wasn't here for the delivery." A nurse pushed another syringe into my arm.

"But where is he? Where?"

The nurses just looked at each other.

Finally, an orderly said, "I think he's with his parents."

"Do you mean I'm alone?"

"You have all of us."

"Where is my baby?" It was hard to keep my voice from slurring.

At this the nurses walked away. I yelled and pushed over a tray. They returned and held me down as another warm flood came back over me, and I fell asleep.

The next day, I opened my eyes to see roses and carnations sent by Valentin. I tried to talk some more but couldn't. Consciousness was a slippery cliff. Where were they sending me? With anesthesia they were mailing my arms, my legs, away again.

Deep dread came over me. Why wasn't Valentin here? When I woke up I called him at home, but no one answered. What kind of husband could do this? A bad husband, a husband afraid of his responsibilities, would have been out drinking. But what kind of husband would have been with his parents?

I realized that from now on my baby could depend only on me. Like so many women before me, I grew up on the day my child was born.

"Where is my baby?" I said. "It's been three days. Who dares to keep a baby from her mother for three days?" I could hear other children crying in a nearby room, and my breasts were very sore. I fell to a low crying, because I knew that my baby was already dead.

What was happening to me? I'd been a spoiled child, but did I deserve this? I half dreamed of my son's face flickering in a mirror.

Then the door opened. Shapes came toward me. I struggled up to my elbows to see.

The tall doctor was already in the hall, talking to the senior doctor. Their voices rose, but it was already too late for them to stop him. My doctor strode in to me holding my baby adorned in a tiny hood, his head snuggled into the collar of his shirt.

"I haven't let him out of my sight," he said. "Many people heard you scream. I explained it was too late for natural child-birth. They'll get over it." He placed Dani in my outstretched arms.

And with joy I saw my baby for the first time, a beautiful child from the meadow, with moss and great trees spreading everywhere in every direction. Dani was perfect, dear mother and father, my poor dead father who loved me so much–already with gentle soft hair on his–

I caught my breath.

To my great shock I saw the child in my arms now regarded me piercingly with Valentin's eyes, Ceausescu eyes. I shivered to think the resemblance would bring sorrow instead of happiness to the sweetest young life on earth.

"DANI!" Valentin stepped into the room. "My baby! My wife! They finally let me see you!"

He told me he'd been in to see us several times in the past three days, but I'd been too weak to recognize him. He took the two of us home and was all the husband I'd ever dreamed of, hardly leaving my side. And what a proud father he was! Sometimes I thought he'd never put Dani down.

FOR the next four months after Dani's birth I saw nothing of my in-laws until I bumped into Elena while waiting to pick up Valentin in front of the Ceausescus' private recreational center, Club Bazin, across from the presidential palace. This hall was constructed to prevent any visitors from actually setting foot in the Primaverii. On the same side of the street, there'd been a grocery store and butcher shop Elena ordered closed because He and She couldn't bear to see the lines of people forming in front of it.

This wasn't the only business they closed to promote their own agenda. When Nicolae's father, Andruta (who named not one but two of his sons Nicolae in a drunken stupor, not realizing the duplication), went to his favorite bar one day, he found it had been transformed overnight into a creamery, "The Lacto Bar".

I looked up. There was Elena, herpes zoster lesions on her forehead barely covered by a big silk Hermes scarf, heading across the street. She didn't seem to recognize me at first; then she stopped for a moment and sniffed at Dani, whose diapers I was changing inside a white blanket.

"You're actually able to change him? I'm surprised you can do even this, little fool," she said, and then walked away without looking at her grandson.

I watched her clumsy figure head down the walk and then anxiously looked through the windows to try to see Valentin's face. Finally he emerged, full of high spirits and good cheer.

"What's wrong now?" He laughed.

I covered Dani's head and started for the car.

"What is it?" he said. "You should have come in. Why don't you ever come in?"

I told him about Elena, and he frowned for a moment. "But we don't want their interference. This is perfect."

We drove home without saying another word.

WE were in the Seagull late that August when we saw The Cat and Ludmila, always Liuda to me. They had two male friends with them, Horia and Radu, who were full of questions about Nicu and Zoia, particularly Nicu. Everyone was talking about Nicu, who at thirty was heir-apparent and who was now linked with Nadia Comaneci, barely eighteen and the gold medal winner at the Moscow Olympics. Rumors were flying everywhere that Nicu had just spent some summer days with Nadia in Neptune.

"She's a little on the young side, isn't she?" Radu said. "But then the Securitate are great matchmakers."

"I hear she loves him," Horia said.

"I haven't kept a candle near their bed." Valentin shrugged as a little blue cup of Chinese tea was settled in front of him on the white tablecloth. "I don't know about my brother. For all I know they're in Neptune now."

"Doesn't she weigh only eighty-five pounds?" Radu was a shameless gossip.

"She's nimble, though. She can avoid him. She's made something of a reputation as a tumbler, you know," Horia said.

Nadia looked like a child Holocaust victim, with slender shoulders and big brown curls around her sunken eyes. This was her unnerving charm, the look that made her, in spite of her dazzling spins and jumps, seem so very old and sad. We all felt like godparents to her. For Nicu to take advantage of his power and conduct a Zeus-like seduction of her, under the auspices of the Securitate... Could this be true?

"Did they meet at a party?"

"They met on some youth sports council together." Valentin turned his cup slowly in his hands.

"He doesn't need the Securitate to secure his dates," Horia said. "Why should he? Look who he is. He's brilliant, naturally attractive. I admit he's rough with women. He finds them himself, or friends introduce him to some. What do you want me to say?"

"Did he rape her?" Liuda asked.

"No," Horia said, blasé. "I've seen this. Since you've asked me a man's question, I'll tell you I know him. Many times, he'll come up to a woman at a party, take her hand, and say, 'Come on. I want to fuck you.' Please excuse the language. 'If you don't fuck right, I'll beat you,' he says. Considering who he is, women are often excited to be with him. He's very direct, yes, but a rapist, no. I know he never raped Nadia, I know this."

With a funny look on his face, Catalin now enunciated into the flower arrangement at the center of the table, "There are real feelings between them. I've heard it was *she* who was looking for Nicu in the beginning. She was hoping to get involved with him."

BEREFT of Nicu, Nadia was on her own over the next few months, eating. No one said there was a connection between her relationship with Nicu and her gaining thirty or forty pounds, but in a short time she transformed herself into an entirely different human being.

IT was also in late 1981 that Catalin and Liuda surprised us all by emigrating to the United States. They were allowed this by Nicolae, who traded human rights reforms for economic assistance from the Reagan administration.

WELL into 1982, I gave in to Valentin's plea that we present Dani to his grandparents at the Primaverii.

Elena looked right through me and acted as if I were crazy to have imagined she'd ever been my opponent. Studying me as if I were a new species of beetle and wondering where I'd fit in her insect collection, she said, "What is that silly thing you're wearing?"

I didn't know what I was wearing.

"How is it you come to see me dressed like this? And why aren't you working yet?" she said. "I never stopped working night or day while I had my children. I studied at night school to get my degrees in chemistry. Are you too good ever to act like a true Romanian woman?"

Outside the window was what I took for six Arabian men walking on the other side of the street with Kalashnikov semi-automatic rifles lazily strapped around their shoulders outside the huge villa kept for guests.

Elena took no notice of them, but instead regarded me over her desk. Then she swiveled her head. "You," she called to a cleaner who, like all of her servants, wore felt slip-ons to protect the floors.

The servant, who was working in a bathroom, halted and regarded us through a door, terrified. She padded over to Elena's entry table.

"Be sure not to rub too hard on the fixtures, or the gold will come off." Elena didn't say another word to me, and when she pretended to read papers on her desk again, I got up to leave.

FOLLOWING orders, I went back to work, but things got even worse at the museum. We shared the same heating system with the Sala Palatului, so the only time we were warm was during the times when the party met. Otherwise, we and the paintings froze. As usual, we wore our overcoats and mittens at our desks while typists wore fingerless wool gloves so their hands wouldn't stiffen while their fingertips kept their precision on the keys. When someone told our minister the cold air was bad for the art, he said, "No, we're trying out a new concept of museography in revolutionary times."

Then one of the bravest of my friends stood up and said, "But look at these paintings! They're cracking. It's criminal."

"*They* will survive."

She was quickly moved to the sector down the hall with the rest of the crazy ones. One of these ladies kept coming to me every day saying she'd been raped with a thermometer. Full days they'd dream and do nothing, but the director kept them on—because nobody was unemployed in Romania, though our paychecks had no meaning as inflation skyrocketed.

To preserve our privacy while we complained of such things, we learned the trick of sticking pencils into the dials of our telephones as we talked, circling them back and forth to disrupt the signal.

WE all whispered Elena was going gently insane, pushing her husband to the limits, but I knew in my heart my own Valentin was beginning to change, too. Ilie Nastase and some other friends met us in late 1984 for lunch at the Fratii Chivu. Ileana was there, as well as Radu. And there was the lovely, serene Roxana Duna, whose long hair spilled down like a waterfall. She and her husband, an engineer, had spoken with Valentin and me a few times at parties, but we didn't know them very well. No, he couldn't possibly be interested in someone as uncomplex as Roxana.

Nastase was down on Romania at the moment, and what he said must really have shocked the ears of the Securitate waiters. "What is Nicolae doing kissing Qaddafi and all these Palestinians all the time in these meetings? Why is Qaddafi visiting Nicolae this week?" Ilie swallowed some beer while our waiter refilled our glasses with water. "Visiting Bucharest. What will they eat tonight, these two? Corpses? I can see it now—'Bring me another hand from the refrigerator.'"

Ileana eyed Ilie. "So you don't like Nicolae's allies and his political schemes."

"What do you know about political schemes, Ileana?" Radu asked. He nodded to the rest of us and smirked. "'Oh, she stays near the ocean and she writes the Romanian history!'"

Ileana blew smoke in his face. Radu's hypocritical attitude was all too common among men in Romania. Since 1944 we women had been called comrades and were declared equal partners in the *revolutia continua*, but often this seemed to be more for show and we were relegated to the role of handmaidens to communism, forever in the dark.

"Yes," Ilie said. "I'm so very happy in this surferless nation. But you know, no one's really evil by intent, not even the Ceausescus. What gets very dangerous is when Nicolae and Elena try to be the best they can be."

A few more people in the restaurant turned around in their chairs to look at Nastase.

"You know the saying, 'Everyone is starring in the movie of his own life'?" he said. "Everyone is playing center court? Oh, how that's true with your parents, Valentin. I know they believe in what they're doing. They're a loving couple, devoted to their children, aren't they?"

Valentin looked down at his plate. "My father feels we disappoint him."

"Disappoint? Hell, he's disowned you. This evil is a crystallization of abstract rationalizations about being very, very good. You become evil slowly by believing there is only one way to be good. It's a chemical change."

"It's Nicolae's greatest feat to make our country appear to be moving away from Moscow in order to secure investment and technology from the West, when in fact he's channeling all the information he's getting directly to the KGB," Radu said.

"Hey, I know a chemical change—there's Pepsi in Bucharest now," Ileana said.

"Yes," Valentin cut in, "but who can buy it? It's more precious than champagne. It's such a mystery. You can't buy the second bottle unless you've returned the first. And where does that first bottle come from?"

"It's an exquisite change from good to evil," Ilie persisted. "It's a slide."

"Let it go," Valentin said. "You're right, okay? Let it go."

"And your brother Nicu, he's sitting on top of that slide."

"Have you heard from Catalin?" I asked Radu to relieve the tension.

"Who's he?"

"Why have you turned on him?" I chased Radu's eyes as he looked away from me. "Hasn't he done a lot for you? He's our friend. Liuda, too."

"It just seems funny," Radu said. "The way he left."

"Funny?"

"The circumstances."

"What? What's wrong with—"

"A Jewish capitalist in league with Reagan. There. And what about the talk about automotive and industrial secrets? There's a funny business going on there."

"Oh, you know Catalin," I said. "He's always up to something new. You liked him well enough while he was helping you. He's an entrepreneur."

Valentin and I left, walking out into Herastrau together through a square that no longer had older people in it.

The park was abandoned and getting colder since there were no more streetlights and the benches were removed. Empty shelves gaped in every window, and the hunger was like that in Zaire. On the news, publicists rushed the same carloads of meat and vegetables to first one photo opportunity, then another, showing Nicolae making "surprise" visits to Bucharest stores and saying, "Do you see? There's more than enough for everyone."

Far from there being enough, gangsters raced through Bucharest in dark cars at night with produce marked for the black market, pursued by the police. Just a few weeks earlier, a friend, a young engineer, had disappeared during a visit with me. "Where have you gone?" I asked when she got back.

My guest shrugged. "I've bought black." She'd been to such a car for tomatoes.

"But it's dangerous at night," I said.

For many months the streetlights had been shut off in Bucharest, spawning mobs of robbers and thieves in a world black as pitch. It was purple and green out there, a nightmare, *Rémálom* from my mother's Hungarian. Streets were no longer cleaned. There was no toilet paper. The level of poverty reported in Romania was not European, but rather "African". The standard joke went, "If things were any better, it would be like wartime."

And still the Ceausescus remained in power. Oh, we had elections, but only the Central Committee could vote in a new general secretary, so even though voting was compulsory, our ballots included choices only for the lower positions. If you failed to show up to vote, as I often did, a party member with a list in his hand arrived at your house and jovially but firmly escorted you to your civic duty. "I would have thought you'd have been among the first ones," a neighbor, pressed into this activity, encouraged me as he took my arm. After the elections, *Scinteia* invariably published articles about the millions of letters mailed by everyday Romanians to the government begging for our rulers' names to be included on ballots so that they could have voted for them. "If only we could," the newspapers wrote, "but the first family insists upon the strictest adherence to the rules..."

BECAUSE luxuries couldn't be bought now at any price, goods were becoming worth far more than money.

Doctors, working triple shifts, refused to see us out of sheer exhaustion, so we brought what we could to swap for treatment, even if we had nothing.

"Bars of soap?" I asked my mother about her friend. "For an appendectomy?"

"That's all she had."

I closed my eyes. "Where does she live?"

The next day after work, I went to this woman's flat with a bottle of Fuji perfume that Valentin had bought for me on a trip.

"Here," I said after I told her who my mother was. "Give this to your doctor."

She cradled the bottle in her hands like a jewel. "You can do this? I don't–"

"This," I said, "is something I should have done a long time ago."

I plunged in. Whereas I'd haughtily refused presents and privileges from the Gospodaria-de-Partid up until now, all of a sudden I accepted everything they'd give me to use for my own black-market currency. Everything in my house had trade value. A bottle of Cinzano bought another lady chemotherapy. A pack of real coffee was a big treat that allowed a friend at the museum to see a urologist. In this case I went to the office with him and waited in the hall while he presented it to the doctor.

"No, thank you!" I could hear the doctor saying. "Give us something real to drink. Don't give us this *posirca*." Our Romanian coffee substitute, made out of petroleum byproducts and black herbs, was junk, very diluted. "It gives me headaches. It has a bitter taste."

"Oh, no, this is different. From Italy. Compliments of my boss, just for you."

The doctor was out in the hall in a second. He wagged his finger at me and grinned. "Ah, *Tovarasa* Dana. What do you think, I work for cigarettes or snacks?"

"The real thing. Good to the last drop." I felt the warmth of this good man, just a regular old crank with a line of fifty people outside. A teaspoon of even instant coffee was now the gold standard, and he'd certainly earned it. "I hope you'll enjoy it." It had been months since we'd had any at the museum.

He nodded, went back inside, and began the treatment. As we left, I saw him beckon to his colleagues to come smell the dark, fresh coffee in the package.

WORD got around. Sometimes people came to my house, sometimes to the museum. A liter of Martini and Rossi secured a friend's sister-in-law an appointment with a good ophthalmologist so she could get new lenses for her glasses. In a twinkle, a box of chocolates transformed itself into nitroglycerine pills for a heart patient. There, Elena–I was finally willing to accept your chocolates.

"They'll persecute you," friends said. "Someone's going to inform on you."

"Many others are doing far more."

"One day I'll inform on you that you're on the black market, you and your medicines," a woman said at work. She nodded toward the window. "Maybe you'll grow wings." But later on she asked me if I were able to get her some antibiotics for her asthmatic child.

"Here." I handed her the package the following morning.

"I'm sorry," she said, and I breathed a sigh of relief.

To the grouchiest doctor of all I sent that most hated of scents, even in the Soviet Bloc–some Charlie perfume for his wife that Valentin had "selected" especially for me, probably at an airport duty-free shop.

Vans from the Gospodaria now rolled in with ten times the coffee, cigarettes, liquor, meat, and ricotta cheese we needed, and twenty times the baby formula Dani needed. The raw cotton we had to use for feminine hygiene had degraded until box after box turned up nothing but gray, harsh fiber filled with leaves, seeds, and sticks. You had to go through 20 boxes in order to get clean, white cotton, so I did—for my friends.

"You want more?" The driver blinked.

"Of course. How could you bring me these?" No doubt he figured I was ripening into a real Ceausescu. "And next time, bring me two of the good turkeys."

After a while, I even started trading directly for medicine with some staff doctors I knew at Elias. After visiting my father there for so many years, I knew quite a few of them. I dropped these prescribed medicines on people's doorsteps. Others I delivered on the streets at night.

There was a time when a certain doctor who'd used his paycheck to buy foreign medicines for his patients did need money, so I went in with someone who needed to see him and handed him a small volume of poems with a wad of bills inside it. "We'd like you to have this book. It's a very good one."

He threw it against the wall. "What can I do with a book? You want me to read?" The money fluttered out, and then he said, "Reading is okay."

"No one else will answer our letters," Liuda wrote to us. Catalin never complained in the notes he scribbled as postscripts, but I sensed the hurt he felt when he asked about his other friends.

We told him everything we knew and helped to keep his contacts alive in Bucharest. Then Liuda's brother took ill, and she and Catalin flew over to visit him.

"Dana," Catalin said, calling from the airport. "We're here."

"In Bucharest?"

"Yes, at Baneasa. But they say I can't go. Liuda can."

"I'll be right over."

No matter what I said, the immigration agents had orders not to let Catalin into the country. "You're here, but you're not here," they told him and handed him his bags. "You're flying somewhere else."

"Where am I going?"

"We don't care. Go to Paris, just not here."

"He's coming with me," I said.

"No, *Tovarasa*," an agent said. "We know that your husband has called, but we have our orders." He looked at Liuda. "*She* can come in. Do you want her?"

Catalin nodded to me.

"You bet. Come on." I took the very upset Liuda by car to her brother, who in the coming weeks made a full recovery.

Later, Catalin was allowed to visit Bucharest on business, but his position remained precarious, and Valentin often had to bribe some officials to ensure his safe entry and exit.

"Why do you do this for us?" he said. "No one else will talk to us. We've been frozen out."

"How long have I known you and Liuda? Since first grade?" I laughed.

"We've been told to stay away from *you*," he said with a smile. "You and your private pharmacy, Valentin with the passports he gets for everybody. But Valentin, I've heard that many of your scientist friends who get passports from you don't return after their studies abroad are complete. What's going on there?"

"I've got nothing to do with that," Valentin said. "What they do after they arrive somewhere is their business. I sure as hell don't want them to leave. But unless they've got unrestricted access to further study here, what's going to make them come back?" He stiffened and said, "How's the car business? Do Americans really want those ARO utility vehicles we're making, designed for Soviet troops?"

"Want them? They're uglier than Land Rovers. They adore them!"

WE KEPT writing to Catalin and Liuda and sending them news of Bucharest, but few beyond us and Ilie, when he was around, would ever communicate with them.

I LOOKED FORWARD to attending Zoia's wedding, since she'd been so crucial to our romance. I slipped out of the house before daylight, went to the black market at the Strada Lipscani, and bought a wedding bouquet of white freesias–Zoia's favorites.

When I went home, Valentin had a surprise for me. At the last minute, he asked me feverishly to stay home. "You can't come," he'd said with a haunted look in his eyes.

I was crushed. "But she's invited both of us." I was so humiliated. I was all dressed, ready to go. He made me believe nobody was going to miss me. I technically didn't exist.

Even though this was none of my choice, I felt our sisterly relationship cool.

VALENTIN was named Scientific Secretary of the Institutul de Fizica Atomica. Many pressured us to move to a better place. Friends said, "Look at Nicu, look at Zoia. They're living well. Move! Move!" Valentin began to be affected by this.

Some friends.

Then Valentin found a house he liked on 16 Grigore Cerchez, named for the architect. My mother said, "Don't do it. It's too much for you. You can't afford it." And we couldn't. Valentin spent long nights making calculations to prove we could, but what it really came down to was he was now beginning to accept favors from the Gospodaria-de-Partid and other agencies through his parents.

By 1985, I was unpacking boxes in a stucco and red-tiled duplex with its own modest garden and garage. We lived on the first floor, while the actress daughter of the famous poet Tudor Arghizi lived on the second.

Built in the 1940s, this house was grand enough to make me nervous. The living room had an ornate plaster mantelpiece cut by the same hand of excess that was building the huge palaces in the Centru Civic in the central political district. "All in the name of modernization," The Danube of Thought had proclaimed, wiping out fifty blocks of buildings dating from the old Turkish inns and *caravanserai* of the sixteenth century to the mansions that Parisian architects designed when remodeling the city in the 1890s.

"How can we live here?" I asked Valentin. "Mitzura upstairs is helped out by royalties from her father's poems. But what about us?"

I'd been rushed into this too-luxurious house too quickly: this custom woolen wall-to-wall carpet seemed too voluptuous, the kitchen too Western-convenient. For years we'd refused any presents from my in-laws, but now, as my eyes rested on each of the gifts, my guilt increased as the rattling of a Geiger counter increases in the presence of something radioactive. I'd been rushed—or had I allowed myself to be rushed?

Yes, I was part of it. I couldn't lie to myself anymore.

It hit home one afternoon when I drove to a village near Sibiu to inspect some artifacts recently discovered in an old farmhouse by a delightful old couple of Transylvanian peasants. Our car had splashed through puddles during a muddy rainstorm the day before, and a friend at the museum, teasing me, had written "Wash me" on the trunk. Barely remembering it was there, I enjoyed a nice conversation with the old couple in their home, took some notes, and emerged back into the sunlight.

"What is this?"

The terrified villagers had washed the car spotlessly clean.

THAT next spring, Valentin left early on yet another junket with his parents, leaving me, Nanny, who'd joined our household, and Dani with many unspoken thoughts.

Whenever my husband said, "I'm on the way home" now, we didn't know if he were on the way to our house or the presidential palace.

I didn't nag him about his absences because I'd promised myself I was a good trusting wife who could take care of herself, and I wanted to show him I believed in him. Besides, didn't we have this beautiful child?

For Dani was beautiful, with smooth skin and genius in his nimble fingers. He was so much fun to be with. He'd learned to speak very early and began to show his own take on everything. He had a profound way of considering a house alive or dead, depending on its state of occupancy. When our neighbors went to Neptune, he was concerned. "Aren't they away on vacation?"

"Yes."

"But they've left three windows open."

He wasn't concerned about the weather; it was about dignity. Windows were eyes. If the owners were gone, the eyes should be closed.

Now that most Western shows were banned on television, we had to be content with Chinese, Korean, and Romanian films "spiced" with political speeches made by Nicolae. Once, when Nicolae was on the screen, Dani said, "Why is Father Vale shouting? Where are his dogs? Why does he just say the same thing over and over? Why is he so loud? It's boring."

Nanny, terrified, quickly clamped her hand over his mouth.

Another time he delighted me when he asked, "Momma, can we invite her over for dinner?"

"Who?"

Dani, then age four, didn't know he was in love for the first time.

In fact, he was sweetly in love, not with one of his little schoolmates in preschool, as I would have imagined, but rather, to my astonishment, with her mother. I couldn't help but smile as I said gently, "Yes, Dani, but I can't invite her without inviting her daughter. Otherwise the little girl's feelings will be hurt."

"She must come alone," he said. This was a sweet young mother whom I'd met only once, and even then it was during a rainstorm as I was dropping Dani off at school. What was I going to do? I looked at Dani, who was now considering the matter with a good deal of gravity. He walked slowly to the window. Finally he turned with his brows unknitting themselves and gave me a wonderful smile, his chestnut hair glowing in baby curls as he let his arms fall to his sides. "Okay," he said. "Her daughter can come, too."

Then he changed his mind. "Wait a minute. I don't want Mrs Georgescu to come. If Daddy sees her, he'll like her also, and you'll be pushed aside."

No matter how hard I tried, his childhood could never be completely normal. He was playing in the schoolyard one day with a few little friends when "crazy" Dr Tudoran drove by. The veterinarian leaned out his car window and frightened the other children by yelling, "Don't touch him. Do you know who he is? He's like gold."

Dani's pals jeered. A few backed away.

The washed-up vet's obsession with everything Ceausescu had extended beyond the Labradors to include my son. Was this another sign of a growing national neurosis? I would never again feel comfortable leaving Dani alone.

Chapter 13

Dead dogs bite not

To celebrate the First of May, 1986, Valentin, Dani, and I were invited to a family party at the Ceausescus' villa on Lake Snagov. I was surprised, since such invitations came only to Valentin, and he and I had long since stopped pretending it was otherwise.

Before I could make a decision to accept, I got a terse note from Zoia suggesting it would be rude of me to not attend when I was expected to be there. So she still didn't understand why I'd skipped her wedding and still hadn't forgiven me. Or had I simply been made the fall guy for this, too?

"Quit worrying," Valentin said, "and have some fun. Do you always have to worry like this?"

"It's my fault. I should have told her I had really wanted to go to her wedding. She helped us so when you were in London."

"She hasn't said anything. You're imagining things."

So Valentin had even forgotten his part in it.

"That's right. And my imagination is improving. Do you see how she's still angry?"

Or was it me?

SINCE THIS WAS my first visit to the Lake Snagov villa, Valentin offered a quick tour. He waved at "his" room–all brocade hangings and silk wallpaper. I was surprised to see a terrycloth robe, slippers, and tennis gear thrown on the expensive furniture by someone very obviously settled in. How often had Valentin been here when he was away on business?

Because the Ceausescus were now being openly paranoiac, in each room of this palace was a sink with a special transparent bottle of alcohol where everyone had to wash her hands upon entering. Securitate officials swept the rooms for bugs and changed telephones there daily, as they did in all the presidential villas. We passed through miles of icy opulence to the terrace. Nicolae was on a patio beside the lake, with his prize vineyards and orchards in full view, carving up a barbecued pig the size of a fourteen-year-old child. Zoia lounged on the terrace wall, dressed in a close-cut leopard suit with a shockingly short skirt, while Elena sat stonily fingering her pearls–a "gift" from Cartier. Nicu was there, drunk as usual but amiable tonight, and he patted Dani on the head as we headed toward the umbrella tables. Zoia pretended not to see me.

This was far from being just a family affair. Official photographers snapped away while the *Stabi*–big shots–"licked" Elena by praising the soirée and calling her "The Queen of the First May Dance and the Queen of Science, Recognized By 124 Worldwide Scientific Institutions," from Rio de Janeiro to Chicago to Britain's Royal Institute of Chemistry. This was absurd hyperbole to the few of us who knew she'd never finished fifth grade. The creature before me now stood with her blocky hips twitching, her wrinkled lips disappearing in a smile. The world had created this monster, not just Romania. According to international media accounts, she and Rosalynn Carter were "great friends".

During unguarded moments she'd stare *ca vitelul la poarta noua*, "like a calf at a new gate", legs apart, her mouth slack, ignorant, open, her eyes looking dull, uncomprehending, and even slightly confused. And here was Nicolae, doing his part for the "worldwide revolution of proletarian peoples", sawing away at the beast as the charcoal hissed below the dripping fat.

During the private part of the celebration, more shutterbugs snapped away at Dani in group photographs and with Nicu and Zoia, running around and having fun. The table was resplendent with venison, trout, lobster, pheasant, frogs' legs.

I sat under an umbrella across the terrace, my head spinning. Valentin showed Dani to anybody who'd look. Then, with the photographers shooed away and aides finishing with the meat, Nicolae, without a stammer, addressed the family:

"I am so glad to have us all together, to see Zoia and her husband so happy in their marriage; my son Nicu now doing his duty at Sibiu, following in the political tradition of our family; and Valentin, who is trying to be a better son. There would be only one thing that could make this occasion more grand," he said. "For one of you to make me my first grandchild. The one who will give me this grandson will receive an apartment bought by me as a present."

Light in my head, I stood and looked at him with my father's eyes. I wasn't going to listen to this. I tore Dani out of Valentin's arms and, not caring how much I embarrassed Valentin, stalked out of the terrace and over the flowers Nicolae prized so much he'd installed several sets of lights for them, his favorites the tiny pathway lights that made them glow in little patterns when he walked there at night.

I didn't care if they shot me in the back. Angry tears spilled down my face, and I hugged Dani so hard that he cried too, our breaths rushing in and out of our diaphragms roughly, the groomed earth stinging with our tears. Dani was coughing. How would we get away? There was an alternate gate, but it was patrolled. We ran across the lawn beside the lake toward the freedom of our guest house. The guard didn't see us, and as we reached the bushes that curved toward our walkway I wondered how it was going to end. Would I be poisoned? I felt a premonitory tingle in my stomach while Dani yowled. What evil had I committed to cause all this trouble for my son? How had love brought me to the center of one of the most satanic empires ever to rule the earth?

I jumped as I felt a hand on my shoulder. "You!"

Elena had an unearthly smile on now, ethereally calming. She looked composed in her matching turquoise outfit and Charles Jordan shoes, her diamond and sapphire bracelet dangling from her spotted arm as she reached out to stroke my *Boanghen* hair. "He shouldn't have said that. I'm so sorry. As a mother I know that Nicule should never have said that with you there. Come back with me now."

"No. Please let me be."

"Come on, come back," she said. "At least you're loyal to Valentin, a trait I admire. You're a fool, but you have this one quality. You'll have to work on the others."

She took me by the arm, and we headed indoors first, and then across the lawn.

But the evening was not finished. As the hours wore on, Dani and I huddled in the corner. Why didn't I leave Valentin and his family now? I was exactly like the rest of Romania–stirred but not awakened.

Valentin, enraged only for the moment, was now back with Nicu, laughing. Nicu had his customary glass of Johnnie Walker Black Label in his hand, refilling it again and again even as he complained of pains in his liver. Nicu was smart. Nicu was doing everything he could to kill himself.

Servants now brought out a sterling silver dish filled with specially roasted, juicy steaks that weren't available in any store now for any amount of money. Nicolae turned to the dish during the same moment Dani broke away from me and asked, "Could I have some of that, please?"

"No," Nicolae said. "These are for my dogs. They love it. You can see if they have any more in the kitchen. Corbu! Sharona!"

Dani and I both knew our relative place now. We watched as the two black dogs tore ravenously at the meat, snarling and shaking their tails.

Zoia shouted at Nicolae, "Why in hell do you expect me to have a family?"

The perfect end to the perfect day.

THE NEXT time I saw them all was at Nicolae's birthday celebration at the Primaverii in January 1987. On our way to the dining room, we passed through a maze of all the gifts sent to Him, as was the custom, for each of His or Her birthdays. Every agency, every factory, every institute in the entire country felt obligated to send tributes: TVs, VCRs, flower arrangements, clothing, paintings, synthetic and industrial diamonds, hunting gear, leather jackets, even cars–all competed for space with innumerable portraits of the couple in oil, on videotape, on china, on silk scarves, and carved in wood. Conspicuously absent were computers. Computers put Nicolae in a rage.

Stepping within earshot of him, I overheard the Supreme Commander bragging–after ordering another bottle of pink Dom Perignon champagne–about the great prosperity Romanians were enjoying and how we should all pull together to take our place as the rightful leaders of the world.

Nicolae was in a continuous revolution in his mind. Where this revolution led, nobody knew. Over and over Elena said, *"Asa e, Niculae.* That's how it is, Nicolae." The champagne also loosened the tongues of Valentin, Nicu, and Zoia, who complained about their work and money problems as a response to everything.

It was late in the evening, and we were seated at a massive table with Nicolae at the head, Nicu at one side of him, Elena at the other. The rest of us were scattered below the salt, with three or four empty spaces separating this trio from the next human being. Zoia now piped up and said, "Mother, you are destroying Science, Culture, and along with that, me." From my distant seat I saw Nicolae shake his head at his daughter, cutting the air with his hands as he spoke. "First, you must learn to work and then maybe I'll put down my ear to listen to you. Even Petre Borila worked in his way," he said, as if to indicate a respectful disdain for my father, the man he'd tossed aside. "Even Stalin did good things. He would have given us back the part of Moldavia the Soviet Union has stolen from us by now." He turned to me, unsmiling.

Zoia got up to walk away. I took a breath and spoke.

"Everywhere I go, I see people are hungry because there's no food to buy. I know you have great developments planned for Romania, great advancements in science, but aren't the people starving now? I've never seen anything like this." I hoped Elena, who was talking to Zoia, couldn't hear. I really wanted Nicolae's answer to this.

Giving me The Look, he frowned for a moment while forming his reply. I tried not to stare at his bright yellow necktie.

"Our scientists at the academy have determined what it takes to keep a worker alive," he said with an automatic cadence, quoting from 1982's ominous Program of Scientific Nourishment, which had determined that average Romanians were overfed compared to their value to the state. "It takes so many grams of carbohydrates, so many grams of fat and protein, so many grams of vegetables. Do you think we don't consider these things when we ask for sacrifices from our people? The finest minds in Romania work on this, including Elena. What other nation has pensions, guaranteed housing, and guaranteed health care for all its people? What other nation has no political prisoners and has no people sleeping under bridges and in parks, the way they do in America? Did you hear these things from your mother?"

"My mother won't speak to me, Supreme Comrade."

"You've never worked, other than arranging paintings in the museum. I grew up in the farmland and was the youngest communist in this country. I was in jail, where I was beaten until I was unconscious again and again. I rose through the ranks of our armies until I was a full general," he said softly. "Elena washed our floors herself with two or three children. She now has honorary degrees from many countries of the world. No one cares for the people more than we. We have entire modern factory cities now, with shops, apartments, and schools bringing together Hungarians, Germans, and Romanians, people who once fought each other, now working together in close harmony to build an industry synonymous with quality. We have economic and cultural relations with over 130 countries. Nobody gets hungry here. They are only greedy. They don't know what's good for them. We must teach them about the modern scientific approach to a healthy mind and body. *Revolutie continua*. We are living in a continuous revolution."

I'd heard these exact words so many times before, in movies and documentaries, that I knew them by heart. How odd it was for him to breathe them back to me now–to hear them over supper. These words were straight out of the red book of his speeches every individual was required to display at all times, our only bible.

"But there aren't any lights on the streets. Our Hungarian immigrants have been taken from the north and relocated all over our country, away from their culture and families. The Transylvanian–"

"I'm talking about the Romanian people," he said, friendly and expansive. "We're all brothers. There are no people but the Romanian people in our culture. Look who is doing the work. Aren't you impressed with the breadth of these contributions? Do you want more privileges?"

"No."

Nicolae rose to his full height of five feet six inches. He seemed to be finished with me. Zoia was talking to Elena and pointing toward the drapes, where I saw my son peeking out.

On the way home, Valentin was jovial as ever and didn't mention my confrontation with Nicolae. But we were both aware of how little consideration He and She gave to arguments by their own educated children and how they listened only to the toadies who surrounded them.

FOR the next two years, Dani grew taller and more voluble while Valentin grew more distant. Dani and I went everywhere together, and I'd almost forgotten what it was like to go out for a day with some girlfriends when I got a call from Ileana.

"You never want to go anywhere."

"I just don't have time." It was a flimsy excuse, since all she was asking me to do was ride on Bucharest's new subway. The truth was, I wanted less and less to be part of the Nomenclatura and was disgusted by the subway, afraid of the dark air that rushed up from vents on the sidewalk. What was down there was the accumulated misery of millions of slave laborers turned into a shaft and a gleaming rail. This Underground was everywhere now, with stations popping up along Herastrau at Statuia Aviatorilor, in front of the National Museum, near my house. No, I wasn't going down there.

"Tomorrow," Ileana said. "The four of us. You'll simply try it. It's not dark down there."

"It should be dark." Connected to innumerable tunnels built to support the secret activities of the Securitate, including rooms where people were detained, interrogated, and tortured, the Underground was something I didn't trust, I told her, because "people with broken hearts made it".

But the next morning, there she was, running around Nanny and barking beside my bed–not my dog, but Ileana. I walked down to the street with her and joined Nora and Anca, bubbling with talk and heading for the door at the Aviatorilor Station that swung open much too quickly for me. We descended into the shaft of the Blue Line.

Anca, wearing some clothes that looked a little ragged, went down the stone steps alongside Nora, whose father was still a member of the Central Committee. Ileana and I followed.

"I don't want to go." I looked back up at the square of sunny sidewalk behind us.

"There's nothing up there anymore," Ileana said. "People are starving. Let's see what's down here."

Anca was still ingenuous enough to be shocked by Ileana, but the rest of us were accustomed to her reckless complaining by now, especially when we were out of our homes and free, for the moment, from the monitoring devices of the Securitate that could instantly place a name and a face with a voice.

"This is wrong. I feel it." I descended warily with them as we went down fifty, then one hundred, feet with just a single set of lights to distinguish it from a mine shaft. "Look. They're not finished." Everywhere around us were the signs of eternal construction, lanterns reflected in the rudely excavated rocks, the black sweat of the Metro, but there were no workers around today. I gasped as we hit the dark floor and the shaft around us opened a thousand feet on every side, revealing a ticket booth and a palatial station black against the glass, numinous in their own subterranean reflections. This was Pharaonic. This was pure Ceausescu. "It's like Avernus. Look at how the limestone runs against what man has carved. It's as if Nature's trying to make this cave her own."

Still, there was more of a sense of *not* seeing than seeing. The sublime feeling you got when you stood in the Alps was here, reversed and in darkness.

The Yellow Line snaked toward Stefan Cel Mare and finally around the city to the Militari Drumul Taberei. We waited by the rail.

"Where are all the people?" I asked.

"You're among the first to visit this gift from our Grand Creator," Anca said.

"Where's the next stop?"

Before long the train, engineered from an original Romanian design, appeared, its green trim flashing against the black. Though it could carry a thousand people, we were the only passengers. I looked out the window at the dark walls as we whizzed by and watched the reflection of our faces bouncing along the jagged cut of the rocks. For a moment I didn't recognize them as our own. Were they the faces of dead souls? Piata Romana. Universitatii, Tineretului. The train started to close in. I stood up.

"What is it?"

"I need some air."

"Some time you choose to need air."

I didn't answer. We saw no attendants, no drivers, nothing but blackness. "Look, really, why is no one else using this train?"

Anca looked down and shook her head.

"Is it a tomb? Why are we down here?" I felt more claustrophobic, as if these friends were pall bearers chatting away while they lowered me deeper and deeper into the earth. It was Religion, not Science, that hurt people, we'd always been taught at school. This subway was supposed to be a great idea. Why did it feel so horrible? I wanted to go. I wanted to be with Dani.

The train plunged ahead, as bright inside as an operating room, making the dark tube we traveled through under the street all the more black. The Red Line. Grozavesti. Semanatoarea. Gara de Nord. Boulevard of the Centrul Civic. Any superstitious Romanians from the villages would have known what was bad about this place. Bucharest needed better transportation, but at what cost? The train slowed while others blew past us, inches away.

Then we seemed to go lower and saw an empty tunnel apparently descending to the right, where I could see water.

"What's that? Where's it heading?"

Nora stared. "Those are the two unfinished metro stations that sank below the water table, below the lake. Nobody said this metro was easy to make."

"Two stations? How many people died?" You could make out the details of one of the stations, and then in the distance the other, the water black and waveless above them, some of the lights still flickering in the distance. Even Radio Free Europe had only mentioned the human toll in general terms. I wouldn't have expected to see it in *Scinteia* or *Romania Libera*, which boasted that, "This massive project was completed in record time, while barely disturbing the bustling activity of the streets above."

Ileana laughed. "You have to drown a few people to make a metro. But they fished them out."

"So this is what passes for the new sophisticated humor," I said. "That's not even a little bit funny." I felt sick inside. Horrible. Responsible. I knew I had a part in their deaths and wished I remembered how to pray so I could pray for them individually. Or was this, too, a self-serving delusional affectation? After all this, was I still consoling myself? Were their wallets still down there? The tongues of their shoes?

"Hey. Who killed Elena and made you the arbiter of taste?" Ileana said.

The surfaces of the rocks perspired as we rattled through the dark like change in the Devil's pocket, and in the glow the eyes of my friends lit up like the archetypal figures in the paintings of Margareta Sterian. What a left-footed underworld of lost souls it was. It took my breath away with its unhappiness.

In a while we got the feeling of coming close to something red. We slowed to a series of lights a thousand feet from the end of the line. Stepping off the train, we ascended on an escalator to a brand-new piazza. The sudden sunlight hurt my eyes. A heap of incomplete marble and stone on an unimaginable scale surrounded us, and once again there were no people. Empty fountains were everywhere—the mute mouths of swans gaped at the sky. My friends were oohing and aahing, animated with disbelief, but I'd never seen so much death in a single place. It was an entire empty city. Stairs rose and vanished under arches that a million people had built.

Before us rose the largest building in the world. The Palace of the People was aptly named because everything we'd ever owned, made, or grown had been taken to build it. It might as well have been built with our bones.

"Where do those stairs go?" I asked.

"To offices of the Securitate and Department of International Espionage," Nora said. "To the foreign service division. Every single office of the government is going to be located here."

"It looks as if an atomic bomb has been dropped here, destroying nothing but vaporizing anything living." I saw a flash of everything in its place, and polished. Oh, it was going to happen. Something was going to happen to all of us.

Ileana tried to cheer me up. "What would your dog do here?"

My spaniel was funny. "She'd bark at all of you." She'd let anyone into my house but would bark if any of my friends had to leave. And in the end, many did leave–forever.

"Have you seen Nicu?" Nora asked out of the blue as our footsteps echoed through the halls of the silent Palace.

"No," I said. "He's a big shot in Sibiu now, the party chief."

"Just like his father," Anca said. "I hear people have more to eat in his province than in Bucharest now."

"He's a pig," Nora said. "Didn't you hear what Nadia did after he finished with her? She drank a bottle of bleach to kill herself."

"With her mother a cleaning woman, I suppose there was a ready supply," Ileana said.

"Stop it. She's a sweet girl," I said. "I was going to tell you something nice about Nicu."

"Go on. Has he been up your skirt, too?"

The black depths of the subterranean palaces echoed in all directions. I lowered my eyes. "Nicu's just a diabolically frustrated child. He heard Dani's feet were hurting and that he needed special shoes. But when our pediatrician took Dani to a medical convention and found an Italian doctor who volunteered to send him a few pairs, Elena scolded me with, 'Do you seek special privileges? Your son should have shoes like any other Romanian, made in Romania.' We'd given up when, two days later, there was a knock on the door.

Nicu. He had a big smile on his face as he handed us two pairs of the shoes while holding his fingers to his mouth."

"Did Nicu also find a specialist for his liver? I hear he's killing himself with drink, nearly as fast as people say he's killing others," Ileana said.

"Last year, Nicu bought Dani an Italian tricycle for Christmas. When Nicu saw that the tricycle was too big, he got angry. We said thank you, Dani was delighted. But the next day, there was Nicu, back with a new, smaller one."

What I didn't say was that sometimes he'd catch sight of Dani playing and then, without warning, say, "I disinherit you." No doubt this was the way he'd learned to speak to a child.

Ileana looked at me. "So," she said.

The others giggled.

"So? Has the playboy gone up into your skirt?"

We walked down the stairs to the mall below the Palace of the People, all six of us smoking like true Romanians. There were coffee kiosks, but no one was there to take our order.

I TOLD Valentin about the subway when I got home, but he laughed. "You're hallucinating."

"It was a nightmare."

"You're sick."

"Like my father."

"Like your mother. You describe it like a painting," he said. "A painting is not real life. Don't you understand that?"

I was beginning to understand it. Automatically I picked up Dani. "You've never been there, have you?"

"No," he said. "It's terrible about the workers who died, and I've talked to my father again and again about that. But this is nothing like the Moscow subway. With a more difficult engineering challenge, we lost a fraction of the workers, and that's still unforgiveable. It's terrible, but it's nonetheless a wonder. All Romanians should be proud."

Yes, it was circus, sure. But wasn't the formula bread and circus? I looked into his eyes, calm as the water that stood over the sunken metro stations. No. I couldn't bear to think my husband was savoring fruit of the rotten apple.

"You're a good man." I smiled as Dani reached for his neck. "'Pollyanna,' like your friends call you. To you, everything can come out good, even when it's bad. I'll love you forever."

With Dani still clinging to him, Valentin turned on the stereo. Leonard Cohen's growl filled the room. Valentin took my hand, lifting me off the couch, and the three of us did a family tango to "Dance Me to the End of Love". When the record stopped, so did we.

"Won't you ever grow up, my Dana?"

His whisper brought back that first sweet night, in Ionel's basement. There was a silence. Then we both laughed.

THE BIG CRASH was coming, and the Nomenclatura were dressing up for Armageddon as best they could. There was something frantic in the air. With the collapse upon us, senior officials threw nervous parties late into the evenings while people outside starved and became more sullen. Everyone acted as if something had to give, restlessly seeking diversion after diversion. They were cats preparing for a tornado. It was already a cliché in America to allude to "Yuppies", so the clever twist applied to our generation by certain members of the foreign press, "Yummies"–Young, Upwardly Mobile Marxists–was very apropos. At some of these parties, I actually saw men drinking from women's slippers and laughing over-loudly as if to convince themselves they were really having fun.

It was a horrible summer. Like all the other elites, Valentin went from party to party, sometimes returning after sunrise. Nanny had gone back to Brasov to rest, so I stayed at home with Dani. Some of my friends told me it wasn't a good idea to let Valentin go out alone, but I needed so much to trust his nobler impulses. Ileana even criticized me for allowing him to come home after the first night away, but I always thought he'd wake up from this bad dream. I felt guilty for hurting my parents, so I had to trust him and make our marriage work so that at least I hadn't hurt them in vain. I didn't want to believe that if Romeo and Juliet had survived, they'd have ended up falling out of love.

Valentin threw a final all-night party at our house, the largest we'd ever planned—he even hired a waiter for the evening. When my mother called to say that my brother's car was broken and she needed a ride to the hospital for her eye surgery, it was nearly 7am. Valentin was enjoying the party and rolled his eyes when I told him I had to leave.

Just then, someone dropped our song on the stereo: *Dance me to the end of love.*

I turned toward Valentin and smiled.

He rose up from his chair, took the untroubled Roxana Duna by the hand, pulled her close, and the two danced away.

It was all I could do to stop myself from screaming, "Is this how you treat the mother of your son?" because I didn't want to live in a world where my Valentin could turn Juliet into the Shrew.

IT WAS ONLY a few days after I returned with my mother from the hospital that I learned from a friend that my husband was spending more time with Roxana. With her smooth hair and guilelessly sexy smile, she was beautiful and so much taller than I. Upset, I didn't call Valentin at work but rather looked in the mirror. Waiting for hours for him to come home, I'd taken up smoking again in secret. I looked old and so worried. I was thin but didn't have the body of a girl who was fourteen years younger. Roxana could have been my daughter. My hair was attractive, but not so fine and silken. My God, this girl was resplendent as a Christmas ornament. Anyone would have been attracted to her, except my Valentin. She was not even a scientist! I began to have nightmares that I was chasing a train in the dark subway, crossing over still water that reflected my face. By day, I tortured myself with brooding. Maybe I could have lost Valentin to a researcher or someone he'd met in the laboratory, an accomplished ballerina or a celebrated actress, some long, smoking thing with long legs from a different world, an Asian girl, maybe, from his trip to Japan or some deep-cover agent his parents had sent to him to disrupt our marriage, but not someone so ordinarily beautiful–like this.

So simple, frankly. Had I gone mad? In what world would I get to choose my husband's second wife! From my circle of so-called friends.

It wasn't long ago that we'd had lunch with this "friend". I was angered to think that perhaps even then she'd been feeling the memory of Valentin inside her. With all of Valentin's soccer games and the research he did at the Institute, how could he have ever found time for her? And why? Hadn't I given him this son?

At nightfall, I heard his key in the lock. He entered the foyer, and I waited for him to call to me, *Buna*. But he was silent. I stepped into the hallway to see what was wrong, in spite of my dread.

"Dana, I've fallen in love with someone else. I want a life with someone else. I am so sorry. Laughter was missing from my life. She brought it back."

Horrified by what he saw in my eyes, he went out to get some cigarettes, like a child who couldn't stand to see the vase he'd just broken.

I reached for a bottle of whiskey. I think I poured it into a glass. He came back.

I burst into tears.

He cried with me for most of the night, and talked in long, elliptical sentences that all led to the same conclusion. She was fun and I wasn't. At all.

"Never?"

"No, not ever." He rolled away.

I lit a cigarette, went out for a walk, and found him slumbering when I got back. I watched him smile in his sleep and wondered if he was dreaming of her. The rat bastard. He'd gotten more handsome during our marriage, and astonishingly less worried. She was younger, yes, and she didn't have to look after Dani, though Valentin had always loved Dani.

I tried to remember the first time I embraced Valentin, warm and intimate in the lake, so many years before. Then, in a moment of illumination, I tried to remember what was around us, beyond the Asian water lilies and the laminar surface of the lake, which glistened like black caviar, on to the villas on the far side of the lake. I lit another cigarette. My mind floated to one particular house on the far side of that memory, the Versailles-like gardens and artesian fountains in front of it, the long pier. His house. I'd never been very far away from his house.

I walked over to the bed and watched him breathing, in complete repose. I leaned forward and smelled his incredibly familiar smell. Then I slapped him. His eyes flew open. He covered his face and cried out as I said, "How could you leave us? You will not leave us."

"I won't," he said, nervous and crying.

We talked for an hour, lighting one cigarette after another, all dry inside. Foolishly, I was sure things would get better because we'd had that talk, and I was able finally to express how much I needed him.

"I'll always love you," he said. "Don't you know what you mean to me? Aren't you my 'Juliet'? Do you see how I love our son?"

I gave him a kiss with my head all hot.

"I can't imagine you without me," he said. "I'll never leave you, Dana. Even if I'm with another woman."

In the morning he was gone for good. The end of love had come.

OVER the next few days, Valentin came over ostensibly to make plans but really only to fight. He couldn't sleep, nobody could. It was humid and hot, more than thirty-six degrees Celsius. You couldn't sleep, you couldn't breathe, you couldn't keep clothes on. He seemed so agitated. And now he was trying to explain to me, "I want to remake my life with someone else. Why are you looking like that?"

"Like what?"

"Now that I'm leaving you, you look beautiful again."

He was tormented, afraid. It shocked him that he could love both of us but that he was *in* love only with her.

ALL OF A SUDDEN I wanted to see the planes at Baneasa Airport, taking off and landing. "I want to see them fly," I said to myself, "the lights moving up and down." With Dani asleep and again in Nanny's care, I called my friend Gabi. She was so sweet she piled me into her Oltcit and started for Baneasa, but we were stopped by the police, who asked us why we were driving at night. They weren't satisfied that I just wanted to see the airport, and I felt lucky when they didn't detain us but rather sent us home.

"YOUR PARENTS don't want Dani or me, and now you don't want us," I said during the ensuing months as Valentin went through his predictable cycles of remorse and reconciliation with me. Often he denied being with Roxana and said he just needed time alone. Then I'd hear from friends that they were seen together again.

Her husband came to see me. "What are we going to do? We can't leave things like this."

"Who says there has to be a resolution? Why do we have to take revenge?"

"We can't do *nothing*."

"Why not?" I said. "What's the use?"

Valentin arranged for us to stay in the house out of regard for Dani, leftover love for me, and fear of losing face. In a way, he was with us during the daytime even more than before. Dani wasn't told about the other woman. He wasn't told anything; he just saw his father a good deal more. But for me, it was like a wound that kept being opened up. I began to dread the visits.

"He's busy at his research," I told Dani about his absence at night. "He'll be back soon."

Valentin slept in his bedroom at the Primaverii, his mother's dream. Now, whenever Nicu visited from Sibiu, she had all three of her children together, fighting with them like a good mother and teenagers. Except that they were pushing forty now and responsible for the lives of others.

My life settled in to raising Dani, my work, watching news via satellite, and listening to Radio Free Europe when it wasn't scrambled. It was a little late to start a new life now, but I'd wake up each day and have no alternative but to do just that: breakfast, Dani, small talk with Nanny, driving to the museum.

Valentin, upon winning the final divorce papers, presented me with a brand-new white Ford Escort. I wanted to shove the keys down his throat. He was more excited about divorcing me than marrying me. "You left me. I don't want anything from you." How unlucky this car would be. But I took the keys anyway.

"Everything's taken care of."

"What are you saying?" I asked him so softly. I looked down. "Look what you've done."

He stroked my hair.

If I don't move, maybe you'll fall in love with me again. How I hate you. Was I addressing Valentin or myself?

I waited for him to get bored with his mistress and come back to me. This, I tried to believe, would certainly happen. But instead he drew further away from me toward a new life that I was unable to understand.

I visited my mother, who, her predictions having come true, was free to love me again. Ironically she chose this time to give me the hope chest she'd denied me while I was married.

"When are you leaving?" Nanny asked me as I packed for an art-objects inventory I was supposed to make in the district of Prahova, nearly due north of Bucharest, early in 1988.

"In ten minutes. Will you be all right with Dani?"

"Yes." Nanny and I rarely spoke about Valentin. There was no need to speak. I was the girl who'd grown up after religion was banished in the 1950s, the unlucky one. I knew no traditions. There wasn't much hope, she felt, for me and my kind.

I got into my car and headed out of Bucharest, where the roads were clear because people couldn't obtain gas anymore. Leaving the city, I saw the trees starting to get taller and rougher and people just lining the roads with shoulders hunched and their mouths open. I headed past square after square until I reached the ancient village of Snagov, only two miles away from the opulent resort of the same name. This scenic place was one of the villages that had received the most benefits from Nicolae's Systematization. And, sure enough, as I approached the town, I saw the wattle-and-clay buildings, white with furze roofs, climbing up a gentle slope to the village square where out of the trees an astonishingly regular series of apartments shot into the blue sky with perfect, fearful white edges, pure Soviet gigantism.

I hadn't seen these buildings driving past here three months earlier. Was I seeing more clearly now? How many people could you put in there? A thousand? Two?

So these were some of the white residential apartment buildings for workers and pensioners that had so impressed the Western media. With the straight, rigid poplars uniformly surrounding them, they looked like something out of a fairy tale. The closer I got, the more easily I could make out individual windows instead of a blue glaze, each exactly symmetrical with the next. Driving toward the first of the monoliths, I saw that, far from having a grand entrance, it had only small blank doors at its unlandscaped base to let villagers in and out.

Curiosity got the better of me, so I pulled over to the side of the road and stepped out of the car. Surrounding the apartment buildings was what was left of the village, cottages with pitched roofs made of the same *stuf* reeds I'd seen around Lake Snagov. Trimmed with nasturtiums, the gardens around them were tiny, since the big lands had been taken by the state and nationalized and there were no more private lands where independent farmers could grow produce. Now farmers all worked in factories while the fields were tended by army draftees.

Splash.

What was that sound?

Splash, splash.

Was it birds? I looked up and saw several Romanians throwing pots of brackish, stinking slop out the windows of the apartment complex. I drew back.

The stench was overwhelming. I looked down around the buildings, and the moat of filth answered my question. There was no plumbing. Garbage was piled everywhere between rows of flowers. I started for my car.

Then a hand touched me.

"Leave me alone!"

A man of about forty, missing an arm, laughed with rancid breath and shook his head. "The people fuck and shit like pets and don't bathe." He studied me. "Come inside."

"I can't. I'm sorry. I'm driving to Prahova. This is terrible. I'll report it."

"There's no heat," he said. "We build fires inside, in our old stoves. It's hard to keep clean."

Splash. I held my nose from the inside. My inventory would take over a full day, with an overnight in a hotel, but I considered the invitation. Who could stop me from seeing this monstrosity– my in-laws? "Commies love concrete," the international press had marveled. Maybe there was time for a look. "All right."

My interrogator growled, nodded, and motioned away the growing crowd that had drawn near since my arrival. I wanted to lock my car but was afraid it would offend them. Stepping around the damp mud, I followed him to the door. "Will you be getting plumbing later?"

"I'm sure plumbing is just around the corner. Nothing is lacking." He perfectly imitated Nicolae's Oltenian accent.

On the first floor, ice was frozen in pools around the cast cement, with more grime smudged on the walls by children. "There is sickness here," I said. "I can't go in."

The man, alone in the dark with me, grabbed me by the arm. Why had I agreed to go in at all?

He looked at me with great disdain and pushed me up the stairs. "There. Come and see where my family lives."

Wind whirled and whistled through the broken windows. There was no comrade here to supervise things, no one to report to. Floor by floor, the rest of the building was the same. I saw the smoke-blackened walls, the rooms bleakly furnished, a scrap of a rag tacked up–the only color in the room–the human spirit crumpled like a jacket thrown against a wall.

"They're made only to look beautiful *from the air*, to impress foreign nations!" he said.

When I reached my car, children's handprints were all over it. The little ones were lined up like little soldiers as I opened the door, their hands outstretched.

"IT'S BUILT LIKE a cheap barbecue pit of cement blocks," I told the state arts official who met me later in Ploesti. "Only there are people inside, instead of a fire."

"Thank you for coming, *Tovarasa* Iordana," he said neutrally.

"But have you seen this place, where there is no heat or electricity, no bathrooms or kitchens? Do you know what happens then?"

"No, and I don't want to know."

I was taken to curate and examine a number of objects from former royalists' houses, some in good condition, some too decayed to have any historical value. This was the part of my job I really hated. We were required to check the houses of old dentists, lawyers, merchants, and monasteries to ensure they were "providing good locations for the preservation of antiquities". This was to ensure compliance with a Ceausescu edict that, in addition to registering their typewriters with the Securitate, all Romanian citizens had to declare their *objets d'art*. We were sent to scour the country for these items–anyone who didn't declare an object was subject to being turned in by a neighbor and having all his possessions confiscated. In accordance with the *Lagea Patrimoniului*

National, our formal state commission inventoried these objects nationwide and "relocated" the finest to "a safer place" in our museums (even though our national galleries provided neither heat nor air-conditioning for our collections).

I was, I realized, one of the slender fingers of this law. I was sent to houses ravaged by earthquakes or floods and had been present when my associate had taken a ring off a dead man to see if it were of value. We were like crows looking for something shiny. Poor villagers would open their doors and beg us to buy their family icons, some of them hundreds of years old, in old felt bags.

ON the way home I drove back through the village of Snagov, late at night, the mammoth apartment buildings backlit by a complex of radio towers against the starry sky. There were red lights at roof-top level to alert aircraft of the high obstacles, but no electricity inside. Some windows flickered faintly with firelight. The clean decency of the trees swallowed everything as I kept driving.

Chapter 14

There's no such thing as fun
for the whole family

As spring warmed, Elena became somewhat civil to me. Roxana Duna was now her target, and we had a common enemy. Roxana was a suspected bridge player, a game Elena had banned nationwide years before when she decided that Valentin, once a championship player himself, was wasting his life on the game. Elena said, "Bridge brings dangerous intellectuals together," because you need a good memory to play bridge, and it was better not to have a good memory in Romania.

I found myself invited to family functions, including movies such as *Two for the Seesaw* in the Primaverii screening room that Valentin didn't want me to go to. Just to spite him, I went, knowing he'd feel uncomfortable if his mistress were there at the same time. Meanwhile, Elena monitored Roxana's every breath. Now *she* knew what it was like to be hunted, and I tried not to enjoy myself too much at her expense.

Valentin began to bring Dani and me a number of costly presents, often leaving them inside my house when I wasn't there, just as his mother used to do when we were a couple. Breaking in is still breaking in. It was still about power.

AT THE MUSEUM, we had a growing sense of *haz de necaz*, rueful laughter, as it was decreed that any artist who wanted to have a show had first to paint portraits of our leaders, even if he or she were an abstract painter. This led to some strange work, including images of Nicolae and Elena as angels, luminous and craven in front of a Dali-blue sky. Even renowned poets such as Adrian Pauncscu and Vadim Tudor became courtesans in order to be published, writing in praise of their leaders. All new books or songs carried the visage of Nicolae or Elena on their covers. And certainly our next museum catalogue and show on French, Russian, English, and Austrian decorative arts, which I was to curate, would not be free of tributes to Nicolae and Elena, even though I'd refused to write the dedication. Comrade Alexandru Cebuc, my museum director, and I had our predictable cat-and-mouse talk about that.

"I honor Supreme Comrade Nicolae and his Internationally Renowned Scientist Wife, Elena, but this is a branch of scholarship too insignificant to be associated with them," I said. "Wouldn't it trivialize their patriotic achievements to include a chapter on them at the beginning of this catalog solely about decorative arts? We could do a different catalog in praise of Romanian art instead, later, couldn't we, Comrade?"

Cebuc slit his eyes at me and laughed silently with the same *haz de necaz*. He'd suspected me for years as the daughter-in-law of our Leaders, even while I was reviled by them. He warmed to me after my divorce, and I admit I enjoyed taking advantage of his never really knowing what to make of me. "Are you saying they cannot appreciate these things, *Tovarasa* Dana?" he said for the benefit of the hidden tape recorders.

"Far from that–I feel these things are too insignificant for them to consider compared to the great deeds of state they must perform. They rely on us to document the inferior collections and keep them intact as a growing monument to the state."

"And as a testimony to the state, don't you think it appropriate to include their pictures and a brief biographical note on their achievements? What do you have against these things?"

"There's no amount of recognition our leaders don't deserve," I said. "I just feel their interests, which do not include relics such as these, apart from gifts forced upon them by other nations, are more purely Romanian and should be the center of a different study. In fact, why haven't you commissioned more people to document their appreciation for native Romanian art and antiques?"

He smirked at me and our games, because we both knew there was no way to avoid mentioning them in the introduction to anything we produced.

SHADOWS gathered over the *ani lumina*, Nicolae's and Elena's twenty-four "years of light", as 1989 opened.

The first nuclear plant at Cernavoda on the Danube was falling apart as fast as it could be built. According to *Maclean's* magazine, at least thirty percent of the original welding was going to have to be stripped off and redone. The Romanian army conscripts and near-slaves who worked on the project were exhausted and performed "substandard labor" while working out of "unheated cardboard buildings with open urinals".

Canada's Stanley Hatcher, vice president of Whiteshell Nuclear Research, bragged that "Canada's exports of reactors will only be limited by our ability to make them fast enough." Toronto's Norman Rubin, director of research at Energy Probe, announced that "there is little chance that Romania's reactors will ever work safely". Romania borrowed over $1 billion US dollars for this project but had nothing to show for it.

When I asked Valentin about it, he, having accepted a post as a Supplemental Member of the Central Committee, now acted as if he'd barely even heard of Cernavoda, though I could detect some signs of strain on his face.

TOWARD the fall of 1989, Dani, Nanny, and I enjoyed what few others had—a satellite dish that Valentin and his engineer friends rigged up on our roof. Most Romanians had to settle for just two state channels at best, with the rest of the signals scrambled by the giant complex of towers posing as a radio station near Snagov. Via this contraption, we were able to receive Western news that was re-broadcast from Germany. While neighbors watched two-decade-old reruns or propaganda, Dani and I saw the latest celebrity gossip from London and Paris as well as *Perfect Strangers* on ten different channels and new episodes of *Kojak*, Nicolae's favorite show.

Now, when the satellite dish worked, we saw Valentin's new world from both the outside and the inside: from the inside, Nicolae forever kissing Muslims on semi-official state visits, and, from the outside, Nicolae for the first time admitting there was nationwide hunger by obliquely blaming the Central Committee for "problems". This was a huge departure from his earlier positions.

From this remote post, we also saw Czechoslovakia and Bulgaria declare their independence from the Soviet Union, and we watched the beginning of the end of the world as we knew it.

On 16 December 1989, an incident regarding a rebel Hungarian priest named Tokes erupted in the tiny city of Timisoara, twenty miles west of the Yugoslavian border. The brave priest had spoken out against the "cultural genocide" of Transylvanian minorities in Romania, the brutal plan of Nicolae's to "systematize" 6,700 rural villages, raze their central squares, and replace them with 1,500 concrete living structures while relocating over 100,000 of their sons and daughters to remote parts of the country in order to homogenize us all and promote his "one Romania, one culture" ideal.

Nicolae's Securitate had hounded this priest Tokes until he'd become a hero, until spontaneous demonstrations occurred around his house even after he'd called them off, with young people smashing framed Ceausescu photographs and ripping up "history" books about Nicolae and Elena in stores. Fire, glass, lost shoes, and death were the only reforms offered. The final, symbolic circle of children holding hands around Tokes's house was an image Romanians were not to forget, including the Ceausescus, who ordered fire upon them with automatic weapons.

In all, an estimated 4,500 "revolutionaries" were tortured, mutilated, and murdered by the Securitate, their bodies trucked to nearby Transylvanian forests and buried in mass graves. Then the truck drivers themselves were shot by the Special Brigade, to ensure no witnesses.

But this time, there *had* been witnesses. This time, the world was watching. Timisoara might have escaped worldwide condemnation, and things might have continued as they were, had not a couple of international journalists been killed covering the event. This set the world media on fire.

More than in the dead children or the forest burial pits, the international press seemed interested in the injuries of a *New York Times* reporter named John Tagliabue; an Associated Press reporter named John Daniszewski; and a Yugoslavian reporter who was injured in the gunfire. Bernard Gwertzman, the overseas editor of the *New York Times*, described the horror of his associate Tagliabue being "wounded in the back by a sniper who fired on a car carrying him and other reporters".

"(Zeljko) Sajin," the bizarre AP release continued, "a reporter for Zagreb television, was slightly wounded in the chest, and Slobodan Kreckovic, vice consul at the Yugoslav Consulate in Timisoara, was grazed."

A few Romanians were "grazed" as well. Hundreds of thousands in all, if you count the diaspora from Hungary and the persecutions of Transylvanians during the past forty-five years.

ON THE EIGHTEENTH of December, I came home from work to find Valentin inside our living room.

"What do you do? Do you just come in here whenever you like?" I put down my valise.

Nanny melted into another room. Dani, happy as always, was even happier when his father was home.

"What do you mean?" Valentin asked. "I'm here to see Dani. How are you doing?"

He wasn't here to fight with me.

"Let's go for a walk," he said.

This was our signal to speak about his parents, far from the ears of the Securitate and from Dani. As we descended the stairs, I saw *Casa Scinteii* glowing like a thousand coals in the chilly December sky.

Then I saw Valentin's car–white, fast, and brazenly Western– with a small dark figure inside it. I could see Roxana's hair, those green eyes, and I smiled. I didn't have to be the one in the car now, waiting. I stopped myself from grinning. "So you have a new person to be ashamed about."

"What?" Valentin noisily lit a cigarette in his mouth, quite a production.

He gave it to me and I tasted his old taste on the paper. I inhaled it deeply into my chest. "Nothing," I said. "Have you seen all of this about Timisoara?"

"I have."

"And your parents are still going to Iran?"

"Sure. How many times can the Ayatollah die? My father feels he has to be there. His connections to the Middle East are useful to the whole world. In time, he could bring peace, as a mediator."

We walked through the park of our childhood love, where we'd kissed so many times and been scolded by the policemen. I could even see the bench where we'd been stopped. "Did he give the orders to kill all those people?"

"Of course not. The murderers were rogue members of the Securitate."

"How could they shoot our own people? So much for the 'one Romania'."

Valentin's eyes glistened. "It's horrible. I can't believe it happened."

"Did Nicu have anything to do with it? His district is so close…"

"What could Nicu do from Sibiu? Papa said thugs and hooligans started the unrest, possibly instigated by the CIA. Everything's changing so much now, with only Romania still the bright Communist state. I'll bet Gorbachev knows a little about it, too. That's really why he's meeting Bush at Malta."

You sound just like a Ceausescu now. I'm free.

"This meeting with Bush is about *everything*. After all these years, it's so bizarre. But I don't think my parents are worried about it."

Asa e, Valentin. Whatever you say. You are a part of the lies. I no longer had a dictator, and with *scinteia* of my own I knew that someday neither would my Romania.

Far from us, at the edge of the water, was the Pescarusul, our old café, with the statue of the seagull. Behind us was our house. I felt the warmth of Valentin, but I no longer felt the ache connected to it.

I'd never made it to the airport with Gabi, but I'd gone back alone, later, on other nights. I'd seen the tiniest specks of light turn daringly into silver spears dropped from the sky. Then there'd be a great roar and the spears would dramatically rise again, headed for London or Paris or Madrid or Naples, and disappear.

I couldn't fly away like that. I was a daughter of Bucharest. I'd spent my life in the city I loved. My mother was here. My father was buried here. I felt a dark shiver run down my back and looked up at Valentin. I lit a cigarette for myself with the lighter he'd given me so long ago. "Do you remember this?"

"Of course, Dana," he said. "I'll see you soon, after the soccer game."

"Sure. Come back in and say goodbye to Dani."

He kissed me on the cheek. "Take care of yourself. You are still my 'girl-near'." He went down the stairs and walked through the darkness to the car. There she was. The car started up, glowing in the night's moisture. And then I saw her face look up from her window at me.

I held my ground.

The car pulled slowly away, along the park, and now she was looking back at me through the rear windshield.

I held her glance.

The car grew smaller and smaller as it headed toward the greatest lights of the city, until I couldn't see the windshield at all.

Oh, Valentin! My chest contracted. I'd had such a great love. It was truly over.

Chapter 15

Palace Square, Bucharest, "The City of Pleasure" December 21, 1989, 8.17am

Reform will come when poplar trees grow pears

"GOOD MORNING," the car radio said. "Our Supreme Comrade, Nicolae Ceausescu, will be addressing crowds of workers and party members assembled from all Romania on Palace Square to announce new triumphs of our state."

If I were Lidia I might have seen the coming storm in my coffee, felt the ill wind blowing against my cheek. But all I could see was sunshine through my window as I drove to work, a trick of nature that made me shrug off the hint of a breeze.

Work was certainly normal. I had only to check the final proofs before sending my catalog to the printers. I still liked working at the museum, even though all art had to reflect the magnificence of The Danube of Thought.

But how would I get to work? Along Magheru Boulevard, a crowd of over 100,000 was assembling at Palace Square to cheer Nicolae's latest words. As usual, the avenues were swept clean of the *traficanti*, the whores and beggars. But today workers sulked as they listlessly held giant posters of the ruling couple, while others, wearing traditional *costume populare*, were oddly not dancing. So often everyone held hands and tripped the *hora*, but today every man, woman, and child stood still. What was this strained silence?

The autumn-like sun was a magnifying glass turned on something about to burn. There was something in the air, but I didn't know if it was my mood or the country's. For weeks now, I'd been sleeping restlessly and was unable to shut my eyes while taking a bath. Even driving was more difficult, because my Escort seemed to require more control. Cars and people alike cut me off, blocking my passage as onlookers wheeled and looked at me with *strapunge*, stares strong enough to punch a hole in my chest. "Who could afford this car?" their eyes signaled.

Something was gravely wrong. Something told me to go home. Even I was astonished there was a force strong enough to make me turn my car around. With no traffic headed in the other direction, I wheeled into the empty lane and headed away from the thousands, away from Palace Square. *Da-i romanului mintea cea din urma.* "Give the Romanian her last flash of wisdom from what she'll know at the end of her life to deal with this now."

This couldn't be happening. I squeezed my knuckles white on the steering wheel.

I was turning around.

"YOU'RE back?" Nanny said. *You've returned unbidden when you'd normally be at work?* The old ones considered it near insanity to do this. *Better to let the house burn down from a forgotten cigarette,* Lidia used to say. Returning unbidden might put me a half-hour off my good luck for the rest of my life.

"Just for a second. Has Dani had breakfast?"

"Yes," Nanny said, as if breakfast—bread and honey from the presidential bee farm—were part of a rocket countdown in this almighty Before.

How Nanny was looking at me now. I turned on the television. The screen was suddenly awash with oceans of people in Palace Square. Nicolae stepped into the cameras, nodded his head, and started to speak. The white heads of the Central Committee bobbed around him. He shouted his familiar exhortations, his right arm pumping like an oil derrick as he bludgeoned each point.

Why had he gone to Iran when some had said it was too dangerous to leave the country?

Nanny served me coffee, and I sipped from the ornate cup Valentin had brought back from his parents' mission to China.

Across the wide avenue from the National Museum of Art, outside the Palace of the Central Committee, Nicolae was saying everything was okay. On a balcony suspended over the people, he said nothing was lacking. He talked glowingly of foreign powers, trade agreements, freighters. There was no human consideration in his speech. They were supposed to applaud, but they didn't applaud. You couldn't talk to a hungry people like that. He talked his way into a black alley where strangers could hurt him *cu mina lui,* with his own hand. In the unapplauding vastness above

Palace Square he began barking his words and moving his arm faster. Then the barking became a shout. All along, doctors had whispered that the movement of his hands was paranoiac, the manifestation of a mental illness.

And then I saw something on television that made my stomach tighten. Nicolae, unable to perspire even though the television lights smoked around his head, continued to shout. His nostrils flared, but his forehead remained dry. But now I saw something actually human steal into his eyes, almost a flicker of regret. He couldn't believe the crowd's growing disrespectful murmur. He just stopped moving, so Elena stepped in front of the microphones and started to talk to the people as if they were members of her household, she a mother figure scolding a nation. My head reeled. Romania was a country with its brakes loose! There was a crackling sound.

The screen went red as the live telecast was mysteriously interrupted.

I heard Valentin's key rattle in the door. He started to talk about the Steaua army soccer team he was coaching in an uneasy alliance with his uncle, Gen. Ilie Ceausescu. He was in a good mood, casual, laughing, actually whistling.

Then he saw my face. "What's wrong, Dana?"

"It happened."

It was my *Rémálom*, my nightmare, come to life. I'd had premonitions of red television screens, of seeing Valentin's finally frightened face as he saw his world turned upside down. This dictatorship, like all others from South America to Cuba to the Soviet Union, was run from a tiny state television station, not a marble capital. Valentin, who certainly should have known better, seemed astonished it could be unplugged.

And then military helicopters, throwing pieces of sound all over the rooftops, wopped overhead. This was impossible, because Palace Square was a flight exclusion area. The wineglass poplar and chestnut trees outside the window vibrated. The air itself vibrated. Were the helicopters beating down that sullen crowd I'd left behind along Magheru Boulevard?

I lit the wrong end of a cigarette. I watched with fascination as the nightmare engulfed us.

Valentin was already on the phone, trying to call his parents. The Maximum Leader and his wife were leaving, ousted. Nicolae and Elena were being snuffed out like a shout in the street. Things were losing their center. There was no more order.

The helicopters circled over the Bulevardul Poporului, which Nicolae and Elena insisted be exactly one meter larger on each side than the Avenue des Champs-Elysees. They landed on the flat roof of the Central Committee. Usually helicopters flew to the grass fields and gardens of the old palace, a more gracious entrance, but now they were abrupt, and low as taxis. Beginning as a faraway *zumzet*, a distant buzz, the noise now thundered at window level and shook the trees with a mind-shattering *uruit* on its way to the Central Committee. Close-up parts of Alouette, Puma, and Soviet-built MI-8 Hip helicopters rumbled past our window—nose wheels, tail rotors, the after fuselages—some of them deluxe white Salon versions built for eleven passengers.

Dorin, a computer systems engineer who was a good friend of ours, burst into the house, straight from Palace Square. "I can't believe it," he said. "It's the first time." Then he made a low sound in his throat, "Huuuuoooo," the ancient jeer, the ultimate sound of disrespect. "They actually said it. Huuuuoooo. Assassin." He covered his ears. "There was noise from gunshots at the meeting." He looked at Dani, standing with his fingers in his mouth. "Maybe they were firecrackers. After all, it's Christmas!"

Without another word, Valentin and Dorin ran out the door.

FOR the next twenty-four hours, as Nicolae and Elena hid inside a bunker inside the Central Committee, conferring with Securitate officials who raced to their side through their network of tunnels, I huddled with Nanny and Dani, making telephone calls, gathering information. Valentin and Dorin rushed in and out a lot of times before disappearing altogether as the chopper sounds increased.

Then, late the next morning, Dorin returned. Tiny beads of perspiration formed below his dark hair. "There are army tanks everywhere, barricading the roads," he said. "It's not safe here. Come to my house."

I reached for my son, feeling dizzy. Where was Valentin?

"Where are we going?" little Dani asked, his eyes widening as a helicopter flew directly overhead.

"Come on." I forced a big smile. "We're going out to play in the great wind."

I grabbed a few of the clothes I'd packed for a mountain vacation we'd been planning, pajamas for Dani and some sweaters on top of the pile. I didn't even have time to find my glasses. Out of breath, I steered Dani to the Escort parked outside, but Dorin grabbed me and shook his head.

"We'll take mine." He pointed to a black car that looked like so many others.

Dani and I tumbled into Dorin's back seat, and we drove off, tires squealing. Screaming crowds made the ten-minute trip to

Dorin's house take nearly two hours. Rotor wash in the trees told the story. When would Romania introduce reform? "When poplar trees grow pears," Nicolae had said just weeks before.

DURING these hours, Nicu, the pride of his father, was caught near the television station in Bucharest. By now, many in the country believed that whenever Nicu, party chief of the city of Sibiu, saw a girl he liked, he had only to ask the 160,000-member Securitate to beat up her boyfriend, and then he'd rape her. Stories of his conquests and Las Vegas gambling were to multiply in the whirl-wind of this disaster–this *revolutia*–that was beginning to rage on.

Sixteen-year-old Transylvanians in factories and fields, abducted from their families to weaken the village gene pools, had huffed about Nicu above their shovels.

Angry servants and merchants fanned the fire, and a desperate anger arose from the people now filling the streets. "The army is with us! The dictator has fallen! Death to the Antichrist! We are the people! We will be heard!"

NORTH of Bucharest, at the TV station, Nicu was stabbed by the furious crowd as the national television cameras rolled. Blood spilled down the front of his blue and black shirt and hand-sewn sport jacket worth a year's salary made by seamstresses who'd worked exclusively for the family. Paraded in front of the crowd, my brother-in-law said, "I didn't give the orders to shoot anyone." Army officers and civilians were dead all around him. Revolutionary commentators reported that Nicu had lied about coming to give himself up and that he was suspected of killing ninety-seven people in Sibiu after putting poison in the city's drinking water. Nicu's eyes lunged back and forth, but he was quiet as a wolf now.

For the moment, no one knew where Nicolae and Elena were. They'd disappeared from the presidential palace "like candles in a cuckoo's nest", as the Romanian song goes.

"What's this noise, Mama?" little Dani asked as I rushed him into Dorin's house from the car.

"It must be a Christmas celebration." I smiled. "We must really have caught God by the leg." Nicu would be killed, and surely Zoia. But what of Valentin? I didn't love anybody the way I loved my son—and through him my ex-husband. I cared for Valentin still, in spite of what he'd done to me, and would always love him. Nicolae and Elena had so often ridiculed me for being only "emotionally ambitious". "She is nothing," they said, "of no importance." My needing Valentin now made me shake my head as I saw him in Dorin's kitchen on the telephone, no doubt calling his girlfriend.

I'd seen the hesitation and then the frenzy of Timisoara many times in my nightmares. And now in Bucharest crowds were fomenting violence in cities, in a fever, crushing themselves like grapes into new revolutionary wine. "Give us back our dead," they cried. "Give us the children of Timisoara! Death to the Ceausescus! Death to the Great Conducator!"

At this moment, Nicolae's brother Marin, head of the Romanian Trade Delegation, hanged himself with his silk pajamas at the embassy in Vienna, the left leg looped around his neck. Marin had helped Nicolae siphon millions into Swiss bank accounts while

He had forced Romania to pay $10 billion in foreign debt at an accelerated schedule. Like the communist climber he was, Nicolae had exported the entire Romanian gross national product to pay foreign creditors for the Palace of the People, the systematization of villages, the Bucharest Underground, and his ill-starred canal built to connect the Danube to the Black Sea at the cost of over 100,000 lives. There was no meat, coffee, chocolate, oil, no tangerines, only rationed bread with no butter. No fruit in a country renowned for black cherries, apples, peaches, and strawberries. No medical equipment or supplies were available at any cost. Gypsy and Transylvanian songs, legends, curses, and jokes–so much of our history–had been stamped out, forced underground. This particular bad luck had a suffocating stench. Somebody was going to get it.

In all, thirty relatives of the Ceausescus enjoyed high government positions. Valentin, the last to fall into such privilege, was still on the telephone, counting off "Arad, Cluj, Brasov, Iasi, Constanta, Sibiu, Timisoara, Ploiesti." Revolution in all the cities; workers marching out of factories; a frenzied dance. Listening, he turned to me. "The Central University Library is on fire!"

Then he whispered something to Catalin Tutunaru, who'd just burst in, and with hasty apologies ran out the door.

Because I'd been sure he was still in the West, I was surprised to see Catalin but had no time to ask him when or how he'd arrived. He rushed Dani and me into his car. I thought I could see foreigners outside the windshield now. I heard the crowd shouting, "Arabs! Arabs!" Whoever they were, these intruders seemed comfortable in entropy, rushing like ants to something spilled. In the confusion I saw the beards, the turbans, the camouflage clothing. Were they

Syrians, Libyans, or from the Palestine Liberation Organization? They'd always backed Ceausescu. Whose side could they be on now? Oh, God, God, were we all going to die?

I shivered with confused fear of, yet sympathy for, the crowds. "Get down," I whispered to my baby.

"Kill the Ceausescus!"

"Death to the family!"

Dani moved over and leaned against me, trembling. Then he shifted and raised his head.

"No, get down!" I snapped, my heart breaking.

"But why me, Mama? Why is everybody so angry? What does it have to do with me?" His eyes were getting larger and larger. He slid slightly away from the spot where I considered him safest; I pulled him back to my side.

Then a woman in a white lab coat jumped on the hood of our car. She had dark hair cut like a boy's and was shouting, pointing a gas-operated Simonov SKS 7.62-mm carbine at Catalin's head. "Where are you going? Who are you?"

"To the hospital," Catalin shouted to her above the roar. "I have to get my sister."

We drove slowly through the crowd while the somewhat beautiful woman kept her feet atop our car like a hood ornament. This woman looked in charge in a world where no one was in charge.

"Quickly, open your window! Tell them to let me through," Catalin cried. "Say it's an emergency."

The crowd was rocking cars over on the same block. I was paralyzed with fear. Catalin threw a glance back at me, then called out to her himself. "The hospital," he said. "Help us."

Was this what death looked like?

The woman regarded me impatiently, swung her leg down through the passenger window I'd just opened, leaned back, yelled "Death to the Tyrants," and motioned the car ahead, down a different street. She had so much hate you could touch it.

"Death to the Tyrants." I'd found my voice.

"You, did you hear?" She sucked in the air. "Ceausescu said it was 'hooligans and fascists from abroad' who began our great event in Timisoara when it was children. It was us! They buried a whole generation, but we've been reborn. Everything they touched was deformed."

"Deformed." Catalin drove to her instructions.

Incredibly, we were moving forward now, though people pounded on our roof.

"Listen to me breathing," the young woman said.

Sick with worry, I looked at her rib cage rising and falling, looked at her carbine.

"It's like making love." She took a rough gulp of air.

"Did you see what happened to any of the monsters?" Catalin asked.

"I saw Nicu. Drunken with cruelty. He's dead by now. So are his parents, the despots who didn't even like their own son. Not a dog, not a maid, not anybody was good. They weren't racists."

"No?" Catalin glanced back at me.

"No." Between her teeth she said, "You have to *like* somebody to be a racist. The Ceausescus didn't like anybody. Oh, it wasn't so much him. It was *her*. But they all must die." She began a Gypsy song that went, "I have oil but I don't have potatoes to eat." She sang loudly when she came to "Digger, please open the grave, I want to be near the corpse.

"Galle tables," she went on. "We've found them in the Primaverii where the tyrants lived. Rosenthal china, silver, tableaux, gold dinnerware, countless works of art, rare books, even bearskins. Have you heard about the Persian carpets, the kilometers of tapestries collected while the people starved? We found a whole underground nightclub filled with rare alcohols for Nicu and dolls and sex toys for Zoia.

"And can you believe Janina Matei, the cabaret singer? Another of Nicu's conquests. His own friends say they were sent out of a hotel dining room while Nicu ordered the orchestra to face the wall and play while he made her dance naked for him. Can you imagine the sweat dripping down the brows of these men and boys playing and looking at the wallpaper while *that* was going on behind them? Blind orchestra, blind nation! And then was she taken out of circulation–disappeared? Is she dead, or not dead? No one knows. Ask the Securitate. But we have Nicu. Yes, I was there at the barricade where he was stopped in his Dacia 1310 five-speed with his new lover, Daniela Vladescu, the opera singer. What luck to have a son so much like his father. 'Our country has gold, but we beg from door to door.'"

"But what of Valentin?" I cupped my hands over Dani's ears. "He's not like Nicu, is he?"

"Oh, Valentin, the scientist, the indispensable man," the young woman said. "The graveyards are full of indispensable men. The 'human, warm-blooded one' who shared a secret stipend of 20 million lei for the Ceausescu children channeled out of the Office of Representation in the Central Committee. The nuclear scientist. He's at large, but we'll find him. The children are accomplices all. They carry a hated name. And surely Zoia is innocent, too?

Oh, yes, with her nude Mercedes convertible and her Renault Fuego GTS and 'salary' of 5,000 lei. For doing what? We have no penicillin and she has her trips to Spain. Well, she's run aground. We had to hustle her off into a little truck to keep people from lynching her. For this crime she will undoubtedly pay."

My heart turned over at the sound of a car's gas tank exploding. Flames leapt around us. We got closer to the hospital and the woman scrambled off.

"Why'd they let us pass?" I asked.

"You didn't see?" Catalin said. "She was showing her papers—she's a doctor. She'd kill herself if she knew who she was helping."

I watched the doctor go, her white coat disappearing into a stream of people moving away from the hospital. She joined a group of soldiers shooting toward the top of a building—where the Securitate were returning fire—and opened fire herself.

We were stopped again, numerous times, with Catalin driving expertly through gaps of people. Behind us was the city in flames. Above it was a special pattern of clouds that my Nanny called "The Eye of God". It was a central sun, looking down on things. Under the eye the clouds were making something of a hand.

If God was with us, what was he to tell us with a hand and eye? It was very clear, a hand below the clouds from the elbow down, this hand out of Michelangelo's Rome. Was the hand reaching down to steal my baby?

"Get back," I screamed at Dani as we approached the jolt of a small bridge. I felt faint, a hunted animal with my child. *And then I saw four bullet holes appear noiselessly beside me in the fabric of the car, exactly in the spot where I'd ordered Dani to sit.* When bullets are shot at someone else, you hear the loud *phat, phat, phats.*

The conventional world is used to such things.

But in the world of *Rémálom*, when *you* are the target, when machinegun bursts are directed at you and your baby, there is no pop. They just... *appear*, there, and there, and there, arriving without the luggage of noise. Dani trembled wildly but kept his seat. With *zarea*, a glimpse that lingers, a kind of temporal distortion setting in, my mind replayed with infrared clarity the Palestinians crouched at either end of the bridge we'd just passed, the automatic weapons, the smiles. Had we been recognized? Were pro-government forces sent out to murder us in addition to the revolutionaries?

Rémálom.

It wasn't merely *Rémálom*, the old Hungarian nightmare, was it, Nicolae? It was *Lidérc Álom*, worse than a nightmare, where you couldn't breathe and you had a horrible headache. It was *Szörny Álom*, the worst of all.

"Kill the Ceausescus!" thousands of people yelled around us. "An eye for an eye! Kill them all!"

Why did Catalin drive so fast? I didn't know what was happening to Dani and me, but I had the confusion of chemicals of the fight-or-flight reflex coursing through my veins as I descended into a state of fully conscious hibernative shock. This wasn't supposed to be how I celebrated my forty-third year.

Out of the corner of my eye I saw a beautiful woman waving wildly in the crowd. Catalin suddenly pulled over to the curb, reached over to the passenger side, and shoved the door open. It was Mariuca—an artist friend of ours, older than I but very excitable. She was both laughing and crying as she jumped into the car and breathlessly parodied the crowd's slogans to Catalin. As we pulled away, she leaned over the back seat to say something to us.

Suddenly, the windshield exploded and hit us like a wave of water. I screamed in pain as shards of glass hit my cheek and forehead, instinctively covering Dani with my body. The car lurched forward and then stopped for an instant as I felt a soft bump.

Catalin whistled and muttered, "I hope I haven't hit someone."

I opened my eyes and saw that Mariuca had been shot by the burst of the automatic weapon that had broken the windshield. Blood spurted out of her neck, drenching her dark brown hair and spilling down the back of her seat.

Outside, the rest of the crowd was under fire as fresh air ripped into the car and I simultaneously saw the head disappear from the shoulders of a man pounding on our windshield. In the spasm of bullets, a human arm in a white shirt fragment hit our hood and exploded, torn from its owner.

"Watch out!" Catalin shouted to us another hundred meters down the road as a shell crashed into a building beside us.

People near the explosion hit the ground. Carefully I draped my sweater over Mariuca's face so Dani couldn't see. He shook.

Still driving with one hand on the wheel, and without taking his foot off the accelerator, Catalin swerved until my vision went gray. The car nearly tipped over, but with a quick jerk and the rpms screaming, he righted it. Ever the Cat. His skill as a racer was certainly paying off.

I held Dani's head into my chest while Catalin drove, shifted, drove.

"Is the lady all right?" Dani said.

"Oh yes, her nose is bleeding. Do you remember when your nose was bleeding a few weeks ago?"

"Yes, Mama. She looks very hurt."

"She'll be all right. They'll take her to the hospital and fix her up."

"That's not her nose."

"But you had a nosebleed, didn't you? And everything was fine once we cleaned it up, wasn't it?"

"Yes." He was trembling again. "Mama, stop my heart."

"What?"

"Stop my heart."

I could actually hear–and not just see–his trembling. I hoped his memory would block this out, that what Dani was seeing would never come back to him again. Oddly, the expressions "to forget" and "to look at something" end in the same way, *am uitat*. Here, in this new Romania, seeing and forgetting were becoming inextricably entwined.

I shivered as we drove through a wall of flame red with death, the wide, sky-blue dome of the Sala Palatului concert hall and the twenty-two floors of the Intercontinental Hotel magnified in smoke behind us along the Stirbei-Voda.

TOON.

I jumped at the strange, musically percussive sound of a tank firing, but at whom?

Pulling up to a stucco house beyond the airport, Catalin motioned for us to get out, and we stumbled onto the walkway. "I'll be back as soon as I can." He roared out of view.

I could hear the gate opening down in the courtyard as we approached our hiding place. Airplanes and helicopters were still everywhere, but we could barely hear them over the growl of the tanks. We exchanged hellos with a middle-aged woman servant who with a frightened smile guided us through the garden to the modest villa.

This woman, so poor she had to wash her one pair of panties each night to wear again the next day, and so profoundly poor she didn't think to complain of this, began to sweep the floor as if nothing were happening. Then she looked up at me in an unsettling way, like a very old cat. For an instant she seemed to weigh alternatives, and then she rushed us, still picking glass out of our hair, into a bathroom, shutting the door behind us.

From what I could make out, we were just beyond the airport now, in a house Catalin owned on the outskirts of Bucharest. There were willow trees outside, visible from a high bathroom window covered with bars, as was Lake Snagov. That night, with Bucharest in flames, people joyous with the revolution would skate out there, laughing, drunk, riding bicycles slipping on the ice...

So this would be our Secret Annex. Little Dani and I would hide with the revolution raging around us for the next seventy-two hours. Servants knew we were here—would they tell? How could they be sympathetic? Valentin had disappeared. Was he alive now?

NICOLAE Ceausescu sat in front of a quickly placed folding table, his silver hair in disarray, his chest heaving inside a fur-lined black overcoat. "I don't recognize this jury. I can be judged only by the National Assembly."

"Shame! You don't know what you're doing! You are children," said Elena, the Genius of Chemistry. My mother-in-law had never graduated from high school or college, so hers was most assuredly talent in the rough. The country's leading chemists and researchers had been rounded up, regardless of heritage, their ideas pooled and published under her name.

The mock trial lasted less than two hours, with revolutionaries invoking the names of "more than 60,000 victims". The dictators' court-appointed defense attorney said just one or two phrases. He wrapped up his defense by wheeling upon his clients and shouting, "You're guilty!"

Elena whispered, "Don't speak, don't speak." They were confident that pro-government forces would liberate them. They thought they were immortal, as if they lived in another world. But there was no order. Even Nicolae's watch, itself a radar beacon with a special radio band to send a distress signal to the Securitate, could call no one.

Before the firing squad had begun to get into position, ten or twelve of the 300 volunteers started shooting. Like popping corn, the volleys of bullets massed, and massed, tumbling from those first few errant shots. The Ceausescus were *zdobiti*, shot everywhere they could be shot. A river of purple blood streamed from Elena's head.

"Don't hit their faces! Don't hit their faces! They have to be recognized," the commander shouted.

Blood oozed from Nicolae's mouth and eyes onto the television screens. Some reporters understated simply that they were disfigured, while others whispered that all 300 shots had missed Nicolae's heart. Safe in his chest, it lay quiet now, awash with dark red unclotted blood. Rigor mortis tightened his jaw; purple livor mortis appeared like a map on his back. Black blood spilled from the idols' eyes and mouths.

This was not Bucharest, but the Bolshevik Revolution of 1917, Paris in 1789, wrote the world's press. Obscure bureau reporters couldn't believe their luck as they filed their stories: "Pro-government forces... are plunging the country into civil war... Members of the security forces have reportedly burst into a meeting of demonstrators at the Opera House and sprayed the room with submachine guns. The Yugoslavian news agency Tanjug now reports estimates of at least 80,000 Romanians dead."

Frightened by the cheers of crowds audible from the fire-scorched presidential palace in the distance and more profoundly by the machinery of tanks on pavement and cobblestones, I believed that my in-laws, even if overthrown, would never be caught because they'd be protected by the Securitate. I believed we were shown dummies of Nicolae and Elena, and that their execution had been orchestrated by the Securitate in order to quiet things down. I believed they were still alive, possibly in a car, the helicopters the perfect diversion, rushing to asylum in Korea, home of the despot Kim Il Sung, or Iran, where days before Nicolae had carried a wreath to the tomb of the Ayatollah Khomeini.

TOON

Locked in the bathroom, I felt the dread animal fear of being hunted. How could I be innocent if I'd given birth to the monster's heir? How could I be a Ceausescu and fear Ceausescus at the same time? Details shut down to a peach-colored couch that for many hours became like a rock in the woods. Dani and I became one being with four eyes, four lungs, and four arms.

The world closed in.

Chapter 16

Fear gives wings

Toon. Artillery shells from an old World War II gun appropriated by the National Salvation Front were now turned on a nearby bridge, shaking our safe house with its thunder from a position not fifty meters away. The gun was actually named Tun, after the sound it made.

Toon.

Little by little the room got darker, and we dared a look out the single window where we could see the frost outside, and the dull ice of the lake.

"*Ole, ole, Ceausescu nu mai e,*" the crowds sang in the background. We could just make out the words, "Ole, ole, Ceausescu is no more."

"Why are they singing about Father Vale?"

Toon. Toon.

So many people in the street. So much singing.

Night fell completely, but the bathroom was lit by gunfire, rockets, gas guns, and flames.

A tree crashed to the ground outside the window, and we both jumped. I craved a cigarette but was afraid to light up, because I could hear the thunk of boots outside the window.

Toon.

A sword of light sliced my face as Catalin opened the door a crack and slipped in, closing the door behind him. "Valentin's here, too. He's brought Roxana with him and asks if you and Dani can stay downstairs."

Really? The basement? Valentin was the one who'd sunk low. I summoned every ounce of grace I had. What did it matter now? I grasped Dani's hand and followed Catalin downstairs. I couldn't wait to join the other things that were kept in storage. The door at the top of the stairs latched discreetly behind us. It was a nice apartment, perhaps something for a student—one of those living rooms that disappeared into a dining room and bedroom and bath.

Moments later a hurried bustle above told me that our new guest was being established above us.

Toon.

There was a lot of talking. I heard Valentin on the telephone.

"Free them! Free them! Please free her!" I heard him shout into the telephone upstairs to Securitate personnel about his administrative assistant at the lab. "Don't shoot anybody!" he said on private lines to the palace. "Tell them to resign! Don't hurt anybody!" He stammered, started to say something, sighed, and hung up.

Then he came down and sat on the bottom stair, looking up at me. He spoke haltingly, in a low voice, devastated now and in shock that what he'd always feared had come to pass. I'd never seen him so worried. I looked at him in morbid fascination. Valentin, my ex and forever, was at a loss for words.

"People are going from house to house," he said finally, "breaking in. They don't know what they're looking for, but they'll be here soon."

We looked over at Dani, who was playing with a Donkey Kong Nintendo game and some Crayola crayons. What would the revolutionaries do if they found him with these decadent things?

"My parents went to Snagov," Valentin said.

I knew this already, from the radio Catalin was playing upstairs. They'd flown away with Nicolae's brother-in-law (and former prime minister) Manea Manescu and former labor minister Emil Bobu, and had deserted them at Snagov after saying goodbye. Before they parted, Bobu and Manescu kissed their hands and wished them luck. In Romania, to kiss a man's hand is a humiliating act of self-abasement. Till the last moment, these men were so afraid that they still kissed that hand.

"Why didn't they pick you up in the helicopter?" I asked him. "Even animals care for their young. Please don't say your usual 'Don't worry'! Isn't it time to worry now?"

"Dana, Dana, people will help us."

Valentin had so many friends. He'd risked his position with his parents so many times to use his influence to help friends in trouble. But I could see in his eyes that it was dawning on him now that everyone who owed him a favor could already be dead.

"Valentin," I said. "Do you think that's why your father went to Iran last week, to set up asylum? That's what some are saying now on TV."

"I can't believe this." Walking to the window, he placed his cheek on the glass of our tiny basement window so that he could see the crowds massing on the other side of the lake. "This is not true." Then he saw me shaking my head. "In bad things, there's always a good thing. Perhaps it's good now that we're divorced, because they won't kill you for being married to me. Every one of us has a better chance." He blinked down some tears. "It's good also that I haven't married Roxana Duna."

"What about her husband?" I said. "Where is he?"

Valentin shrugged and danced around a bit, gnawing at his nails. "Goodbye," he said after a long silence. "Don't go upstairs." He went back up to sleep with her.

I didn't know this Valentin anymore.

Don't go upstairs.

Upstairs.

Upstairs, the two of them together amid all this havoc. Caviar in a snowstorm.

I didn't sleep that night. In spite of our great danger, I irrationally thought of the woman above me. Was there anything to keep Dani from knowing who this woman was? Then a murderous curiosity got the better of me and I needed to take a look at them. I'd just go upstairs barefoot and watch them sleep for a minute. I was fascinated with her, in love with my hate for her. My bonds with this woman were infinitely greater than hers were with Valentin. They were only lovers. The feeling ran much deeper in me. This was undocumented territory, what we had with each other.

With Dani asleep in some *plapuma*, comforters, I tiptoed up the stairs. I could feel my breath going lower and higher in my chest than it had ever gone before as I reached the door to the basement and eased it open. I felt like a young child in the Christmas of seeing something bad.

The sound of distant gunfire barely rattled the blinds. I crossed the kitchen, feeling my way over the dark smoothness of a table that dropped off into nothing. Over there was the dark silhouette of Catalin, snoring on his couch. Tiny flashes of light from far away danced on the other side of his blinds, occasionally holding still in a glow.

I stumbled into another table in the dining room as I crossed the hall and headed to the other side. Feeling coldness everywhere, I left the table and drifted off into space, everything black now, me a cosmonaut fumbling around as I reached the other side and saw the blackness of the guest room and the two shapes asleep in an embrace.

I was discovering something new about myself, daring to see them like this. I meant them no harm. In fact, they were beautiful. Stars were visible through a skylight in this modern house, and then the blinds rattled faintly again with another explosion.

Toon.

Catalin, my old friend, rushed to my side now, quiet as a deer. I smiled to let him know there was nothing to worry about, and he, with one brow raised, smiled back. I trembled. This was a ballet, without music. I felt the flashes soft on the windows, the blinds answering, the night clouds twinkling above the glow of the city. I disappeared back downstairs.

I had seen them.

ONCE, when we were sneaking around, just starting to be a couple, I actually slapped a girl in Valentin's grandparents' house. Valentin had invited some friends there for his birthday party, and I saw one of the girls looking at him. Even though it was hot in the house, she suddenly went to him and said, "I'm so cold. Let me wear your coat." Valentin took off his jacket and wrapped it around her shoulders. I went right up to her and slapped her.

Whatever happened to that girl—me? Why did I say nothing just now when Valentin went upstairs? Maybe because it was finally beginning to mean nothing.

I fell asleep until, just before morning, my son nudged me with a tiny hand. "Mommy, there's a stranger upstairs."

I shot bolt upright. "Where were you?"

"Upstairs. There's someone having breakfast with Daddy."

"Nobody in this house will hurt you," I said. "Was it a man or a woman?"

"I don't know."

"Do you know who it is?"

"No, Mommy."

He'd seen Roxana often enough at dinner parties at our house when Valentin and I were still together. Dani had even danced with her, but I was glad he didn't recognize her now.

"I'm sorry about this," Valentin said when he came down to see us close to 11am.

I said nothing back to him.

He walked over and hugged me hard.

ZOIA was seized at the Primaverii, the Ceausescus' White House. She stood there and looked at her captors like a stewardess from a really mean airline, in an airplane that was crashing. She tapped her right leg incessantly. Her two dogs, unaccustomed to people touching her, snarled as she was led away by troops who dragged and stuffed her into a *blindat*, a military armored car, awash in crowds. Television cameras from the international press corps flickered and clicked as soldiers opened her atta-ché case. Lenses zoomed in. They opened the valise into the eyes of the TV cameras. It was loaded with jewelry and foreign currency.

So now the twice-married *Domnisoara* "Miss" Zoia had plenty of attention. People jeered at the truck and threatened her as it sped away, but didn't dare touch it. Zoia had always been protected *pina la piele*–to the skin–by the Securitate. Once imprisoned, she began a hunger strike, living on coffee and Pall Mall cigarettes.

A national search would be conducted for Valentin, who'd tried to stop his father's murderous policies. Bullets, insanity, tanks.

And in the confusion a voice had come onto the radio, broadcasting from central security to an astonished world, a low, revolutionary voice with murderous pride in its accents, saying, "I am telling you this from the Den of the Wolf."

A voice from the end of the world.

"I HAVE to go," Valentin said. "Everyone's dying. My parents have been betrayed and captured. They're calling for the death of Nicu, Zoia, and all the rest of us. Nicu has been stabbed at the airport. They're accusing him of killing people in Sibiu–of poisoning the water when he left. Too many people know I'm here. I've got to find somewhere else to stay." His moan, so much like his singing, could still break my heart. I had no time now to resent the woman upstairs, but Valentin kept mentioning her.

"You will keep Dani down here?" Valentin asked.

"Is that a question or a request?" I said. "How could you treat us like this?"

He jumped up and down in a little dance of anxiety. "I have to go. You'll be taken care of. I will come back, but I have to go." He touched my hand and then kissed Dani.

He ran upstairs and made some telephone calls, asking insiders he knew on both sides where his parents were, and then, from our window, I saw Valentin and Roxana running out the door.

I asked Dani to come over to me, and I held him.

"Where's Daddy going?"

"He's just going back to town." I vowed this was the last time I'd ever lie to him about his father.

"Oh, can I go too?"

We stayed down there for another two days amid the gunfire and shouts of crowds, the helicopters beating everywhere over our heads.

"Do you know what's happening?" I asked Dani. What was I going to tell him about his grandparents when he asked? Weren't we all to blame?

"The city is on fire."

CATALIN'S servants brought us food. We had lamb, some steaks, a lot of french fries, some salami and cheese. In this basement apartment, in the hours suspended below the closed door, my feelings overwhelmed me. Valentin. My mother.

Dani saw me crying and came up to me. "What is it, Mother? Will we have a Christmas tree down here? When are we going to the mountains?"

Catalin went in and out, telling us news. I smoked what cigarettes I had left; then I was embarrassed to ask Catalin for more. I ran my fingers through my hair until Catalin teased me with the old phrase, "With the world on fire she combs her hair."

During the killing outside, many people just wandered about in a fugue state. There was no relief from hunger for many, and the electrical service was very sporadic, so by night things got even worse. Airports nationwide were closed to cheering crowds while other Romanians continued the rage of killing. People were stopped everywhere and accused of being Securitate. No place and no one was safe–patients were even murdered in their hospital beds for their clothing and blankets.

I tried to assemble my thoughts, but failed. I picked lint off my sweater. I quietly scratched my nose. My autonomic nervous system had taken charge of my senses while I was this deep in fear and treated me to such odd reactions as an itching need to urinate as well as tingles under my arms and on the back of my neck, which made me squeeze Dani instead of comfort him. I went a little mad, just as one might transfer reactions when the telephone's ringing and the soup's boiling over on the stove at the same time. You answer the soup! You telephone the stove!

Doors opened and closed above me, with everyone calling *Ceausescu, Ceausescu* now, on the TV, radio, outside, everywhere. The name of a target. I decided I'd never call Dani "Ceausescu", ever.

THE NEXT morning, the gate rattled again and then more glass broke. How could so many people be out there, whooping, playing so early in the morning out on the ice of the lake?

I just held my son and smelled the sweet young smell behind his ears.

The noise went away.

An hour passed, with other friends and acquaintances coming and going from the floor above us. Some would stop by as if to take a last look at the two of us, out of kindness but also possibly to say they'd seen us "just before".

While Dani took a nap, I watched TV and saw that the Securitate was trying to retake the airport, even though the army was supporting the National Salvation Front, the revolutionaries who were taking over. New leaders called for the arrest of Valentin and Dani, any Ceausescu. "*We want the whole gang.*" They ordered a national search.

I wondered if it were too late to talk about heaven to my son. *I'll give my life for him. If I have to die, I'll die. But leave my son alone. What has he done?*

"They've seen the pictures of him taken from the palace," Catalin said. "They're showing them everywhere. He's the only grandchild."

Catalin continued to go in and out. The nice couple upstairs took great pains to make everything seem normal, even bringing Dani a Christmas tree, which we stuck into a spare tire. Yes, we celebrated the holidays... severed from religion.

Unfortunately, Catalin himself did not spend Christmas with us. On the night of December 23, he roared into the mayhem and distributed water, bread, and fruit to the army, who were desperately trying to protect civilians during firefights between the Front and the Securitate. Many of the soldiers were so hungry they ate the oranges he lobbed to them right through the skin, not bothering to peel them. He ferried a number of senior soldiers back and forth between the army and the headquarters of the National Salvation Front.

Finally, just after 3am, as he crashed his car through a barrier, a burst of automatic weapons gunfire hit him twice an inch from his spinal cord as gas guns whined overhead. His Ford was so recognizable that troops swarmed the car immediately. News flashed over television screens nationwide that Catalin had been gravely wounded, calling him the first American civilian casualty in Bucharest. I choked down tears for the man who'd risked so much for so many, and vowed that I'd live to tell Liuda and his children how brave he'd been.

Without further word, we stayed alone downstairs for hours while I pondered our next move. Sometimes I could hear the maid and her husband rattling pans and talking upstairs. I played Monopoly with Dani, a game that, oddly, was perfectly acceptable in Communist Romania. In fact, I'd seen many children of devout Nomenclatura members squabble ardently over Ventnor Avenue and Marvin Gardens. Dani's favorite piece was a car, but he changed his piece with each roll of the dice to have more luck.

"Why do you do this?" I smiled at my little puppy. Just now I had to know why he

did it.

"I don't know, Mother," he said. "Wouldn't you like to try?"

When he wasn't looking up, I turned the TV on but quickly turned it off if I caught him watching. Reports showed the members of the new government, the faces of these familiar men appearing sporadically, spliced with scenes from Timisoara and street fights. Each report contradicted the last.

Then the programmers began to show *Judgment at Nuremberg* over and over again. I watched the stern brow of Spencer Tracy having to choose between evils but unhesitating in his condemnation of Nazi war criminals. This was a new American face for me, a man pondering and considering right and wrong.

Between showings of the film I watched footage of Zoia and Nicu's capture. Watching my in-laws being led away in handcuffs was like watching my own funeral. I knew Dani would be killed if we were discovered, so I smothered him with hugs.

Dani shouldn't have been held responsible for what his grand-parents did, or for the privileges his parents enjoyed or what we neglected to do, but the crowds were so wild and people were so angry that we could be killed even by accident if we ventured outside, in a frenzy or by a stray bullet, like Mariuca.

The gate kept rattling. Mobs streamed from one house to another, delirious with freedom. After lifetimes of repression, these people were like drunks on a binge.

ON the third day, hooligans who called themselves revolutionaries came into the house to loot. In an absurd way, I was relieved, because it meant we had to leave our basement. When we heard shouting upstairs, Dani and I slipped through the terrace window and around the garden to the house next door. Glass was all over the ground, and smoke burned my nostrils.

"Where are we going?" Dani asked.

I contracted my muscles and raised my shoulders as I felt a hand touch me. I turned to see Caezar Lascarescu, Catalin's sec-retary, whom I'd watched the day before announcing Catalin's near-death to reporters on TV.

"Here. Over here." Caezar motioned us toward a car waiting behind the house.

"Thank God. How is Catalin?" I said.

"Oh, he'll be okay. No one can kill him. He's got the hide of a bear. The American Embassy is arranging to transfer him to a hospital in Germany." He jumped into the car, zoomed up over the curb, and pushed open the door to let us in. "Where can I take you?"

"Paula's." I was glad to be going to her house. She was a good friend, someone we could trust. Paula had no involvement in politics, wouldn't judge us, and seemed a lucky person. Her house was closer to the fires, but I didn't care. Somehow this felt good. We drove through the people-crushed streets in a thankfully rusty and battered car, and no one challenged us. Instead, people pounded on the car doors and windows and waved. We waved back.

Caezar turned onto Cocarasu, then left on Golescu Iordache G., and then finally onto Strada Gala Galation. The Hebrew cemetery, where many victims of the Iron Guard lay at rest, wavered in the background. Heedless of the graves, people were running through the cemetery, jubilant. We turned left and followed Bulevardul 1 Mai to Strada V. Mironiuc, where my friend lived. We pulled up to her driveway. People were everywhere, spilling over the ruins where a house had once been.

"Where is it?" I blinked. I'd been there maybe twelve or fifteen times.

"It's gone, burned." Caezar rested his chin on the steering wheel.

There was only the black foundation where the house *wasn't*, a window hanging onto what was left of a wall. People came up through the smoke to the car and pounded on the glass again, malicious smiles on their faces.

"Look!" a woman with all-brown lower teeth said. "Look! Boom!" Her arms were filled with Paula's clothes, one a blue knitted shawl I was sure I recognized.

Dani was under my feet, with a blanket over his head. *Help me think. I've got to be calm so we won't be killed.* More people approached our car, so I smiled again and threw my arms up in triumph.

"Where do you want to go?" Caezar's job was over; it was time for him to get to his family.

"I don't know," I said, holding Dani down.

"Decide."

"I don't know."

We absolutely couldn't go to my mother's house. It was crazily near the center of the fighting. Because it was within the security periphery of the towering state television station, the heart of Bucharest, the area was still being fought over, filled with roadblocks. There was a lot of gunfire, bursts and deadly silences mingled with the rending of metal as the tanks repositioned. I glanced at Piata Victorei, where my mother's house was surrounded by smoke.

"Where?"

I found it hard to speak. I croaked out my mother's address and leaned over to hug Dani. Holding his head, I looked out at the insanity of people outside as we flashed from street to street. And then in the blur it struck me, as we passed the mouths of the gigantean shafts that descended into the subway from every station in the city.

On the filthy tile walls, large "WANTED" posters had been hastily pasted. The car stopped short to avoid hitting a running girl brandishing a magic marker. I was suddenly confronted with a grainy image of my sweet baby's face. *The enemy of the people, last of the evil Ceausescus.* "Dracu Grandson! Kill them all!" she'd scrawled across his cheek. What would this crowd do if they knew Dani were just feet away?

With all Romania hunting for us, my little son and I dropped into a rabbit hole and disappeared.

IT was twilight when we arrived in my mother's neighborhood. Crowds were still fighting over the television station behind her house, and thousands of people were on the Piata Victorei, screaming and cheering as young men in black took turns speaking. The National Salvation Front—who exactly were they saving now?

Caezar drove us closer than I thought he'd dare, reached from the driver's seat to pull the door closed after we got out, pushed a basket of food toward us through the car window, and screeched away after we exchanged abbreviated goodbyes and good lucks. We stepped into live gunfire as twenty men pushed past us in the semi-darkness. Looking back, I saw the headlights of Caezar's car turning in the distance and making it to safety. We slipped and slid on snow as we followed the shadows along the stairs and bushes of the final houses that took us around the back of the television station and the last apartment building that we had to run around before we got to our "safe haven".

We were surrounded by violence. Securitate men crashed through my mother's garden and ran on the tops of buildings. I saw one neighbor slyly eye us as we ran across the little courtyard that led to my mother's stairs. There were no lights on in anybody's house. Would she tell? There was more gunfire as we beat our fists against my mother's door, but I was afraid to turn around to see how close it was.

MY MOTHER, barely able to see us and breathless with the deadly ecstasy of the revolution, finally opened the door as two men ran over a roof two houses away and slid down to the other side, firing. "I am glad you've come," she said. I hugged her wildly. It seemed like something very normal, the right thing to do. I hadn't seen her so sweet in a long time.

Dani and I walked inside and felt a wave of warm air hit our legs. Like a miracle, from the inside Mama's house seemed untouched. Twilight sky shrieked through the bombed-out remains of many surrounding homes, and the setting sun was reflected in millions of shards of broken glass.

We could watch World War II from our dining room—my mother had finally made it back to World War II. The view! This was what Nero must have seen from his balcony so long ago, these lights, these fires. Over the rooftops, beyond the Strada Teheran and Tolstoi, was the smoking lawn of the Ceausescu Palace on the Primaverii, with still more cars parked recklessly around it. Once, no car but Nicolae's Mercedes or his midnight blue Dacia had been allowed to travel on that road. Tanks and great crowds swarmed all around us in the explosions of fire; swelling, throbbing, they came along the Bulevardul Aviatorilor and over to the Piata Dorobanti.

Mama had both the radio and television on. She wore only an old nightdress and looked like a little girl, not a grandmother. She seemed only slightly distracted that we were here and interrupting her while she was so busy with the end of the world. "What?" she said back to me as a rocket went directly over her house, slamming into the station. "What?"

"We might as well end up here," I shouted.

My mother ignored me and stood on the front porch for a minute, night clouds and stars behind her whipping her dress. "Hide under the table to avoid stray bullets." She crept over to the window again, busy watching the mayhem from below her shade. "Go in here," she said. She pointed to the bathroom.

Before we could enter it, Nanny came into the house. I was elated to see her, but she looked past me and talked only to my mother.

I looked around. Whatever was left of my life was in here, but it wasn't much, beyond the opportunity to weather these hours with the partially blind old woman whose life I'd ruined. This was fine, but how could I save Dani? Everything was disappearing. What would we do?

Mama wasn't so much my mother anymore as she was a kind stranger. "They've already been here, looking for you," she said. "Do you know what they'll do to us if they catch him here?"

She had no food in the house except two pieces of black bread, so the three of us shared them and the contents of the basket. We savored it all.

"Go down there now," Mama said. We stayed in the bedroom at the far end of a long, narrow hall, behind a bed that we pulled slightly away from the wall.

Valentin, where were you? Were you going to come help your family? You disappeared from us. Caught up with your family and the Central Committee, you were taken away as by a hurricane, so that nothing was left but for you but sports and... that was another life.

Concentrate on Dani.

It's never too late to be who you might have been. It's never too late to be brave.

SINCE Christmas Day, the television had been flashing the executed purple heads of Nicolae and Elena. Without modifications or updates these pictures appeared again and again, *zdobit*, green-lipped, the life run out of them. This was all the light my mother allowed in the house.

"Turn that off, foolish one," she said when I switched on a sconce three or four nights into our stay.

Mama fed us meatballs that were mostly bread and mashed potatoes, anything Nanny could find. Sometimes she let us in the kitchen to eat, but for the most part during the weeks of hiding that followed, we had to stay in her bedroom down the hall, huddled against the wall. One morning we woke to hear a scraping sound.

"What are you doing, Mother?"

"Help me."

She was barricading one window with an armoire so the bullets wouldn't come in.

At night, with the windows and cracks in the wall covered, we huddled by candles under a table and prayed for the gas to stay on to keep our radiators warm.

Many of my friends came looking for us, but my mother told them I wasn't there.

"Can't we trust her?" I said of one.

"They came in here and said they were looking for terrorists," she said. "They made me put my arms against the wall. But having found me, they kept looking for you, tearing everything apart. They pushed me, screamed at me. Who knows who they are, Securitate or revolutionaries."

"They were looking only for us?"

"Daughter, haven't you seen the television? 'Anyone Ceausescu should die.' They say, 'Where is Valentin? Where are you? Where are these people, Valentin and those around him? Anyone

Ceausescu should be punished.' Now they're saying, 'Everyone Communist should die.'"

One day I heard the voice of a colleague from the museum. Absurdly, she'd brought some forms to be forwarded to me, wherever I was, so that I could officially request a leave of absence from work. I was so lonely I walked right up to her from our hiding room just as my mother was denying I'd ever been there.

"I'm so happy to see you're all right!" she said. "Thank God you're all right! We hoped you'd escaped! There are crazy people out there, ruffians. How can I help you? So many of us thought you'd been killed or imprisoned. There's so much hate about this family."

"But I'm not part of the family."

"Oh, but you are!" She nodded her head quickly. "You know what they'll say. 'For twenty years you ate better than us. You had nice clothes, nice houses—you enjoyed yourself. It was a good thing for Valentin to divorce you as a facade to protect you!' It's a little late to be saying you're not part of the family! You've got to get out of here! Your husband has turned himself in! You've got to get Dani out of here! Do you know that *Paris Match* has printed that you and Dani are the only two Ceausescus left at large—you two alone? There's an international manhunt for you!"

Unable to speak, I just stared at her. She was right, about everything. But was she repeating only what she'd heard, or what she felt herself?

"At Dorin's house, some so-called revolutionaries came to look for you," she said. "They looked in the attic, in the basement and bathrooms. They asked for Valentin, Nicu, and you. At Dorin's office, someone came in with a gun. 'You are no longer working here,' they said. 'You're finished.'"

I looked back at the room where I'd told Dani to stay, and her eyes followed mine.

"You've got to get away from this TV station neighborhood–as far away as you can." She lit a cigarette and studied me. "Look, maybe I shouldn't tell you this, but I was named to a commission to go to your house and make inventories of your possessions. I refused, but that doesn't mean everyone else at work did." She blew an expert smoke ring. "Hey, by the way, you were right about all the wiretaps under your desk. A shell destroyed your work center. All you can see of the floor is a bunch of melted wires and enough microphones for a professional stage company!" I hugged her. "Goodbye," she said. "Go to another country!"

Also unnerving us during these days was the sound of the once-gentle Silviu Brucan, my schoolmate Anca's father whom Nicolae had placed under house arrest as a dissident during the final nine months, laughing like a devil amid scenes of the executions. He was a neighbor and an intellectual, an associate of my mother's, a former Central Committee member and a colleague in the press. He laughed with joy when reporters asked how he felt about the Ceausescus being dead. But he said, what happened to the Romanian people? How could we have been broken like this, brainwashed? How could we have accepted outrageous invasions of our privacy? When did we lose our ability to respond in a proper way? It was as if we were a disabled people.

On the 9th of January, Brucan, once the acting editor of *Scinteia* and now in charge of International Affairs for the National Salvation Front, amended the statistics from 60,000 dead to

10,000 dead in the revolution, but 60,000 since the beginning of communism. More disinformation, Nicolae style! *Before* we'd been told, "We have a gigantic wheat crop this year." It was a lie. "There was so much corn." A lie. Now the Front had said, "So, so many dead," then, "Oh, not so many dead." It was the same kind of lie.

Mama allowed only her old friend Zina to come see us regularly, and she often brought us apples, milk, and news.

"Maybe they think you're gone," Zina said.

"Why?" I brightened for an instant.

"Because they're saying, 'Every Ceausescu is dead.' Maybe they think they've drowned you. Did you know they filled your basement with water? They filled the whole house." Zina bit her lips and looked down. "My cousin was at the execution of your in-laws. The television shows them dead together, but as they took them into the drilling yard to be shot, they separated Elena from Nicolae."

"Why'd they do this?" My mother now took an interest. Nanny leaned closer to hear.

"To humiliate her. They called her a whore."

"She's a murderess, but not a whore," my mother said. "She was true only to–"

"At the end she was brave," Zina said.

My mother nodded slowly.

"My cousin was there. He told me," Zina said. "She was proud at first and even disdainful of the troops until they separated her from Nicolae. You could tell she was sure she'd be rescued until they pulled her from His side. 'There are no bank accounts. Go look for them. I brought you up like a mother!' She begged them to let her stay with her husband. She smiled, she screamed, she wrenched, she pleaded, but this they wouldn't do. They called her a bitch and told Nicolae she'd been with many other men. Enjoying her pain, they slapped her and pulled her from him. They dragged them to separate corners of the parade ground until Elena broke free. She called out to Nicolae and ran toward him like a young woman before they gunned her down. The soldiers were amazed. She'd over-powered two men and made it to within five feet of him, arms outstretched. They let Nicolae see this before they gunned him down, and then they just kept pumping thousands of shots through them till there was almost no flesh left. My cousin said Elena's running to her husband was the noblest thing he had ever seen. It's what all the soldiers are talking about. He said that's why they kept shooting."

"Bah!" Nanny said.

Every evening, the contending crowds of the National Salvation Front met, and their brave new leaders made speeches to great applause. They lit torches and searchlights and made decisions they'd reverse the next night. On two nights the crowds were there until morning. Riots broke out between differing factions. Many waved pine boughs or carried Romanian flags with the communist emblem cut out of the center, "a hole in the flag" that unnerved the world. Now nearly a million people were out there.

Who were these "new" leaders? Many of the voices I heard were familiar murmurs I remembered from receptions during my childhood in my parents' home. In fact, I'd grown up knowing many of the "new faces" that Vladimir Tismaneanu would reveal to the world in the *New Republic*:

Ion Iliescu, our new president, had often attended Central Committee meetings with my father. As a young man, he'd gone to college in Moscow with Mikhail Gorbachev, a lifelong friend. When I was ten, he'd shown his colors early on by persecuting Romanian students when they tried to demonstrate after Soviets tanks rolled into Hungary. How gentle was that? And Tismaneanu was right in pointing out that Iliescu had never dared to criticize Nicolae before December 22, 1989. Far from it, Nicu had actually been this man's protégé. In this free Romania, how could he now be in charge?

Our new prime minister was Petre Roman, a former schoolmate of mine who was also born into the Nomenclatura. Newly married to our ambassador to Switzerland's daughter, he'd worked as a hydrology professor at the Polytechnic Institute in Bucharest before bursting onto the international scene. Petre's father had fought with mine in the Spanish Civil War and been a member of the Central Committee until 1983. In spite of that, these nights, Petre seemed the very image of a dissident. I'm sure he wasn't reminding anyone of the time he dated Zoia now!

Our new vice president was Dumitru Mazilu–a Securitate colonel who'd written many of Nicolae's fist-thumping speeches. He'd turned against Nicolae during the final years, even slipping a memorandum on Nicolae's human rights violations to the United Nations, for which he was slammed in jail, but how strange it was–a former Securitate man shouting "Death to Communism" so loudly in that odd little voice each night to the crowds below us!

Corneliu Manescu seemed to be the only one who could touch anyone's heart. Freshly released after having been under house arrest since March, he spoke a lot, blinking and shielding his eyes, his frail blue body illuminated by the floodlights. Nicolae had denied the seventy-three-year-old any medical attention during his nine-month imprisonment, though he'd once been known to the world as president of the United Nations General Assembly. Now he had a voice, but on the other hand, no one was giving him a position of authority.

Everybody wanted a piece of Romania now, including Britain and the US, whose State Department officials and advisors were infiltrating Bucharest. And what did the National Salvation Front do during these first unsteady months?

One of the first decrees was to ban the death penalty (now that they could be the ones toppled by a coup), legalize abortions, and ban the communist party, the CPR. Passports were issued to everybody. Immediately, like mushrooms after a rain, new parties like the Christian Peasant party and the Romanian Democratic Party were born.

Soon an endless display of furs, furniture, gold dinnerware, diamond-encrusted high heels, and solid gold scales used to measure out food for Zoia's dogs hit the airwaves. The press dug up example after example of the atrocious luxuries they'd found everywhere in the palaces.

They replayed the footage again and again, and now to our horror the scenes included Valentin in chains in a line of people far more involved with the government than he. He had an ironic grin and looked like a condemned man. "Finally we have caught him," they said. Valentin was grouped with an odd lot, among them short, balding Emil Bobu, who pushed his rodent-like cheeks in and out as he stared out of the screen. Under Nicolae, his wife, a judge, had risen to the highest position of the justice system, attorney-general. Ceausescu's chief of personal security, Gen. Neagoie, was in the line, too. He'd been connected with Nicolae and Elena for twenty or thirty years. His obsequious movements were almost birdlike.

Valentin looked if he were mocking everybody, as if he were saying, "You did it again, fools. The leaders are the same types of people in different clothes." He looked contemptuous of the situation. For that reason I began to fear for him.

On the radio, a lot of people spoke against him–people I'd never have thought would condemn him. During interviews of these witnesses on an international station, the most venomous was Mircea Lucescu, a soccer star who played for the Securitate's Dynamo club, arch-rivals of Valentin's Steaua team. Mircea was a friend of Nicu. Now this man was lying about Valentin. This was a bad omen.

ONE OF THE NEW newspapers announced it was compiling a database of Nicu's victims. "All People Who Have Had Affairs With Nicu, Contact Us."

No one responded, the newspaper reported later. Did everyone conclude, then, that Nicu'd had no lovers and had never gone to Las Vegas on gambling sprees with jet-setters such as Armand Hammer?

Safe in the United States, Nadia Comaneci was denying ever having slept with Nicu, and Catalin was recovering from a second set of surgeries to remove bullets from his back.

NANNY came again one morning and told my mother, "I've been to Dana's house."

"Yes?" We all crowded in.

"All the doors are open. Photographs are strewn everywhere, stamped on, and ripped. I saved as many as I could. Here. Everything's been taken out, except your clothes."

My clothes?

My mother turned away.

"Your dresses and underwear have been cut with scissors, right in the drawers, into a thousand pieces."

"Who could be so sick?" I asked. This was a very ancient kind of hatred. "Why didn't they just steal them?"

"Some of your neighbors *are* wearing them," Nanny said, "but the rest are cut up."

So they wanted to punish me, too. What was Nanny thinking as she spat and looked away?

"And you weren't watched, coming here?" My mother concentrated all her questions on her dear old friend.

"Why my underwear? Who'd do this? This wouldn't be the Securitate."

"No," Nanny said.

"Other women?" I couldn't believe it. "Why would other women do this?"

There was a knock at the door, so we returned to our hiding places as a young man spoke in low tones to my mother, then left. She brought papers into the kitchen and spread them on the table. I was being called in for an inquiry, and it was her responsibility to find me and ensure that I appeared.

"Mama, don't worry," I said.

She grew frantic and cried.

"I'm going to see this man, Ghenus, the prosecutor. It's been forty-five days," I said. "We're not going to do this anymore."

"Don't go," Mama said.

"You've done too much already, and I don't want you to get in trouble."

Chapter 17

*One who digs another's grave will be
sure to fall into it himself*

THE WORLD seemed just as it had always been, with early bird-
song. It was quiet outside. Perhaps it was over. Perhaps we'd
be safe. Perhaps not. I could hear melting snow dripping, dripping
from the eaves.

I left the perfect darkness of my hiding place and started out the
door into the dazzling February warmth to turn myself in. It was
the first time in forty-five days I'd seen sunshine. Other people
were walking to work; I fell into this walking as if heading to
work with them and continued along the street toward the central
political district and the courthouse where Prosecutor Ghenus was
waiting to greet me. Buildings were riddled with bullet holes. The
Central Committee was now just a skeleton of girders. Shouldn't
this courthouse have been one of the first fired upon, too?

I was pleased and bewildered that no one recognized me, but I
felt glad Nanny and my mother were back with Dani. We wouldn't
know what was going to happen to us unless we asked, and this
walking felt so good. At least I was going to end the uncertainty.

I smelled the earth blooming under the snow, a fragrance so old and familiar, as the wind blew spring across Lake Herastrau. It felt so good to be outdoors, but what a strange outdoors. There were signs everywhere that this was no longer the Bucharest I knew. More workers in hats, dark coats, and faded dresses walked back and forth between abandoned tanks; there were still offices and deadlines and factories in this new world. I reached the courthouse with the same odd dread I'd felt when seeing my in-laws for the first time–I wasn't supposed to *be* here, was I? The overworked receptionist took no notice of me as I quietly stood in a corner once inside. "Where can I find Mr Ghenus?" I asked. There were armed guards everywhere, not porters and doormen, like there used to be. Maybe things will be all right. Nothing happened for a few minutes while business was conducted with three men ahead of me.

I walked up again. "Borila, Iordana. Mr Ghenus has asked me to come and speak to him."

Uncomprehending, the clerk wrote my name down as I spelled it. "Mr Ghenus is busy."

This was wonderful! I was not snapped up and thrown into jail yet; the comfortable pillows of bureaucracy seemed to be padding everything.

"Here," a young woman said. "Over here."

She gently guided me to the anteroom of the court offices, where a guard checked me for knives by patting my clothing. "In there," he grunted and gave me a shove on the left shoulder.

I tried to get my bearings as I was roughly conducted past an endless series of small cubicles hastily fashioned of wood and cardboard where the "judges" sat. At the end of this cardboard district was a private office where the prosecutor Ghenus was at work on some papers on his desk. When he looked up and recognized me, his malicious smile told me things were not all right. The image of Dani flashed through my mind.

"Comrade Ceausescu." He invited me to sit with a wave of his hand as he ran his eyes down my body. This man had the eyes of everyone I'd ever been afraid of. He didn't smile. Instead, he looked matter-of-fact. Maybe that frightened me the most.

I felt dizzy. "My name is Borila, Iordana, not Ceausescu."

Ghenus shook his head in slow amusement. "Do sit down. Would you like a cigarette?"

"No, thank you." Ridiculously I'd been longing for one.

"No? There must be some way I can make you more comfortable." Ghenus was expansive here in front of me. He was an artist at these questions, he undoubtedly thought. He was having a good time.

"No, thank you."

"Comrade Ceausescu, the first thing I'd like you to do is write down an hour-by-hour account of everywhere you've been and everything you've done from the 16th of December until the moment you walked through this door. Do you know that we're very, very glad to see you?" He crossed the room and stood in front of me so I saw not his face but his belt buckle and the bottom of his necktie. "Very glad. And how is our little boy?"

I focused on his necktie and caught my breath. His necktie—I'd seen it before! Was it Valentin's? My mind raced. No. *I'd seen this tie's match on Nicolae* when he'd washed his hands in alcohol beside me and was telling me how few grams of food it took to keep a Romanian alive. Nicolae!

My eyes grew wider until Ghenus smiled again and took my shoulders in his large hands. "I'm flattered you find my person so interesting. But I've instructed you to fill in this report. Do what you're told." He motioned me up from the chair.

The young woman reappeared and escorted me to what I knew was an observation room, with glass everywhere and nothing but a small desk and chair. I wrote and wrote, thinking of Dani with each word. I'll die before I tell him any more about Dani. "Here," I said when Ghenus came into the room. "This is what happened."

He took it agreeably and began reading with a crafty smile.

I was ready to go to jail now. I watched his eyes travel over the paper. Then he laughed out loud and salaciously looked at my sweater. Did he have a sweater fetish? Where was Valentin? Didn't he promise me I'd never have to face this alone?

"Write it again." Ghenus pushed me back into the room.

An hour later, I handed the papers to Ghenus. I would not cry. Petre Borila's daughter would not cry.

His face grew purple as he read them again. His hair, dark as shoe polish, stood out from his stocky scalp. Then he handed the papers back to me. "This first place where you lived was on Grigore Cerchez," he said. "Write it down. Your house. And so on. Don't you know we've known where you've been every second of time since the revolution began? Excuse me." He picked up a telephone ringing on his desk. "Zoia's husband? What a whiner. Oh, go to his house and pick up some clean underwear for him then. He has no more in prison, and I suppose we could do that much." He hung up and set his eyes on me. "There were many valuable things in your house, Comrade. I've been there. So many wondrous appliances and toys... a satellite dish, rare china. But the paintings, they are the finest in Romania. I should like to compliment you on your choices. Can you tell me about their provenance?"

"These are just some paintings that—"

"Your parents, Nicolae and Elena Ceausescu, gave you." He reached for some carbons and held them up. "Look! The requisition documents!"

It was true. Two or three had been given to Valentin by his parents. I knew these gifts were going to be my undoing... "Some were from my real parents, the Borilas," I said. "Others I've purchased over the years."

"And they were too good for our art museum? You thought instead you'd procure them for yourself?"

What did it matter now? The entire revolutionary army was decamped in the gallery spaces. Bullet holes had ripped through a number of paintings that survived the earthquakes; over 100 paintings were destroyed; many others simply evaporated into thin air.

Ghenus now showed me an inventory with my address on it. In addition to luxuries I'd never seen, some I had seen, and some inexpensive sheets and quilts that were mine, was a detailed list of everything I'd requisitioned to help my friends: cases upon cases of infant formula, precious meats, and liquors that had been my stock in trade. My throat felt dry. There was really nothing to say.

"Your world is about to change, Little One."

"I've committed no crimes against Romania."

"Do you have a lawyer?"

"Yes." I knew someone, but would anyone represent me? I was fascinated with my own trans-objectivity. Could I possibly be guilty for not throwing the furniture and appliances out of our house when Valentin guiltily loaded it up toward the end? I remembered Catalin's prophetic warning in early November to "move your chair to a smaller house", and I wished now that I'd taken his advice.

"I have all the information I need," Ghenus said. "Go home. We'll set up the trial date. Now I must decide where to imprison you."

My throat started to constrict. "But what will happen to Dani? No one can take care of him. My mother's too old."

"After your trial you'll become a prisoner of the state. Your son will be sent to the government orphanage, where he'll grow up like all of the little Romanian children you Ceausescus tore from their mothers' breasts. He deserves to enjoy the 'progressive' programs you designed, doesn't he? *One who digs another's grave will be sure to fall into it himself.*" He told me his sister's family had been victims of Systematization and had lost their home, and their child had been sent to Brasov, where he disappeared. All the records had been destroyed and they still couldn't find his nephew, so his passion here was both justifiable and authentic.

The tears felt gritty behind my eyes. I wouldn't give him the satisfaction.

"And so it will be for your son."

"Why? What has he done to anyone?"

"What have any of the children done, Comrade Ceausescu? It's simple. You'll have to be put in prison like the others. The Little Ceausescu will have a taste of what other children went through. Just bring him to us, and things will go better for both of you. There's nothing to worry about."

"Nothing to worry about!"

"Nothing."

These were not words of justice, but rather revenge. They *were* going to take their vengeance out on Dani, "the Devil's heir". Ghenus was still talking about the years in which my son would come to know the deprivations of the true Romanian workman, a life sentence of penitence and ridicule, when I straightened. I think I even brightened a little when I stood up and said, "That's enough."

"What?" The prosecutor was taken aback.

"Bringing my son in tomorrow. I shall not do this." I tried to sound like Mama. This was my last chance. In spite of the democratic protestations of these new leaders, what was needed for the moment was Ecaterina Borila's daughter. What was needed was a show. "I will present my son on the date of the trial, and not one moment earlier. You have taken up enough of my time, Prosecutor. Good day."

The words were luminous in the air. For this one triumphant moment after all of those dark days under a table; or under a bed; or under the spell of Valentin, my mother, or anyone else who'd made us look down; for this moment Dani and I were incredibly alive. I looked at Ghenus impatiently.

"Thank you," he said. After two heartbeats, he motioned me out of the room.

I left him writing something on his desk and walked outside. An aide emerged and conducted me into a second processing room, where key identification papers of mine were returned. Several other people derisively looked at me but did not speak. To my astonishment they didn't stop me even after I found myself walking on the steps, walking home free, stars bright over my head. In fact, I smiled a little crazily about it. I'd eaten nothing since I'd left home that morning, and it was after 7pm now. I felt light-headed and empty.

The streets were packed with revolutionary celebrants again, just as they had been six weeks ago. I didn't know what was going to happen next, whether they were going to follow me or not, whether they were going to take us all prisoner, but: I'd turned myself in, and I was free. My son was innocent, but he was guilty. I was divorced from Valentin, but never so connected to his family as now. There was no gunfire, but the greatest danger was upon us. The people were free without Communism and the Ceausescus, but they were desperate without someone to blame.

There is an old artistic term called *raccourci*, used by Italian Renaissance painters who tilted perspective on edge and zoomed their foregrounds into their backgrounds. Looking up from a vantage below, you'd see a figure's toes, then his nose. The beginning and the end parts of my life had been foreshortened, and nothing in the middle was important anymore.

BECAUSE of the new dangers from the court, friends of my mother took us into different homes from night to night, returning us to her for short stays only. When we were with her, Mama began to snap at Dani for little things, like playing with the wax on the candle we kept under the table. I was on edge all the time, grinding my teeth and smoking too much, thinking. She paid for a lawyer for me who'd been recommended by a Jewish friend and even talked about going to the Soviet Embassy and asking for asylum for me. "I'm still a captain in the Soviet army," Mama said.

"Why do you even think there's a Soviet Union anymore?" I asked. "Why do you think they could help us?"

Every day now she walked outdoors, picking up the copper shells from gunfire that were spoiling her garden.

I'D SNEAKED out of the house one night to get some air when a car pulled up behind me on the street. Turning around, I was astonished to see Catalin, tanned but thinner than when I last saw him. "How could you–"

"Get in," he said. "Dana, get in."

"I'm so glad you're all right!"

As usual, he got right to the point. "You must leave here. Nobody knows what's going to happen, and it's worse now than it ever was."

"Leave here?"

"Leave here," he said. "It is not safe for you and Dani. My wife wouldn't forgive me if I didn't help you now. Besides," he said with a grin, "since I've already saved your life once I'm responsible for you."

"But what about my work at the museum? What about my pension?" I said insanely.

"Pension! Grow up! What is this about a pension if you're not going to live to see it?"

Up until now, I'd truly never considered leaving. I'd grown up in Bucharest, and my parents had built this country, for better or for worse. They were heroes here. There was so much beauty in this city, and it was the only home I'd ever known. My friends were all here...

"You've got to decide," he said. "I can help you only now."

"But when?"

"Tomorrow morning."

"It's too early. I need more time."

Catalin looked grave for a moment. "There's not going to be any trial," he said. "The Securitate burned all the financial records to hide the money and cover their tracks, so the National Salvation Front is looking for a scapegoat. They're getting ready to pick both you and Dani up. They think you have money stashed away. Ha! Are you willing to wait until Ghenus grabs you? We'll help you, but you must realize the danger you're in. You've got two minutes to think it over."

"Give me a half-hour. After I get home I'll call you, but I need to decide alone. Same number?"

He nodded.

"I can't worry my mother about this, and I can't tell Nanny. When I get there, I'll tell you. I just have to think."

AT HOME, I drew my legs up into my father's chair. We probably won't make it. It will be the worst thing you've ever tried in your life. The borders are crawling with guards, and it's known the Loyalists will kill us if we're caught taking Dani out of the country. These will be the most agonizing moments a human being can go through. We've already lost a lot of people going just this way, and you're so much more recognizable. Just look at him. But it's a chance. Do you want to go or not? Sometimes the only thing left to do is the impossible.

The endings of Gypsy songs and legends are violent, sentimental, dripping with gore and justice. Dani and I had been through so much together. Was I to lose our last chance? Were we to drown "like Gypsies so close to the shore"?

TEN minutes later, on a neighbor's telephone, I spoke with Catalin for just twenty seconds. Then, after midnight, with everybody asleep, I stole into the kitchen, slipped the lighter Valentin had given me as a wedding present out of my purse, and lit a candle. As quietly as I could, I opened a kitchen drawer and drew out my grandmother's carrot knife. I sat on the floor once more. My heart pounding, I plunged that knife into the heel of my boot, and into the deep slit I folded my birth certificate, a tiny triangle. My past disappeared into the heel of that boot.

From that moment I would no longer be afraid.

Feeling powerful for the first time in my life, I grabbed my purse, flicked the lighter on, and burned everything else, including Dani's identification papers and birth certificate, anything marking him a Ceausescu. I burned my green museum pass; my red party card; my blue-gray identification papers with my photograph; my pink driver's license–anything that had the hated name on it, slowly, turning them curiously in my hand. They made a little pile of white ashes. The scientist in Valentin would have been pleased–it was amazing how papers representing momentous personal events conformed to the law of conservation of matter and energy. Finally, I touched the flame to my three-page divorce papers. The hated name Ceausescu was on that, too.

Fool. With so many other records destroyed by the Securitate, this was your only proof that you *weren't* married to Valentin. If you were truly captured and recognized...

But I didn't care. Now I rose to my feet, walked into the living room, and, hoping it was still there, found and pulled from a cabinet my father's wide old star book, in which I'd stashed letters from Valentin since our teenage days, some oversized, others small as florists' cards. One by one, I touched the flame to them, too. I burned excuses from London, apologies from Lake Snagov, assurances from Neptune.

With everything Ceausescu destroyed and nothing remaining but my birth certificate, I was truly Petre Borila's daughter again. I'd burned my fear, my naivete, my childhood, my tentativeness, my irresponsibility, my cowardice, my connections to the Nomenclatura, and now my heart was catching fire. *Rosu ca focul*, blushing with fire, I rose from the ashes as the last of the papers made little blue flames and burned while I looked on, thinking of Gypsy endings entering the sky in flames.

Chapter 18

Praise to the face is open disgrace

I PUT on a tan skirt and a brown sweater. In my pocketbook was the cigarette lighter and a compass my father had given me as a teenager, wrapped in a leather pouch. I carried some photos of my early life; I don't know why. I packed just as few clothes for Dani and stayed awake the rest of the night. It was insane to try to get away now, of all times. I had literally no money and no plan for escape, but I knew where we wanted to go. I'd known it for many years, like an old story my dreams kept telling me.

In the morning, while my mother was sleeping, the blue car arrived. I hurried the surprised Dani into the car.

"Where are we going, Mother?"

"Come on. Keep quiet. I love you."

I turned around to see only Nanny at the door. I didn't say anything, but I didn't have to. The nod she gave me let me know she understood.

"What happened?" Catalin asked with alarm. "What happened to Dani?"

"What do you mean?"

"He's trembling. Has he pneumonia? The whole top of his head is white!"

"He'll be all right." I put my hand on the top of his head to cover the white spot. "He's afraid of all loud noises now, and he's been indoors too long. I'll hold him right here, beside me."

"Will he be all right? Look at him."

"He can make the trip," I snarled. "He'll make it. Get down, Dani, underneath this blanket."

I slunk down myself and closed my eyes a moment.

No one was going to take my child.

Dani was going to get well.

There was an early blue color over my native Bucharest as the car rolled quietly through the first streets, then picked up speed. Because there were rumors of at least fifty roadblocks to the south, Catalin headed north in a lunatic direction. *North!*

I was a denizen of Bucharest who loved the people and my old haunts. No one would have thought me capable of leaving this city; certainly not Valentin or my mother.

We were leaving Bucharest forever.

My stomach and mind were on fire.

"Look behind you," Catalin said half an hour later.

We were on a highway headed for the mountains, the first of which I could see ahead of us in a half-imaginary blue. I turned around and saw a few cars. "What is it?"

Dani tried to poke his head up to see, but I hugged him so he slid back down. Behind our car was a second, decoy car driven by two friends of Catalin, and then a green Dacia.

"What?" I asked.

"Don't look," Catalin said.

"When can I look?"

Catalin was speeding up now, although still staying in the inconspicuous flow of traffic heading northwest of Bucharest. Slowly, the mountains ahead were coming toward us, the near ones rising up to the laps of some more majestic summits, the highest capped in snow.

"All right," he said. "Now, do you see a green Dacia?"

"Yes," I said. "Three cars back."

"That car," Catalin said, "is following us." He kept on driving and flicked on the radio.

"Take this piece of paper," he said at length. He reached down between the seats and gave me a long blue sheet and a pencil. "Write down the license plates and colors of each car behind us."

"Okay," I said cheerfully. "Dani, do you want to help me?"

"Yes, Mother."

"All right. Now what's the license plate of the green car behind us?"

The green car had moved up a car, while the colors of the others had changed, or dropped away. For a moment I couldn't see our decoy car, and a wave of fear washed over me.

Dani told me the license number.

"Good," I said.

"All right," Catalin said. "Do you see any others?"

We kept a tally, which quickly filled up two pages. Wouldn't it have been easier for us to count the cars if they started shooting at us? Otherwise, what could we do? Dani had never been so good, and I felt different, too. I'd do what Catalin had asked, *because* he asked it; I felt comforted that he was the finest driver in Romania. No one could get closer than he would allow.

"I want to know if any of these cars shows up again, many miles from now," he said.

"Dani," I said.

He looked sleepy. "Yes?"

"Are you hungry? I could make some sandwiches." I made salami and cheese on some good black bread and gave them to Dani. "Do you want something?" I asked Catalin.

"Yes," he said. "Sure. The same thing. Now–look slowly around."

I did as he said. The green Dacia had passed our companion car and was moving up along our right quarter panel. I slowly turned back.

"Don't act suspicious," he said. "Don't watch them."

Slowly, with my heart pounding, I saw the green Dacia pull up beside us. I looked down at my son, whose head was in my lap now. His eyes looked up and met mine. He chewed on his sandwich and smiled. The Dacia then pulled further ahead and drew parallel to us while I felt the right side of my face freeze in anticipation of the window exploding with a bullet hole. "Do you know a song?" I asked Dani, still bracing for it. "Sing me a song."

"I know something." He began singing, "We have no food, we have no money, but we have a canal, which the president and his wife have made... for a promenade."

Catalin shook his head.

"Where'd you learn this?" I asked. "Do you know what it means?"

"I heard it outside our house," Dani said. "The people outside liked to sing it."

"Please, Dani, don't sing it anymore. It's not a nice song."

"How much longer are we going to drive?" Dani stirred from my lap.

I looked slowly to the right and saw the green Dacia directly beside us, with two men inside, or their shapes, rather, because I didn't want to see the faces of the men who might kill us. I couldn't bear to do that. So I felt rather than saw them, with my mind racing over the edge. "Speed up," I begged Catalin.

"Why?"

"To get away from them."

"Just relax. They'd have stopped us earlier if they were going to."

"Do you think they're following us?"

Instead of answering, Catalin asked, "Are you writing down the license plates?"

"Yes."

Catalin took a bite out of the sandwich I made him and said, "Yes, I do. Do you see our other car?"

Our companion car was three cars behind us now, while the green Dacia had pulled ahead of us.

Catalin nodded toward the Dacia. "They have an antenna on their car, yes?"

"Yes, sure," I said. "Can't we lose them?"

"Sure. But do you want them to know we're trying to lose them?"

Then I nudged Dani. "Don't get up," I said, "but up ahead is Sibiu."

Our companion car had pulled ahead of us, with the green Dacia falling back and taking another lane. It looked as if it were going to take the first exit to Sibiu, and I relaxed for a minute.

It didn't.

But we did. Catalin hit the brakes hard and veered to the right, with the companion car following, flying over a little bush. The green car, locked up in traffic, impassively continued in the other direction. I kept watching it, expecting the swerve, but it disappeared over a rise as we skidded down into the streets of Sibiu, with Catalin downshifting and turning so many times I lost my bearings.

The cobbled streets were full of the Saxon Sibiuites, Transylvanian Germans who were hungrier and angrier even than the crowds in Bucharest. Sibiu, 800 feet higher in the mountains and far from the prosperity of the Danube, had always been poor.

"Don't look at them," Catalin told us as we slowed behind traffic around two tanks skidded akimbo and abandoned in front of the financial district. There were some old peaked buildings here, the ruins of a once-beautiful city.

But what had Nicu done in Sibiu? I felt as if everyone were looking at us. Scarred by fire and rain, there were still some remnants of posters of Nicolae and Elena, torn and defaced with oaths. What did these people want?

I finally realized they were too hungry or tired to notice us, but Catalin evidently felt we were slowing too much, because he said, "Hang on." He took both hands from the wheel and drove with his knees locked around the steering column straight into a crowd of 400 people. With one hand he rolled down the window, and with the other he reached into a dark corner below his seat and came up with a handful of cellophane-wrapped pink candies. He threw them in lazy arcs, one by one, to his left so that the crowd flew *into* them as if they were reverse grenades. I leaned over and grabbed as many as I could and began throwing them out my window.

Veering through the gap, Catalin accelerated onto an empty road.

"Catalin," I said.

"What?"

The mountains appeared again, a little closer, some vineyards appearing brown and green on the lower hills. "You can drive with your hands now."

A smile crept onto his face. "What for?"

Beyond the city, the rough-peaked mountains that constitute the Transylvanian Alps continued to rise, and I went back to writing down license plate numbers. It was therapeutic, anyway, and kept me busy.

Another hour passed, and I barely paddled conversation along by saying, "Do you see those mountains, Dani?" I continued the fiction that we were going to the mountains for our long-planned vacation. "On the other side of that ridge is Mount Moldoveanu."

Even Catalin looked up at it. Suddenly he got excited. "There! Did you see?"

"What?"

"That flash of blue?"

"We're going over *there*?"

"This strange area which stands before us is just as the last Ice Age left it," he said. "Ancient animals such as the chamois live here, beyond the Muntii Fagarasului range, which cuts itself away from the modern world like a wall."

"What are chamois?" Dani asked.

"A prehistoric goat." He then told Dani about the fruits, chestnuts, and wines of the Calugareasca Valley and Odobesti;

the marbles they mined in Ruschita; the painted monasteries still active in the mountains of northern Moldavia that one can only reach by horse. Everywhere on all these slopes, from 300 to 600 meters, were the ruins of lovely orchards.

"We're not going that way, are we?" Dani said.

"It'll be fun," I said. "But from now on, you are a new person. You must learn a new name." Catalin had friends who'd given us new passports with new identities. "You are 'Bela' now."

When I said this, Dani hugged me hard.

Little angels are so brave when they're in danger. He knew we were at risk, but he seemed so trusting in spite of it. I kissed the white circle on top of his head so many times I worried about rubbing the hair off. "I love you," I told him. "I love you, Dani."

"I love you."

"You must be very tired."

"No," he said. "Are we going over there?" He pointed to some very high mountains that looked as though they were made of iron ore. They were considerably different from the familiar brown and green mountains around Sibiu. Beyond these, to the west, were still more mountains, barely visible in a lighter blue. Would these mountains lead us to freedom?

It was the harshest way out of Romania and the way least taken, because once you were across you were so far from a real city you might as well become a Yugoslavian yourself, a mountain person. But people were crossing everywhere, even going into the Black Sea at night on inner tubes in the hopes of being picked up by the Turkish navy or friendly freighters. Others were hiding in oil drums or walking northwest and attempting to cross into Austria via Hungary.

"Will we try to cross the border tonight?" I said to Catalin, stroking Dani's hair as he slept. It was getting dark now and we were in a part of Romania I'd never seen before, climbing slowly as we turned south toward the small villages so far from the commercial routes that they lived by farming as they had a thousand years before. It was here that people played the lutelike cobza and the tambal, something like a dulcimer. I looked outside as the rough edges of Simena gave way to the more Germanic, fortified buildings of Transylvania. The stone and heavily timbered castles had roofs that were severely hipped and steepled to ward off heavy snow.

With a snare sound, my lighter illuminated the shapes of the three of us in the car as we continued the slow climb, circling like an airplane as we wound higher and higher into the snow country. We had a few cheap candies left and some biscuits, which I fed to Dani. There were great bumps in the roads now, and lance-shaped spruces out of storybooks, and for the first time I let Dani take a long look outside.

The temperature dropped. I could feel the cold in my legs, even though we had the heater on. Dani had never complained or asked to go to the bathroom. I was going to be like him.

The roads were getting narrower and less cared for, swerving between hills. Beside us was Riul Mare now, black and alive. We looked across the river and saw more mountains, savage and inhospitable. "Do you know where we're going?" I asked Catalin.

"Sure, I've been here many times. It's ski country."

"There are no lifts here. No one lives here."

We drove for another hour in the darkness, descending now, and suddenly the Danube appeared in the distance to the left, lit up with small clusters of lights that increasingly told me we were opposite some Yugoslavian farmlands. Far away, we saw a big cargo ship floating, its lights reflected dully on the water obscured by convection fog.

Our car was thick with smoke. Catalin hated smoke and coughed sarcastically every time I lit up. How could we even breathe in here? We kept driving.

Then we came to an area where the trees were very tall with patches of late snow. A group of peasant homes in a semi-circle near a larger structure suggested a roadside inn.

"We're staying here tonight," Catalin said. "I know these people. But don't let them know who you are. Don't even give them a chance to guess. Tell Dani."

I woke Dani and told him his new name and history again.

What did these people do here? There was no industry I could see, no sign of a state farm, just the unencompassable quiet of the forests, and the night, and this simple, two-story house, surrounded by small cottages, which rose from the darkness as we approached the door. Sheep huddled to one side, and I could see the steam from their breath in the light from the window.

"Stay inside," Catalin said. "Remember, you're nobody."

"I'm nobody except by coincidence." I was looking forward to being nobody.

He left the car and went to the door, where a large man with very low eyebrows stood for a moment and then embraced him. In Romania, the only heroes who'd survived the revolution with their reputations intact were sports heroes, it seemed. Catalin was a celebrity who was known even out here, beyond the reach of the cities. Our host wore an oilcloth smock and bellowed out a rough laugh at something Catalin said. Catalin eagerly waved us in.

With Dani holding my hand, we approached the man, who was now backed up by two others who were clearly farmers supplementing their meager incomes with cross-border smuggling. "Tell me, tell me about Bucharest," the oilcloth man said, sweeping us indoors out of the cold.

Inside, the house was almost medieval, with a huge stone fireplace and rough-hewn beams exposed—except for the very thin young man who had an automatic rifle balanced on his knee. A large fire curled around a great iron pot in which was some sort of thick *gulas*. No one had looked at us. They were so familiar and friendly to Catalin that it made us nervous. But then more people came flooding in the door. I looked at Catalin, who looked quickly in the other direction.

"Hello." A young woman gave me a lingering pat on the back. "Welcome. You must be terribly hungry. Sit down and tell us about what's happening in Bucharest."

She introduced herself, and I explained that we were old friends of Catalin from Bulgaria. I saw Catalin in the kitchen, talking in a low voice to the oilcloth man, who was accepting some money.

"Sit down," a woman stirring the stew commanded. "Sit down before we talk."

They didn't know who we were. I'd changed my hair by pulling it behind my ears with a hairband and began acting in a way I never had before—carefree! I sat down and made animated small talk; I was the life of the party. I had to laugh. Wasn't it Ileana who'd changed her hairband like this in school and set out like an arctic explorer? Was I finally able to chart an independent path?

I looked around at this curious village house with luxuries like a color TV set and a ham radio but only a stone floor and straw for a front lawn. "What stations can you pick up on that?" I asked.

"Everything from 50 kilohertz to 1.2 gigahertz," the younger man beamed.

"With no jamming?"

"None whatsoever."

"How could that be?"

"Eat," the woman said. She placed thick bowls of the *gulas* in front of us.

I wasn't hungry. But they had a lot of food, some *tuica*, plum brandy, and some wine. I tried the wine, but it was too strong, so the *tuica* was nice, in a heavy red glass.

"So you've seen the heads?" the woman asked me. "The beautiful purple stinking heads? The Great Conductor and his whore!"

I didn't know what to say. I shook my hair and I let my eyes grow large, animated. "Yes, they were wonderful. There are tanks everywhere. We have a new nation now." It wasn't a new nation. Only the purple heads change, that's all.

"The purple heads," they said over and over. "Like beets. *Zdobit*. Have some stew."

They were overpoweringly generous. I could tell Dani had taken note of this and was wondering why such friendly people were so critical of his grandparents. He hadn't said much of anything all day in the car, and I'd told him not to talk about the revolution, but what could he be thinking now? The damage to him had been incalculable. Usually he was carsick for even the shortest trip, but coming here he'd been unnervingly serene.

The young woman leaned over to me while Dani dipped into the stew and said, "What did they do to him?"

"What do you mean?" I forced my voice to be light.

Behind us washed the silence of the Transylvanian Alps.

"His hair."

It was ghoulish, this white spot. I'd seen the other mountaineers taking quick looks at it amid the clatter of spoons and boisterous talk of the revolution. More people came to the door, the heavy old wood creaking open to show the stars. Dani covered up his tremble with a smile.

"Oh, yes, they're dead." The slim man stood up. "The president and his wife, his sons. Dead. The father, the mother, all the children."

Valentin? This was impossible. I refused to believe it. I gave him my biggest smile and hugged Dani, whose shoulders were sinking.

"I haven't heard this," the driver of our decoy car said.

"Oh, yes, the terrible sons," the woman said. "They've gone the way of the others. Soon they'll execute Zoia, too."

Catalin stared with white eyes. "It isn't true," he whispered to me.

I was trying not to look at Dani and yet held him close to me and rapidly patted his back. His heart was leaping out of his chest. "It's not true," I spoke into his hair. "They're rurals who don't know anything. Smile."

I WARILY allowed myself to be conducted to the guest room upstairs. I felt honored because villagers seldom offered their guest rooms to strangers. The rooms were just for show, never to be slept in except by in-laws. I looked at the fine linen, embroideries, the handmade quilts, modest china, and crystal displayed carefully in this small, clean room and then, with Dani finally inside and the door closed behind me, fell down on the bed. I was exhausted.

Through the bedroom floor I could hear voices by the fire. They spoke to Catalin about the goods–mostly Western clothing–they were smuggling across the border, and which point was best for such a high-risk gamble, where the guards were not so inquisitive when you crossed.

"How'd you get here?" someone asked Catalin. "There are at least fifty roadblocks between here and Bucharest."

"Not the way we went," Catalin said to laughter.

These hill people truly thought of us as tourists. We were just some people "going over". They didn't recognize us because it was too absurd to think of Dani escaping. They didn't care about anything but their smuggling.

While I "slept" in the room, I heard Catalin asking the oilcloth man about yet another route for crossing. We were no more than eleven kilometers from the border. The man ruled out two gates because of scrutiny that had recently been too high and recommended a third, perhaps half an hour away.

IN THE uncertain light of the next morning, we started down the asphalt road which was both dark and light, with islands of ice. It was a gray day, no sun, the beginning of some freakish late sleet that became snow. The highest mountains had disappeared and given way to the tricks and twists of these medium hills.

We had changed cars with our decoy. I continued my job of writing down license plates and asking Dani to keep his head down. Fifteen minutes passed, then twenty.

"Dani," I said on an upslope, "you know we're leaving Romania for a short time, don't you?" We'd never talked about it, but he must have guessed. Why wasn't he talking more? "Dani?"

Trees rose up while Catalin pointed to the right, over a hill. "That's one of the gates."

"Are we going to try to go through that one?"

"No, that's the bad one. Some people were shot there yesterday. We're supposed to go up here."

We climbed again.

"Are those elves?" Dani pointed to some shepherds. One had blue boots and a white beard. "I'm cold."

"The heater is on," Catalin said. He turned to look over our heads through the rear windshield. His eyes widened. "Do you see that?"

Behind us, far away, was a car, a flicker of green.

"Are those lambs?"

"Yes, Dani."

That couldn't be the same car. We were driving around the side of a mountain now, and what was unmistakably a green Dacia disappeared again behind us on the far side of the curve. The snow was pretty heavy now.

"What's the license plate?" Catalin asked.

"How can I see it?" The snow was a whorl, above us and on every side. I was getting tired of pushing Dani's head down. "When will we get to the next gate?"

"We're almost there."

I turned completely around in my seat now, looking for the Dacia.

Pffft.

"Are they shooting?" I asked.

"No. I can't even see them."

"What was that noise?" I asked.

"I don't know. Must be hunters."

"Where is he?"

"I don't know."

Pffft.

Chapter 19

Old sin makes new shame

Racing ahead of the Dacia, we found ourselves caught behind a slow silver car filled with a family. Baggage nearly blocked up their rear window as they moved along so ponderously we couldn't get past. Catalin, generous with his horn, swerved back and forth behind them, screaming.

"It's too narrow," I said. "We don't want to fall there." I looked down a steep ravine that followed the snow down to a tiny stream, far below. There'd be no surviving that kind of fall.

Catalin pounded the wheel and shouted, "Come on!" at the gray touring car ahead of us while I watched behind me for the Dacia, which, though farther away, had now rounded into view.

When I was a little girl, my father and Mocaneata had been caught in traffic once, out in country like this. This was in the early 1950s, on the way back from Brasov. In any case, the car ahead of us wouldn't move to the side of the narrow road to let us pass, in spite of our chauffeur's honking. Wordlessly, Mocaneata stood up, aimed his service pistol at the left rear tire of the offending car, and fired, sending its wide-eyed occupants spinning perfectly to the left and into a soft landing in a snowbank.

WE plowed along behind the silver car all the way down a little valley into the border gate Catalin had selected and waited while the family ahead made their noisy progress.

Amazingly now, there was no sign of the Dacia.

The snow suddenly stopped, and the sun came out for the first time. It was incomprehensibly bright up here in the snow, with these trees, the bright green gate, and sentry posts rising up rough against the unvarnished pine of the processing building and–

Above us.

Again, like we'd seen during the regime change in Bucharest.

The same cloud formation the rustics called "The Eye of God".

"Look," Catalin said.

With the strange spring snow gone as quickly as it came, the guards were looking up there, too. It was the opposite of an eclipse, in a way, where, far from darkening things, everything seemed to get twice as bright.

My brain danced.

Look.

In the brightness, a guard briefly peered in at us through the window. His was a smooth round face in its fifties. He looked at us very quickly and motioned us on.

The decoy car was behind us. Still there was no green Dacia in the line.

Another man walked by, a younger man this time, in a fatigue jacket and an unmatching pair of dress pants, looking quickly at all of us in the car.

Catalin kept driving slowly. He bravely rolled his window down and thumped the door. "What's the holdup?" he called ahead to the younger guard, who shrugged his shoulders and walked toward the gate to see.

Would they recognize me? No. I wouldn't even recognize myself.

As we moved ahead toward the gate, we waited for the customary bump of a trough filled with chemicals that would disinfect our tires upon entry into another nation, but felt none. This really was a quiet gate, with perhaps twenty other gates left behind us closer to Bucharest. Within ten feet of the gate, a third man who'd been going in and out of a wood-and-glass hut beside the gate asked for our papers.

Catalin produced the papers with a flourish. "Get some air," he said to us under his breath. "Get out." He nodded toward the family ahead, who'd gotten out of their car while their papers were being checked. "With them." His hands were white against the wheel.

Why were we separating?

"Okay, 'Bela'?" My son "Bela" and I were out like a shot, instantly incorporating ourselves into the family of five standing ahead of us. I pushed us into the center like a rude cousin and joked with the mother, standing almost on top of her, while Dani jumped around close by and helped to make perfect the human camouflage.

Above us, the Eye of God shone brightly over the scene. Crazy with happiness, I even pointed it out to a guard.

Catalin inched forward in our car.

The silver car was cleared to cross through the 100-meter neutral zone lined with logs to the Yugoslavian gate on the other side. I bumped into the other guard, who at that moment was handing our papers back to Catalin, and laughed. I was finally Iordana Borila again. My shoulders trembled, but I forced myself into another laugh as I scooped 'Bela' into the car and we rolled forward, *past the gate...*

Why was Catalin so tight?

Something was wrong...

I didn't dare ask him, but slowly pushed "Bela" back down as we rolled over the gravel in the incredible brightness. I felt the way I had when I'd run out of the Snagov palace with Elena running behind me. I braced my back for the end, the instantaneous whiteness, the explosion that would end everything.

Bump.

There, finally, was the chemical trough.

They'd never let us through this other gate. Beyond, the countryside of Yugoslavia shone like Oz. Soldiers in brown Yugoslav dress, quite a few more of them than on the Romanian side, intercepted cars and turned them to either side of the road for questioning.

But we drove right through.

Catalin was even less talkative now. He scratched his neck and changed radio stations. He looked around to see our decoy car gliding through as well. Just past the detaining station, Catalin slowed the car and put his head on the wheel. His shoulders shook. Then he began to take deep, slow breaths.

THERE weren't a lot of people here in our new country of Yugoslavia. We waited for the decoy car to catch up with us. This car made it, too, and when our other driver slowed down beside us, he put his head on the wheel and began to cry.

I enjoyed everything I saw. The sun, the sky, everything was so bright. Every piece of rock, of scenery.

We walked into the Yugoslavian welcome cafeteria, our minds aswirl. The men ordered whiskey, and now I cried. We got a Pepsi for Dani, who was very subdued.

WE stopped later in Zagreb for coffee and a sandwich. I knew it was wonderful, but I couldn't taste it. I just knew it was very good ham and butter.

Were we tasting freedom?

We drove through the Alps of Austria toward Vienna. Through the mountains we did again see the green Dacia and confirmed its license plate. We sighted it just after Zagreb and several times more through Austria after that. High up in the Alps there was a blizzard. I remember looking at the car, now as likely to be a friend as a pursuer, and seeing it disappear just before our rear windshield went white. We went around a curve and descended into the steaming, incomparable spring of Vienna, where we stopped for lunch.

"You'd better leave, if you're Romanian," the waitress said. "Do you know what you've done here?" Her eyes flashed with anger. "You've overrun the city. You're stealing everything. Romanians have eaten our swans from the palace of Schönbrunn. Someone will have to pay for this."

We shook our heads in exaggerated sympathy and paid—but only for lunch.

Catalin handed us an envelope of money. "This is from a lot of us. Good luck."

"How can we thank you?"

"Call Liuda when you can. Stay alive. If you need help, you can count on me." He embraced us and took his leave.

Dani was sad as he watched the car turn around a corner and disappear. We saw many Romanian faces, and we hid ours. We fell into a crowd as we walked past newsstands and shops with my in-laws' mutilated heads plastered everywhere. Our next stop was Israel. My old friends from the early days in the Nomenclatura were not going to understand this, but it was where I'd dreamed of going.

Chapter 20

It's a bad plan that can't be changed

DANI and I arrived in Tel Aviv at 11.33pm at Ben-Gurion airport, crowded with thousands of immigrants. It wasn't just a Romanian diaspora; we were coming to this generous country from all over the Eastern Bloc. "Welcome Home," the sign greeted us in Hebrew, English, French, and Russian. Because of my Jewish ancestry I didn't have to ask for political asylum, and no one questioned me about my name. To them, I was just another pilgrim, *oleh hadas.*

In Bucharest there were many speculations about our location, so we continued to live undercover to avoid reprisals from Romania. Valentin, I learned, was still in prison but fine, along with Zoia and Nicu, whose trials would drag on into perpetuity.

After talking to distant relatives I decided I could settle near Haifa. I'd left behind all the family I'd ever known, but I was to discover a new family full of love. An enthusiastic old friend whom I'd known years earlier in Bucharest took us to a kibbutz where the people were among the most gentle I'd ever met. Because I was over forty, I was disappointed to learn, I was too old to join.

I experienced a sense of peace and hope in Israel that I hadn't felt in years, but Dani didn't feel the same. The bold, brave eyes of all the children I met on the streets were a wonder to me–the way they proudly looked directly into my eyes–and I wished Dani's could be as bright and excited. The problem was, Israel seemed always on alert, and Dani, his head still white, had already had enough. Every night there were sirens, bus bombs, or loud noises. With Scud missiles trained on us and the Gulf War at its doorstep, the entire nation had its claws out, as well it might.

Dani couldn't sleep. "What was that, Mother?" he'd say, waking me again and again in the night while civil defense drills kept him from relaxing during the day.

I had hardly any money left, and not a lot of charm at this time to offer my Israeli friends, but they did everything in their power to make my *aliyah* comfortable. At least we were anonymous here.

Until there was a knock on my door early one morning. I looked down at a stranger from our second-floor window. This young man rapped incessantly now, scratching his head and looking up and down the eerily sunshiny street. Finally I went down.

"Iordana Borila?" he said. "Iordana Borila Ceausescu?" He jostled halfway into the door.

A cold hand gripped my heart. I stared down at his hands and at his notebook. *They knew.* They knew where I was. "What do you want?" I answered him casually in Russian, praying he didn't know Russian himself. "What do you want? I don't understand you."

"Mrs Ceausescu, I just wanted to ask you some questions about your family. Do you know how many people are...?"

I spoke faster and faster, and his look became more quizzical. Finally, his hand gestures having failed him, he looked back at his notebook and back at my door number and shrugged his shoulders. Then he walked out to a blue van with a television camera inside, which slowly panned the house as he left.

I was in great turmoil trying to decide the best thing to do for my son. I had to find a more peaceful hiding place.

THE NEXT morning I was torn, thinking about this, when the telephone rang. It was some friends who'd fled to the most insane nation on earth, the United States, urging me to visit. Just like the Israeli people, my old friends seemed so reassuring. Gathering together the last of our funds, I purchased two tickets on El Al airlines and, on a rainy Wednesday, roared up through the cloud levels until we hit the bright blue air. The rain-washed coast of Israel disappeared as the floor of clouds beneath us turned soft and white as Biri, the lamb I'd had as a child.

We were returning with a planeful of tourists who'd seen the Holy Land and were now coming home to New York, Boston, and, in the case of the pretty old lady who shared the seat across the aisle, Sarasota. I was afraid to talk with her and wondered what we could do. I'd brought some oranges and peeled them for Dani, since he seemed suspicious of the microwaved tray of indistinct meat the stewardess slapped in front of him.

How unlikely it was that we were going to America! I'd watched my lovely childhood turn into the murderous coda of a communist world gone awry. The Soviets were finished. My child had been deeply damaged and disturbed by the violence... and I was taking him there? Solzhenitsyn had disappeared into Vermont, but couldn't I have found a safer place in Europe? The plane sped on while the doubts overwhelmed me; beyond the guns everyone carried, I'd always been afraid of the threatening way all Americans hailed each other, with this word "Hi." It wasn't soft, like hello or how do you do, the way they spoke in London. Instead, speakers used this bloodthirsty "hi" to seize people's attention and tell them what to do. In Romania, we also have this word, and it is an abrupt, piercing command that means, "Get over here. Get over here. *Hai*." How frightening it was to be assaulted like this on the plane. What could have happened to these people in the New World?

"Romanians," one man bellowed. "Why aren't you covered with blood?"

"It wasn't so bad," I said. *Not so bad*. Had I really said that? "In fact, there were some really good moments."

"What was good about it?"

At one time, some of us in the Nomenclatura believed in the possibility of... I don't know... a new benevolent royalty. Our generation was so sure we could make a difference. The intellectual elites would lift up the lowliest. Everyone would prosper.

"Hi. Are you Romanians?" asked another younger man. His black leather jacket bulged with a pistol. "Doesn't that make you commies?"

"Do you want your chicken?"

I quickly handed my tray to the demanding man.

There was so much shrieking and laughing in this plane, too.

A man beside us was reading an article in the *International Herald Tribune* about "Firebombing in Canarsie". A real-estate agency who'd sold property to minorities had been targeted in the very country where we were headed. Dani and I needed no more of that. Wherever it was, I'd have to cross that terrible neighborhood off my list.

WE arrived in America all right, like any exiles determined to love it like a woman might love a very short haircut. The seacoast town where we began to hide was lovely, full of dark woods and gulls, and a number of Romanian friends of ours were congregated here in clusters of small families. But what to do? Is there an easy path to happiness in America? So far, Dani loves it here and wants to stay, and I love it, too, though I'm tickled by some of the superficial differences I encounter in this new culture.

For example, here in America, no matter what, you have to smile. Smile to get a job. No matter how good you are, they won't select you if you don't smile. When I ask people how they are, all they say is, "Fine, thank you." It's an unscalable wall. Everything's sleek, wonderful. Americans are bursting with health and happiness. In Romania, in answer to how-are-you questions, we describe the work: "I'm working, I'm washing dishes," but never this enigmatic, "I'm fine." In a grocery store last week, a boy finally let the mask slip. "I must tell you that I'm fine," he confided to me as he stacked some lemons in neat rows, "but really I'm not." I loved him!

Because the concept of God is so much a part of American culture that even the phrase "In God we trust" is on dollar bills, I feel more acutely the lack of my religious upbringing here. It is ironic to read editorials exhorting Americans to put the Christ back in Christmas, because in Romania we celebrated all religious holidays that were by state order disconnected from any history. Sometimes I wish I could give God to my son, but I think it may be too late for him, too.

Another caution in my rough guide to America: Americans drink everything with ice.

I've also learned that no matter where she lives, a single mother has limitations. Imagine what it was like to teach my son to shave! "Don't tell me," he said. "I know what to do." In a few minutes he was back, sheepish. "Tell me."

Yesterday, I walked out to the beach with Dani. In winter, this place is a bit like a deserted Black Sea resort, with the sidewalks rolled up and all the windows covered for a winter storm, a Neptune for disembodied souls. It's romantic here in my refuge on the coast, and very modest, a place where you can stand in front of the ocean and feel the endless wind. We come here to feed the gulls. If I listen to their cries and close my eyes, I feel for a moment as if I'm in Herastrau.

DANI and I are still in hiding because the "evil that men do lives after them". There will always be those who want to seek revenge against the Ceausescu name, and as a result we've taken refuge for a while in the anonymity that America offers. But we have a surprise. "Hi" is the warmest, most wonderful word in the world. It is the simplest, most revealing expression of tenderness we've ever heard.

Our life is so different here, and so is life in Romania. People there still ache for the old communist ways, even planting flowers at the graves of Nicolae and Elena. My mother and Nanny are fine and still living in Bucharest; Valentin is free enough to be able to attend World Cup soccer matches; Zoia's trying to start her own newspaper; Ileana's a marketing director for a fashion magazine in Rome; Dorin is back at the top of the computer field in Bucharest (he recently represented Romanian telecommunications as part of the Iliescu delegation to the US); Catalin and Liuda's ARO sport utility vehicles are known worldwide; Ilie, having unsuccessfully run for mayor of Bucharest, alternates between his homes in New York and Connecticut; and Nicu...

Well, my friends from Romania tell me that until he died of reported liver problems, it was everybody's educated guess that Nicu was going to be a candidate in the next presidential elections in Romania.

Hold on a second—my son has just come in the door with some friends.

"Hi, Mom," he says to me before running back outside to play with them in the trees that look so much like Romania. It's as if this entire country is one great village, uncomplicated and sweet.

"Hi." I smile. "Come here a minute, Dani."

Obediently my son comes, and I give him a deep embrace.

"Come on!" he says. "They're looking." He's so strong now, so happy.

We live in hiding, but we've never been so happy in our lives. We thank God for the peace and the serenity we have here. I hold him for one more second—

"Mom!" More than anything he looks like my father now, in the pictures I remember of him when he was a young man.

"All right, go," I say, no longer looking down but looking up at him as his shiny dark chestnut hair bounces beside his friends' in the sun.

Hi.

Epilogue

Old Orchard Beach,
Maine, USA

WHEN WINTER drifts into this tiny resort, the sidewalks roll up and the swell of visitors vanishes. The "Eye of God" Ferris wheel stops turning. The creatures of the Noah's Ark carousel slow into a deep slumber, and the lights of the pier that stretches into infinity go dark. O.O.B., as we call it, has a population of 8,000 souls, mostly huddled in the town center. The emptied beach seduces you to take a contemplative stroll. It was both a perfect and a dreadful place for Iordana and Dani to disappear. "Only my brooding thoughts," she said, "drown out the boom of the surf."

It was several weeks into our interviews before she risked telling me that her son was still in hiding with her. I had already learned not to press her for details, and it was several more weeks before she told me where they were living. When she seemed more relaxed, I offered to introduce her to my son, and the next time she came to visit, she brought Daniel Ceausescu with her.

"Dani" wore a Chicago Bulls hat. His favorite basketball player was Michael Jordan. My son's favorite basketball player was Shaquille O'Neal. In the early silence I said, "Jordan, meet Shaq. Shaq, meet Jordan." Dani's reply: "I believe they've met."

My son and Dani took quickly to each other. It's quite possible not to understand either one of these two boys, but impossible not to delight in them. Looking back on their meeting, my son says, "Basketball was Dani's cover. Mine, too. Liking Michael Jordan was a brilliant disguise. Jordan was a magician with the basketball. Everyone liked Jordan. You could use that enthusiasm to disappear. To talk about Jordan was to evade, to camouflage yourself."

Iordana once invited us for coffee at the studio she'd rented a block from the beach on East Grand Avenue.

"It isn't much," she said. She lit up a cigarette, which I'd come to realize was her veil. Sometimes she used the smoke as a screen. Other times it was a repellent, like octopus ink. By now she already knew how much I despised it, but because she had so little left of her old life, we had a nicotine truce.

Her cheaply furnished seasonal rental had never been meant to be anything but a way station, a shadow space with white plastic dishes. I got the distinct impression that Iordana and Dani were poised to move out with two hours' notice. It seemed a conscious decision to avoid showier accommodations, as if she were doing some sort of penance. This cinderblock quadrangle was a monk's cell, the walls adorned with faded posters of tropical islands. On an altar in the center of the room sat a small television, the sound turned down.

"Interesting." I caught her eye. "Did you do the renovation yourself?"

"Good one."

We sipped the instant coffee fortified with an extra spoonful of the brown granules, "and a half-teaspoon of sugar," she said, "for the liver." At least nobody was going to try to see the future in Folgers Crystals. Before I'd even finished half the cup, I got the sense it was time for us to leave.

Iordana stopped me as we headed toward the door. "I have something for you." She produced a tissue-wrapped envelope. Perhaps she was fighting the need to show me the contents and hide them at the same time. "Here is a picture of me as a girl wearing my scarf."

"Is this what you wore during the mountain scene?" I asked.

"I hate talking about the mountain scene!"

Was it because the mountain was where it all started with Valentin?

She removed three more photos. "This is my mother at the journal office. This is a photo of my father with his fighters in the woods. And here we are at our house. That's my father looking at me on the porch swing." She turned to me. "Sometimes I'm afraid I've given you the wrong impression. It wasn't all grim!"

The weight of these images knocked me over. What a lonely path they'd taken to get to this strange place. By now I'd guessed that Iordana had landed here because Catalin had met her and Dani in Canada, where it would have been easier to slip in without a passport. At night, he'd driven the two through an unpatrolled stretch of woods across the border into Maine. I'd stopped asking about such an underground passage because I realized they didn't want the pipeline shut down. I like to think she was trying to spare me a charge of collusion by failing to report it.

"I can't accept these," I said. "You'll want them. They're too dear. I will copy these and return them to you."

She relaxed her shoulders.

A seagull swept past her window, blotting out the sun for a second. "A bit scary," I said. "It reminds me of Hitchcock."

"I actually like the gulls. They keep me company when Dani's at school."

Was she blinking back a tear? She would always love the Pescarusul. She would always love Valentin.

"You deserve a change of scenery," my wife said.

So WE PICKED up Iordana and Dani that weekend and took them to a cottage my grandparents had built on the seashore in nearby Kennebunkport.

"Thank you for your kind hospitality." Iordana presented me with a book about Margareta Sterian. When I opened it, a photo I hadn't seen fell out. She picked it up and held it toward me. "This I do want you to have, too."

"I can't accept it."

"You must. It's all I have to give."

"Your mother?"

"No, Mama Mare, Valentin's grandmother, in the gardens outside the Primaverii, which is a resort like this." She pointed to the Colony Hotel across the jetty. "It's yours."

That evening, I dropped the snapshot into the folder with the images I'd Xeroxed. I look forward to the time I can return the snapshot of Mama Mare to Dani.

IT WOULD BE the only meal we shared out in public, and that was only as far out as our front yard. I'd asked Iordana, "I'll be cooking. What do you like to eat?"

She closed her eyes and smiled. "Anything from the sea."

I managed to scorch the haddock into a dried mess. After a polite nibble, she covered her mouth to suppress a laugh.

"Okay, let me have it," I said.

"Anything… but this!"

My wife, my son, and Dani had already fled to the kitchen for hot dogs.

The boys had become a bit of a gang who met up once every few weeks with no need to share what happened outside their friendship. Dani had proven to be a sweet, brilliant kid who felt his mother's broken heart even while bravely trying to take in the rush of fresh air of being alive right now. A teenager with an apocalyptic backstory can seem both vulnerable and hard-shelled at the same time.

My son and Dani, who enrolled in the Old Orchard Beach school system as "David Daniels", were in the same year grade but not the same school. No details of Dani's high school life were ever disclosed to us. Because this was Iordana's tender spot, I never asked. And she made it clear, the story was not to be about him.

Iordana was only able to seek medical and dental care through friends of ours who agreed to ask no questions. Even this was complicated by her reluctance to sit in the waiting room of my wife's dental office. She preferred to sit in a closet. Was it a *tovarasa's* disinclination for being viewed as waiting in line, or was it a real fear of being recognized by other Romanian expatriates as a member of the hated Nomenclatura? She laughed when we asked over cocktails which it was. She let drop that they had no social life outside our visits, as Catalin and his wife had returned to Europe. It became obvious she had the television on all day to keep her company when Dani was at school, so she was learning about life in America from *The Jerry Springer Show*.

She became mesmerized by the 1995 trial of OJ Simpson. She said, "In a way, I'm like OJ. Guilty if I'm guilty, guilty if I'm innocent."

She was still trying to hold her shadow space together in the year 2000. My wife and I attended Dani's high-school graduation with Iordana, and the two came to stay at our house over the summer before they relocated so he could attend Bard College in New York, still under his assumed name. (His senior thesis: "Temperature Transformation and Relativistic Thermodynamics of an Ideal Gas.")

I read the story manuscript to Iordana, and she was moved to tears. She said, "I love it. That was me. How did you know?" and I began to plan sending it off for agency consideration.

I strongly urged her to apply for Immigration Amnesty that year (I'd come to accept that she was not here legally) and had understood she was working toward that. She promised she would, but then I was frustrated to discover she'd ultimately refused, fearing that to apply would be to reveal her identity. This caused a rift in our relationship, which I regret.

Iordana began to be suspicious of everyone, even Catalin. Was she in Maine not to be shielded but to shield Valentin from embarrassment? As nostalgia for the revolution began to set in, was she now nothing but an inconvenience?

When I showed her a polished version of the novel, she began to express concern that she'd been too open with me during our interviews.

"I wish I hadn't told you all that. It sounds so American, so personal. I am now embarrassed. My *legs?*" she said of the Lake Snagov interlude with Valentin. "I only did it for Dani, to make his life easier. Now I realize he has to do that on his own." Finally, "Please don't publish this while I'm alive."

I never saw her again after that summer, but we kept in contact with emails that became less and less frequent. The last time I heard from her was birthday wishes in 2006. I continued to email her Hotmail address without reply. I learned on the internet that she and Dani turned up in Bucharest. Sadly, this is also how I learned she passed away.

SEARCHING FOR the mother and son I had tried to know, I drove to the Old Orchard Beach library. I'll never know if I would have been able to find the courage to do what they had done. If every assumption I'd ever had were ripped away from me–if I were in mourning for myself and my life–could I travel a world away and hide in plain sight the way they had? She told me she felt that everyone in the world was either watching her or watching for her. I tried to imagine Iordana walking in to register her son "David Daniels" for school. Think of what it took to accomplish that. Maybe Iordana walking in alone. That first day. Imagine her practicing being poised for their questions, Catalin coaching her: "You're tensing up. Stop looking suspicious."

"Easy for you to say. I am!"

Imagine her mind running wild. "Where is his birth certificate?" "What is your Social Security number? Are you a US citizen?" "Where does the father work?" "Where do you live?" "What school bus stop will he be using to board?" "Do you want to sign your son up for the lunch supplement?"

Approaching the reference desk, I asked the librarian for the Old Orchard Beach High School yearbook for the Class of 2000. As I took it to a table in the corner, I felt her eyes following me. Now I was the one under suspicion.

I expected to see nothing, or "Not Pictured". But I was wrong. There was Dani, standing tall on the basketball team. Had Iordana ever blended into the crowds to watch him? For an instant I imagined Iordana's story never being told—erased, like so many victims of conflict. She'd never come to Maine, never spoken to me, never gagged on my burned haddock, never shown her heart.

Then I caught my breath. Feeling Iordana looking on, I slowly turned the page to David Daniels's senior class photo. He stares out from it. "David Daniels. Dave." His chosen inscription: "The truth is only what someone chooses to believe."

Acknowledgments

I'd like to thank my wife for her support and my son, who befriended Iordana's son, for his insights. Thanks also to Catalin Tutunaru, a clever storyteller; Johanna Hanaburgh, a sensitive listener; Gwen Thompson, a talented reader as well as writer; and Dr Catherine Baker at the University of Hull for her thoughtful questions. I'm grateful to Martin Goodman for his passion for the novel as an artistic composition of the truth.